FINAL

MW01128043

By Richard Frost

Copyright C 2017 by Richard B. Frost

All rights reserved. No part of this book may be reproduced, distributed, or transmitted in any form or by any electronic or mechanical or other means, including information storage and retrieval systems, without the prior written permission of the author, with the exception of a reviewer quoting brief passages in a review.

This book is a work of fiction. Although some actual figures and events have been included, the principal characters and their interactions with actual persons are derived from the author's imagination. Any similarity of the principal characters to persons living or dead is purely coincidental.

ISBN-13:9781546894001

Library of Congress Control Number: 2017908729
CreateSpace Independent Publishing Platform, North Charleston, SC

For Marty and Zoey,

And for all Baltimore Orioles, and their fans,

past, present, and future

PART ONE

April 30, 1993

The man behind me patiently explained to his son why the runner on first base had already started for second with the pitch. "They call it a hit-and-run, Sammy. See how he got a head start, so that he'd be able to go further? But the batter has to swing at it."

"Dad," Sammy asked. "How would the batter know the runner will be running?"

"Watch that coach down at third base, Sammy. See how he keeps fidgeting and moving around? Well, he's giving signals. To the runner and to the batter."

Sammy squinted. "How can you see a signal? He just keeps moving his hands and yelling. How's the batter figure out what to do?"

"Each coach does it differently. Probably the batter and runner wait for him to do one certain thing, like maybe putting both hands on his head. Whatever he does next is the signal."

Sammy shook his head. "I don't know, Dad. I think maybe I'd have to call time out and go ask what he wanted me to do." I empathized. All those signals could be confusing.

Oriole Park at Camden Yards was full for Baltimore's game against Kansas City, but to me all forty thousand fans were embodied by Sammy. No one cheered louder each time the Orioles scored. He's a kindred spirit to those of us fanatic about our team. Going to ball games wasn't just entertainment. At least for me it wasn't. This team was part of my life. Every contest either gave something to me or took it away.

A little bit later, Sammy noticed the idiosyncrasies of Todd Frohwirth's submarining pitching motion. "Dad!" he said. "You tell me not to throw underhand like that. That I have to throw overhand if I want to play like a big leaguer. How come no one tells him?"

I'm sure if I had turned around, I'd see Dad smiling as he answered. "Well, he's an exception. Trust me, if you ever want to make it to the majors, Sammy, you'd better throw overhand."

Our cheering – Sammy's and mine – paid off. Our team went home victorious.

The Orioles had won nine, lost fourteen so far in the young

season. But they'd taken four out of five since it really started to matter. At least since it started mattering to me.

No one anticipates a physician giving bad news. No one wants the biopsy coming back malignant. No one wants a spinal tap to show meningitis. No one wants an abnormal blood test.

A doctor enters the room, and a strange reflex comes into play. He asks, how are you doing. You respond, oh, pretty good. A moment later you both realize he shouldn't have asked; you shouldn't have answered. You're sick. You're not feeling pretty good. Otherwise, why would you be there? Yet you go through the ritual.

I find it especially loathsome to have a doctor come in and say, so how are "we" doing? As if you're both doing the same. Or that you're going to split the difference on how you're doing. Choose the mean. Which leads you to try yet once more to remember, now which is the mean, which the median, which the mode.

An appointment for follow-up results after treatment is different. You're not sure how you feel. That is, you don't know if, after all the testing, all the radiation, all the chemotherapy, you're ever supposed to feel normal again. How can you, after your body has hosted the individual equivalent of both trench fighting and nuclear attack? You have to be scarred, emotionally if not physically. Maybe, you ponder, there comes a new normal. Then the question becomes one of how you feel compared to what you know now about a life under attack.

It's easy to feel barraged by numbers. Blood counts, liver functions, LDH's, and the like. The patient's equivalent of home runs, stolen bases, and batting average.

Blood tests lack a certain tangibility, though. It's pictures you believe, pictures that are worth a thousand words, pictures generated by the machine whirling around you while you try to ever so briefly hold your breath. Those CT scans hold the clues to your future. You don't feel any different. Your blood work isn't any different. But the computer will spit out a series of images that determines whether you continue your normal life, or instead prepare for its end.

When you get good at this, you see the results on the doctor's face when he greets you.

I'd gone to medical school with Eric. When I left for a family practice residency in Ohio, we lost contact. He did internal medicine in Boston, then stayed on for oncology training. A year after I began practicing in Maryland, I learned that he had joined the Johns Hopkins staff. When I got sick and went to see him, it had been well over a decade since we'd last talked. Now, of course, we saw each other all the time.

Eric wasn't smiling when he entered the room, never a good omen. He wasn't exactly frowning or grimacing. Rather he was forcing himself to make eye contact, as he knew he should, yet somehow not quite looking straight at me. Usually he joined me on the brown leather couch in his consultation room. This time he went behind his desk. When he sat down, he began tapping his toe rhythmically. He'd always done that when he felt uncomfortable.

"Dan, there's no reason to couch this with a bunch of pretty terms. The lymphoma's worse." He paused a moment. At least I think it was a moment. Maybe it was a seventh-inning stretch. "There's some in the liver, plus now it's involving retroperitoneal nodes."

I hadn't let Mary come with me to the visit. We'd been separated for a few months, and I still needed to prove to myself I could handle things on my own. That didn't keep me from reflexively glancing to the other side of the couch, where she would have sat had she been there. She'd have noticed that I still hadn't gained back all my weight, and that my hair was growing in a bit unevenly.

So I had to deal with the bad news myself. I'd already used my lifetime quota of reserve energy the first time around. This time I was prepared to skip the anger and denial stages, maybe even the negotiation stage.

Eric--should I say Dr. Bell, now that things began to take an unhappy turn?--offered little small talk. No comments about the Orioles (he passionately followed the Red Sox, an allegiance best pursued before their annual July swoon), no questions about Mary's garden.

"I may as well be direct. The tumor mass hasn't shrunk as expected. Lab work's fine. Bone marrow has recovered nicely. No liver or renal toxicity. But chemo just didn't do much."

It's rare that I need much of a pause to keep a conversation going, but that day I wished I had one of those ten-second tape delays. "So what comes next?"

"Well, there are options. For one, we're part of a study group testing a new rescue therapy."

Rescue sounded a bit too optimistic. How could it be rescue if I hadn't had a full remission to begin with? "I'm not going into any protocol with a placebo group," I told him.

"The experimental group will be paired with patients getting standard therapy," he said.

I got back to my habit of responding quickly. "Standard therapy which doesn't work, right? No way I'm accepting the flip of a coin."

Eric barely changed expression. He expected my answer. "If you want, we can just give you the experimental protocol and not enter you into the study. Read up on the side effects, call around if you want. How about you come back in a week and we decide?"

I tried to swallow, but my mouth was too dry. "How about some data first?"

He weighed his words carefully, putting a modicum of patient-doctor distance between us. "Some groups are reporting a 20 per cent success rate with adriamycin, BCNU, and cis-platinum."

BCNU sounded a bit too much like "be seeing you". Not the sentiment I wanted for my cancer drugs. "By success, you mean cure?"

"No." That toe was tapping more rapidly. "But it's increasing the one-year survival."

"What's my prognosis without any treatment?" I ventured

"Straight?" he replied.

"You know a better way?"

I felt badly for him. Eric was tall and lean at baseline. Now he looked even more stretched out, lankier, uncomfortably spilling over his chair. I imagined Ichabod Crane looking like this on a horse. He continued to force eye contact, all the while looking for openings to avert his glance. The tapping picked up in frequency.

"You might make it four or five months. It might edge up to a year."

So, at best a one-year survival chance with no therapy. But a shot at twelve months with new– meaning toxic– therapy. Outside of medicine, that's six of one, half dozen of the other.

I'd always preached the lack of validity to the usual parameters of cancer treatment success. Telling someone the drugs, or the radiation, or the surgery, might lengthen life six months, a year, or two years struck me as misleading. All those days of hospitalization, vomiting, postoperative pain, fatigue so overwhelming you couldn't get out of bed– they should be subtracted. Net gain of days feeling good was the better measure, I'd tell medical students. Oncologists complained when I did that, but I always felt compelled to make the data real for the individual patient, not aggregate it to the cohort of a research project.

The journals could say *xyz* treatment or *abc* disease carries a 20% risk or a 40% complication rate. But for an individual patient, it would always be 0% or 100 %.

"Eric, what would you do if this were you instead of me? Or, let's make it, what would you want if it were Ginny?" There was no happier marriage than Eric's and Ginny's. He could never do anything, even hypothetically, not in her best interest.

It bothered me how long it took him to answer. Might have been only twenty seconds, but you could have played the whole Sergeant Pepper album in it.

"I think I'd try the protocol," he finally told me.

"Well, let me ponder it a little," I stammered.

"Okay," he responded. "But you have to come back and tell me in person what you decide."

A day passed before I called Mary and summarized the appointment. We'd gotten along much better since the marriage ended. Her support from a distance buoyed me up much more effectively than when we spent all our time together.

Once I'd finished, she simply asked, "Are you going to get another opinion?"

"No. Eric's as good as anyone anywhere. I wouldn't insult him by asking someone else."

I could sense her fear. She didn't want to ask the next question. I had just started to speak again when her words came out. "What are you going to do?"

Not a millisecond of hesitation. She knew the answer. I'd long proclaimed I would follow the Orioles around the country if I had a disease that couldn't be cured. Instead of worrying about my impending death, and brooding over past failures and regrets, I'd let baseball be the diversion that preserved a sense of sanity. My reason to get up the next morning.

"I think it's time to hit the road."

"Have you told Eric this?" she asked.

"Called him this morning."

That night, Mike Mussina and the Orioles shut out Minnesota, 11-0. I took it as a signal I'd chosen correctly.

No two places are as close as they seem on a map. Certainly not Minnesota and Maryland.

Leaving Baltimore right after the Kansas City game on Sunday got me as far as Wheeling, West Virginia, that night. I should have washed the Camry and done a little interior vacuuming, but who cares about a clean car at a time like this? I threw away the accumulated food containers, napkins, and parking receipts. There were a couple of scorecards on the back seat; I added those to the collection in my bedroom.

I'd planned some sightseeing the next day until I studied my map at Days Inn. I still had over eight hundred miles to go. So much for checking out ancient burial mounds near Chilicothe, Ohio. I figured I should learn about how different societies handled death; maybe I'd get better ideas on dealing with my own. No time now for such niceties.

Instead I got an early wake-up call, skipped taking a shower, and got on the road by seven. By the time I stopped for a late breakfast in Madison, I already had a couple of hundred miles behind me. I found a place near the University of Wisconsin campus. Sat at the counter and ordered my fix of eggs, potatoes, and bacon. Greasing myself up for the last leg into Minnesota, I told myself.

A young girl took the stool next to me and asked if I was a professor. She sought my advice on picking a college. I offered encouragement but generic answers. There was pleasing irony in imparting strategy on beginning a life, while I was working on the plan for ending mine. I got back on the interstate, averaged seventy-five miles an hour all the way into Minneapolis, drove straight to the game.

The team split two games in Minnesota. Mussina won another shutout, but the Orioles lost the second one. I was disappointed, but at least I'd gotten myself onto the road. Until I took off for Minnesota, I wasn't sure I'd carry through with my plan. Always feared this would join so many other ideas left on the cutting room floor. I've never regretted much of what I've done in life, but I do ruminate about opportunities missed. Guess I saw my time watching the Orioles as a last attempt to achieve balance. Making it to Twins Stadium marked an important beginning.

There's no straight line between Minneapolis and Toronto short of finding a surviving voyageur to row across the Great Lakes. Still, the idea of some foreign travel on my circuit appealed to me. Of course, this is English Canada. It'll still be "runs batted in," not "PP" or "points produit," like in Montreal.

Sometimes Mary came along to Toronto. She found plenty to fill her time if she didn't want to spend every hour at the Skydome watching baseball. I vaguely recall her killing one afternoon at a shoe museum. We rode the elevator to the top of the CN Tower, toured the hockey museum, saw the Stanley Cup. Hockey's serious business up here. The Cup gets guarded as closely as the gold in Fort Knox.

I first tried getting tickets here in 1988. A saleswoman told me the Oriole series was sold out. It took two years to get my first seats. That put me onto a priority list, so I bought tickets every year whether I planned to go or not, just to hold my place in line. People benefiting from extra space alongside them owe me some thanks.

Empty seats on both sides right now. Just as well. Climbing to the upper deck left me a bit breathless. I'd come early to watch batting practice, but I was also tired of hanging around the hotel. Everyone in the Royal York lobby seemed to be part of a group, or at least paired off– with spouses, lovers, whatever. Biggest display of public affection emanated from a lesbian couple off in a corner. I assumed I stood out being so obviously by myself.

Maybe staying at the Royal York hadn't been such a good idea. I loved its ambience, the imposing facade, the elegant public spaces, its proximity to the ball park. But it was a place for celebration, like weddings or special vacations. Or for the trappings of commerce, where big business deals would go down. Its

[11]

enormity was too cavernous for someone alone. I didn't need anything to make me feel more insignificant.

I glanced around the stadium, trying to estimate the size of the crowd coming in. The temperature was comfortable, just a minimal breeze that carried the smells of peanuts and beer back from the row in front of me. Watched the outfielders toss the ball back and forth while batters made their swings in the portable cage on the field. Nothing in their actions signaled any urgency. Just men going to work and making their living. No way could they know what the game might mean to one fan in the upper deck.

Thousands of people would soon fill in the space around me. But that wouldn't leave me any less alone.

The original diagnosis six months earlier barely caused me to break stride. I went through denial, anger, and bargaining to acceptance pretty quickly. After all, lymphoma could be cured. Or at least well controlled.

I didn't plan to miss much work. Spent a week in Nova Scotia, where the coastal breezes of Cape Breton boosted my spirits. All that fiddle music might have been therapeutic, too. I welcomed any immunologic enhancement that an improved attitude might bring. Then I returned home for round one of chemotherapy.

I'd briefly pondered going to Boston or the Mayo Clinic. Balancing the benefits of anonymity against the downside of impersonality, I decided if my home town had been good enough to live and practice in, it would be good enough to be treated in. At that point, it hadn't crossed my mind that also meant being good enough to die in.

The hospital staff was solicitous of my welfare. Everyone displayed consummate professionalism. It couldn't be easy. Usually they were taking my orders, or calling me for advice, or stopping to tell me about a new restaurant, or bragging about a kid's high school science project.

I worked hard at being a good patient. Endured extra needle sticks from the new phlebotomists, remained calm while nurses looked frantically for tape to secure intravenous needle sites, honed my skills at delivering pat responses to well-wishers. Kidded around with the x-ray techs who ushered me into the MRI tunnel. I grew to hate that machine, the way it isolated you from your environment. Once on a train, I told a conductor it was too bad we were going through a particularly famous tunnel at night. He retorted "tunnels are just as dark in the daytime." MRI's probably are, too.

For three months I adhered religiously to every order, never voiced the mildest complaint, displayed my optimistic outlook like a merit badge. I ignored the nausea, dealt with the fevers, faithfully drank the nutritional concoctions. When they sent me for the newest-and-greatest spiral CT scan, I joked how its cavity couldn't match those spiral tunnels that trains traverse in the Canadian Rockies. I was the poster boy for dealing with a bad disease.

Maybe that's why the recurrence caught me so off guard.

I was glad the Orioles had a four game series in Toronto. After the trip to Minnesota, then another long drive only two days later, I felt ready to put down some roots, even tenuous ones. It was already clear there was nothing romantic about long stretches of interstate.

I asked the guy next to me if he was from Toronto.

"No, I'm up from Baltimore," he said. Only then did I notice his Oriole T-shirt. "Most of us in this section are from Baltimore."

"I'm impressed the Blue Jays save good seats for out-of-towners," I offered.

"Yeah," he continued, "I sell auto parts down there. Go to all the games I can."

"Season tickets?" I asked.

"A partial package," he said. "Figure if I have tickets to thirty games, I can trade on nights I can't go."

I never bought season tickets myself. Rationalized my work schedule wouldn't permit it. As if mortality rates in the county would have soared if I stopped seeing patients earlier and caught a few extra games.

We stopped talking as the beer vendor made his first run. Not always sure if I dare have alcohol, but that night I felt pretty good. What the hell? Hotel's only a one-block walk.

He picked up where he left off. "You know, when you're there game after game you come away with a different view of those guys."

That made me wonder. "You mean who hustles, who can't

[13]

lay off a high fast ball, and all that?"

"Hey, this one's on me," he exclaimed, sending a ten-dollar bill down the row, meeting the beers from the other direction about halfway. "Well, you get that. But you get a lot from how they behave before and after the game."

I must have looked puzzled.

"Yeah, how they treat the fans and all. I mean, Cal, he kind of keeps to himself. You can see that. No way he can go near the stands without being mobbed. But all of them need to give the fans a break." He paused to pocket the change. "Like Devereaux. There's a good guy. Feel bad he's been in such a slump. He takes time with every kid that comes near him. Signs autographs, talks a little, makes them feel good they came to a game."

"I like to assume most of them are like that," I said.

"You'd be surprised," my new friend continued. "Some look good on television, but when they're not on camera, they won't give you the time of day. That's what I mean. When you're there a lot, you see a whole new side of some guys."

We stood for the "Star Spangled Banner." And for "O Canada." Two anthems when you play north of the border.

Life felt a little better. Pleasant evening. Good pitcher on the mound. A Baltimore fan in the next seat. This game would do more for me than tonight's sleeping pill.

Except that on the field, the Orioles floundered. Team had scored eight runs last night but lost. Tonight proved equally frustrating. Tied 2-2, in the eighth, Fernando Valenzuela was giving his best effort of the young season. Todd Frohwirth came in to lose it, 3-2, in the ninth.

Next morning I slept late, then went downstairs for breakfast. Plenty of time on my hands before that night's game. I wasn't in the mood for a museum, so I drove over to Fort York and walked around. American soldiers attacked the British there during the War of 1812. As they retreated, the British blew up the powder magazine, killing a host of American soldiers. Including their leader, Zebulon Pike. I'd known about Pike's Peak in Colorado. Guess now I sort of knew about Pike's nadir.

I'm sure Pike expected to accomplish a lot more before he died. Who doesn't? Is it better to have life end so quickly and

[14]

unexpectedly, as opposed to getting clues months or even years in advance? Was my own nadir going to be a long plateau rather than a split second? Might there be occasional upswings? If not peaks, at least moments of satisfaction or accomplishment? Am I being unfair in not putting all my training and experience to use here and there? If it doesn't matter to me, does it matter to anyone else?

Baseball took my mind off such ambivalence. The Orioles took the next two to split the four-game series. With those wins, they escaped the American League East cellar. It's nice at least being out of last place. Lets me conclude things are going in the right direction.

I decided to leave my car in Toronto and fly back to Baltimore for the next series. That gave me another night at the Royal York, where I treated myself to a room service dinner and savored the two victories. The extra night let me feel I was on vacation, rather than on evasion.

The following morning, I crammed my suitcase with plastic hotel laundry bags full of dirty clothes, left a few clean things in the trunk, tossed the accumulated coffee cups and newspapers. Amazing how much room that left in the back seat.

Back in Baltimore, the Orioles beat the Red Sox 2-1 on a sacrifice fly by Mark Leonard. Brad Pennington got his first major league save. Who in the world are these guys? I spent years studying this team, yet so many names were now unfamiliar.

I lounged on the sofa, reading the newspaper before the next game. A quick glance around the room showed the usual amount of disarray. A few coffee cups waiting to be washed, a small stack of books on the low table, two weeks worth of newspaper inserts to toss, a couple of dirty shirts on the floor. Everything pointed to the space being inhabited by a single male.

From the newspaper, I learned there were three bank robberies in the city the previous day. That's 44 for the year. On pace to break the record of 96 heists, set in 1980. Later on, as I left the park after the team got shut out by Roger Clemens, it would occur to me the bank robbers are having a better year than the O's. Someone should set up video cameras around town and make that into a spectator sport. Give fans something to follow after they give up on baseball.

As I sipped coffee from my Oriole mug next morning, I read about a guy visiting his wife's grave with his eight-year-old son; he got hit by lightning and died on the spot. Over in Bowie, someone found a piranha in a pond. The Orioles weren't the only ones around Baltimore having bad seasons.

On the other hand, Mr. Rogers would give the commencement address that weekend at Goucher. Everyone will leave college thinking it's going to be a good day in the neighborhood. Wonder what he might have thought about my plan to follow the Orioles.

I flew back to Toronto, picked up my car, and prepared to retrace my previous route to Detroit. The Toyota had picked up the oily smell of the indoor parking garage. I might have done better leaving it outdoors, and praying it wouldn't be stolen. Once outside the city, I pulled off to fill up with gas. The back right tire looked a little soft. I found my gauge in the glove compartment; and went out to measure. Three of the four were low on air. Here I am battling death on the highways of North America and I have to waste time inflating tires.

The route was straightforward, but I refolded the map and left it handy on the passenger seat. Without mountains or other topographic features to break up the view, there was a monotony to the ride. Long and boring horizons, a surfeit of annoying commercials on the car radio, no thoughts but my own to break up the ennui. Maybe this idea of being alone wasn't such a good one. I'd read an article a few months earlier on the adverse effects of solitary confinement on prisoners. Would I be subject to the same ill effects from spending so much time isolated in my Toyota?

Three days in Detroit offered little relief. Team dropped the first two games before salvaging the final one. As I drove east, I reflected on the Orioles. The team's outlook was better than a few weeks ago. But we weren't scoring any runs. Any team whose main offensive weapon is the sacrifice fly needs airtight pitching and flawless defense. Neither happened to be the case. If the team's going to win only one out of every three, it's going to be a long season. Whether I make it to the end myself or not.

It was nice getting back to Baltimore, at least until Oriole castoff Jose Mesa came into town with Cleveland and shut out his former teammates. I wondered, do players cut loose by the O's get better when moving to teams with more ability, or can this coaching staff simply not evaluate talent? Maybe it's as hard to determine who's a really good ballplayer as it is to figure out who's a good doctor. Looking in the yellow pages doesn't cut it.

Rain halted the next game prematurely, letting Valenzuela win a shutout. Then Sutcliffe won despite tiring in the eighth. The team brought up some new pitcher named Jamie Moyer. Not just another retread from the minor leagues, I hoped. Gave up three runs in his first start, one in the next. This being the Orioles, it left him with an 0-2 record.

Back at the condo I opened the *Sun* to find a local lawyer is assembling a group of investors to buy the Orioles. At least he's from Baltimore. It'd be just my luck to have someone move the team to someplace like Oklahoma City days before I die. Another article noted volunteers for drug studies were getting paid good money. There's an idea. Put a volunteer on retainer to try chemotherapy drugs before they're used on me, just as monarchs of old had their food tasted by servants to assure they weren't being poisoned.

The team split the first two against Milwaukee at home. In the final contest of the three-game series, Orioles made five errors and lost 9-1

My friend Sid had warned I didn't realize how bad the team was this year. "As miserable as they look on paper, as inept as they sound on the radio, wait till you see them in the flesh. No spark on the field, no fervor in the stadium." Only April, and fans were deeming them losers.

It was on to New York, to face the Yankees. *Baltimore Sun* reported reopening of the Reptile House at the zoo after extensive renovation. Perhaps I should have stayed in Baltimore with the serpents rather than risk the agony of defeat in New York. But that wouldn't be fair. The team on the field might not notice my absence, but I'd know. And at this point, keeping promises to myself was all that mattered.

[17]

Even for fans of opposing teams, it's awe-inspiring to be in Yankee Stadium. A century of baseball history swirls around this place. It doesn't matter who you root for, you know about Babe Ruth's slugging heroics, Lou Gehrig's emotional efforts, Joe DiMaggio's hitting streak. Had there not been the Yankees and this stadium, there might not be baseball as we know it.

You look at the vast outfield pasture, with those monuments out in center field to Ruth, Gehrig, and Manager Miller Huggins. Other teams' players haven't merited such memorials. Only the Yankees reign bigger than life. Whatever it took to win, this team always seemed to have it. Only Yankees come back and haunt you from the grave. Maybe I'll meet some of them in the afterlife and learn their secrets for success. I'll have time, since apparently I'll be arriving sooner than I'd originally planned.

Orioles won three of the four games, the lone loss being Moyer's 1-0 affair. New Yorkers are never good losers. After a Ripken homer clinched an Olson-saved 8-6 victory, next morning's *New York Times* read— "For Yanks, a bit of everything, except a victory." When Ripken's base hit sparked a five-run eighth inning rally, the sports reporters cited a misplay on the part of the Yankee left fielder. Next night, Mike Devereaux looped a game winner into left field for a tenth-inning win. Sports pages argued the Yankees had the third strike on the previous pitch. Clenched my fists as I read. It just pissed me off. Damned New York writers always assume their teams are so perfect; anything that doesn't work out has to be someone else's fault.

I made the mistake of scanning the *Daily News* and the *Post*. Drive-by shooting of twelve in Baltimore. Another series of shootings in Washington. The usual New York City crime list— three taxi drivers shot in 24 hours; Bronx bar owner robbed and killed; 17-year-old Nigerian immigrant stabbed to death when his basketball rolls onto the neighboring court. It's not only urban society. Two college students were shot after stopping for teenaged girls who flagged them down in an upstate New York county. The malaise has spread to rural America as well.

Was I lucky I just had a lymphoma? My violence was merely on the cellular level.

I checked out of my hotel room and grabbed a cab to JFK. California, here I come.

[18]

For the first time, doubt set in. Maybe it was the loneliness I felt on the West Coast. Especially in Los Angeles. I didn't know anybody. No places to walk around. Too much concrete. Highways, parking lots, stark buildings. New cities once challenged me. I could have visited Hollywood, looked for the La Brea tar pits, checked out the original Disneyland. Instead my time went to motels, quick meals, ball games. And cabs. Cabs to the ball park. Cabs back to the hotel. Cabs to restaurants when I didn't want room service. Cab drivers were about the only people I talked to.

I began thinking I should have stayed in New York. Maybe gone up to the Adirondacks for some clean air and a bit of rejuvenation. Let nature and wilderness replenish my spirit. Show that even in the face of illness, I wouldn't submit to the subjugation of neurasthenia, the defeat under the weight of brain fatigue, the capitulation to stress.

Everything on the springtime mountains and in the forests used to thrill me. The budding out of spruce and fir; clusters of purple violets; the occasional pink-edged trillium. Blossoms on ancient gnarled apple trees signifying the onetime presence of long forgotten farmhouses. Sounds of pileated woodpeckers turning bug-ridden trees into excavation sites. Visions of ducks and herons flying overhead. Chevrons of geese returning north. With my suddenly rose-colored glasses, I forgot about the mud and the torment of black flies.

Too late. I was already in California. Besides, a promise is a promise, even if only to myself. I'd broken enough pledges over the years. I may as well keep my final one.

It didn't help my mood that the Orioles lost all three games to the Angels.

Oakland proved more tolerable, if only for its proximity to San Francisco. I rode cable cars, carefully clinging to the side when we edged uncomfortably close to traffic. At the Cable Car Barn I saw the ingenious mix of wire ropes, gears, and motors powering these trolleys up and down the city's hills. A steep walk along Mason Street convinced me they needed them. Horse-drawn carriages couldn't have made such ascents– not to mention all the manure.

I climbed Coit Tower on Telegraph Hill. From the

[19]

observation area 180 feet above the ground, I saw harbors and piers, the downtown skyline, and the Bay Bridge. Depression-era murals decorated the interior– agricultural and industrial scenes, railroads, urban life complete with an auto accident and a robbery, library with one man reaching for a book on Marxist theory.

Chinatown offered its cacophony of languages and dialects. I learned how the Chinese came for the gold rush, then stayed to build railroads. Roots and herbs in store windows exceeded my powers of identification. Upon my asking, a man identified a spiky, football-shaped fruit as durian– "tastes like heaven but smells like hell," he added. Aromas from open restaurant doors enticed me in for duck curry spooned over jasmine rice.

On Tuesday I took the boat to Alcatraz. The stark, remote prison made my situation look better in comparison. Life imprisonment might be a worse condemnation than death by malignancy. Or was it? I ruminated a bit. Does hope survive better in prison or in the midst of a fatal disease? Likely whichever place you don't find yourself would be better. What's a diagnosis of metastatic tumor if not life without parole? A prisoner at least has a sense of why he ended up there.

The O's won two of three against the Athletics. I boarded a red-eye out of San Francisco International. Like the players, I'd have an off-day to regroup. I wanted to be home.

Suddenly the Orioles began winning. After dropping four of six on the West Coast, the team came home and rolled past Seattle. First three-game series they'd swept all season.

Jack Voigt hit his first major league home run one night, drove in the winning run on another. He told an interviewer, "I'm not a superstar, but I feel I do the job consistently every day." Knows his role, always ready to play. Worthwhile philosophy. If more people thought that way, we'd be a better society.

We won another on two late homers and a wind-blown single by Cal Ripken. Finale was marked by a melee when Mussina hit a Seattle Mariner with a pitch, seemingly in retaliation for an Oriole hit batter. Baseball's version of "an eye for an eye."

The Orioles pushed their streak to seven in a row by beating Oakland. It was enough to make me glad I hadn't died out west.

I considered saving energy– and traffic jams– by taking the

train to Boston. But that would just slow me down (or would it slow me up?) trying to get to Milwaukee for the following series. Besides, a rail trip up the eastern corridor would show off decaying sections of once wealthy and vibrant cities. If I wanted to see decay, all I needed to do was jump on the scale or look at the new hole I'd punched into my belt.

Orioles sailed through the first two games in Boston, Moyer and Mussina both winning. Team was still mired in fourth place, but a nine-game winning streak gave reason for optimism. Optimism seemed to be my basic fuel, replacing ATP in providing energy to fading cells.

Game three was an afternoon one. I slept until ten, grabbed coffee and a bagel, got to Fenway well in advance of the one o'clock start. I watched batting practice, read a *Sporting News* I picked up at the hotel newsstand, wrote down starting line-ups in the scorecard as they were announced, wondered if I dare hope for the winning streak to hit double figures.

"Hey, you look sick, man!"

And nice meeting you, too, I wanted to say in response to the man in the next seat. Black guy, maybe in his fifties, keeping his own score, clearly into the game at Fenway Park. "No, really, you okay, man?"

I swallowed down the fatigue and breathlessness. "Yeah, I'm okay. Just under the weather. Too tough getting tickets for this series. Feel like I better use them."

"Know what you mean," he said. "Where you from?"

Safe to say this in enemy territory? "Baltimore."

"You're brave coming to Fenway. Of course, it's not like you're from New York." He laughed. "Hey, your team's playing pretty well these days."

"Yeah, bunch of untested players still trying to jell into a team," I answered. "Pitching needs to hold up."

He continued. "Baseball's more fun when your team has lots of young players. Kids who aren't used to all the money and hype yet. Kids who play the game like their lives depend on it."

Like my life depended on it.

"Can't argue with you there," I responded. "Wasn't it Sparky Anderson who said they play harder when they're driving

[21]

Fords than when they're driving Cadillacs?"

"Hey, lemme tell you." He vaguely pointed at the outfield as he talked. "I played ball a few years. In the Cardinal system. We had a great time. Might have been Single A, but we played like every game was the World Series. Only a couple of teammates ever made it to the majors, but if desire were the key, they'd all be there." He stopped for a swig of beer. "By the way, Joe Gibbons," offering a handshake.

"Dan Jameson," I managed, my fingers aching a little from his strong grip. "What happened to you? Did you get to the show?"

"Nah," he laughed. "Not enough talent. I banged up my knee before I packed it in, so I get to say that's what kept me down. But I never had more fun in my life than those three years playing pro ball." He was heavyset, probably had gained a few pounds since his baseball days. His arms were still muscular, looked like he could drive the ball a long way.

Red Sox down without a score again in the seventh.

We ducked as a foul ball came our way. "So what do you do now?" I asked.

"Oh, I'd finished three years of college before turning pro," Joe answered. "So I went back to school. I'm teaching science in Roxbury. Decided to teach high school partly so I could coach. They make me help with football in the fall, but that's a fair trade for letting me run baseball in the spring."

"Ever think of coaching or something in the pros?"

"No, not really." He offered me peanuts." "If I could be at the top, I'd probably jump at it. I mean, who'd be able to pass up that chance? But otherwise I'm not up for all the travel. You got to be younger to ride those buses and eat all your meals at the fast food places."

This was a good guy to meet right now. He knew the game, undoubtedly better than I did. Paid attention to the action on the field. Understood I wanted to pay attention, too. Neither of us missed a pitch during our conversation; both scorecards filled in at the same rate.

"Hey," he said, as he pointed to a square on my card, "He struck out swinging."

I looked up at him. "Yeah, I saw it."

He took another swig of his beer then turned back to me.

[22]

"Then why the backwards K?"

I shook my head and laughed. "Everybody asks that. Don't ask me why, but when I learned to score, somehow I got taught, or convinced myself, that a regular K means called out, the backwards one means stuck out swinging."

"Well, that's wrong!" He took a swig from his cup. "Still time to get it right."

He was using a mechanical pencil. Hadn't seen one of those in years; didn't know they were still made. "Guess I've done it so long it's a tough habit to break. Plus I've still got most of my scorecards from over the years. This way at least I know what I meant. If I fix it, how will I remember if the game's from my old system or the new one?"

"I can't say as I go back to look at many old scorecards." He was raising his hand to signal a vendor for another beer. "But I guess if you were to die tomorrow without letting anyone know your secret, someone might compare your cards with the record and think you didn't know how to score!"

"We all take risks, I guess." I shook my head to decline his offer of a beer. "A reputation as a bad scorer isn't my biggest fear."

By the ninth, the Red Sox trailed by four. Brad Pennington held on to win. Ten in a row for the Orioles. Divine recognition for my persistence in following the team to my dying day?

Joe asked if I'd to be in town another night. "I've got two tickets for tomorrow afternoon. My wife hates baseball. Want to join me?"

I had planned to leave and get a jump on the trip to Milwaukee for Monday's game. But I'm not turning down an offer to watch a game with another true fan. Even if he roots for the opposition. "Sure, if you really don't have someone else to bring."

"Nah, I'd rather be able to talk baseball the whole time," he said. "Plus you're an Oriole fan. I can work on correcting some of the misconceptions you've got."

"Don't take this wrong," I reminded, "but isn't it the Red Sox who haven't won the Series since forever?"

"Our day will come," he said. "God knows we're a patient breed up here. We're waiting for the Second Coming of Ted Williams."

We set a meeting place. Just before melding into the exiting crowd, he called out. "Hey, hope you feel better!" I walked slowly. No need to hurry. With luck, I'd be back in Boston in September, but still best to see the extra game now. Should I have warned him that any game might be my last? Told him not to wait long if I didn't show up on time?

O's lost that last game in Boston. I guess it's unfair to complain after winning ten in a row. Roger Clemens beat us. He'll be in the Hall of Fame someday. It's nice being able to claim I saw him pitch.

Trip to Milwaukee was long. Long and boring. After the Lord gave mankind the mountains and the seashore, He (She?) must have called in some chits and forced Interstate 90 on them in return. Following the Thruway across New York, I felt time passing more slowly than the mules must have felt pulling boats along the Erie Canal their fifteen miles a day.

I hit Cleveland Sunday night. Got up early, veered back onto I-90. Only when stopping for lunch near the Indiana border was I confident I'd make the first pitch.

Highway driving was already tedious. Radio didn't help. Stations played the same songs over and over. The remaining coffee in my Styrofoam cup went cold. An occasional concealed police car helped keep me alert. So did being passed by the same tractor trailer– cows painted on its side– that I'd seen stopped along the side of the road several miles back. I blinked my lights to acknowledge his need to move back into my lane.

I brooded too much on the way from Boston to Milwaukee. About projects I'd wanted to complete in practice, like the larger free clinic the city needed, or the *Medicine 101* course I thought we could offer the public. Why my marriage broke up. Whether I should have given treatment one last go. Maybe I should be flying on these trips. Then fears of plane crashes could keep my mind off interior demons.

An explosive fifth inning pulled us from behind in Milwaukee, ending the one-game losing streak. The ten game winning streak energized me, but it's also important to win again quickly after such a string ends. I'm finally rooting for a team that's won more games than it's lost this season. As someone said, winning

[24]

may not be everything, but it beats the alternative.

I calculated about five hundred miles from Milwaukee to Cleveland. Open date today, no game till tomorrow night. No time pressure, so I wandered back roads. Passed blue Harvestore silos alongside weathered barns. Slowed down to read Burma Shave signs. Late morning I found myself outside a small Wisconsin town named Ladysmith. Stopped at an old family restaurant, the kind that filled American roads before interstates imposed their homogeneity upon society.

I tried making conversation with the waitress. "So what do people do around here?"

"There's nothing to do. So we don't do nothing." She placed a Pepsi in front of me.

"Did you grow up here?"

She reached into her apron pocket and pulled out a straw. Not the slightest eye contact. "Wouldn't be here if I hadn't, I can tell you that."

When she brought my cheeseburger I ventured one last question. "So how'd Ladysmith get its name?"

She stopped and stared at me. Shrugged her shoulders. Who could care, her demeanor told me. She'd be no happier elsewhere. Yet I'm the one who's dying.

I pulled into the gas station across from the diner, filled up, went inside to pay. I bought Diet Cokes for the road, plus this week's *Sporting News*. I popped open a can, then pulled out my coffee-stained map and spread it over the steering wheel. It was beginning to tear from the frequent folding and refolding.

I'd diverged so much from the tentative route I'd inked out with a black Magic Marker that I was further from Cleveland now than when I started this morning. Would be an hour getting back to Milwaukee. Then 450 miles to Cleveland. Good thing next game isn't until tomorrow night.

A tractor trailer, its diesel fumes giving advance notice, edged into the station. I turned the ignition key. The Toyota engine turned over smoothly. As I began folding up the map, some Coke spilled onto it. I fumbled for a piece of Kleenex to clean it up.

At first I didn't notice the girl leaning against the passenger side window. She tapped on the glass. I pushed the button, and the window slid down.

"Hey, mister. Willing to give a girl a ride?"

PART TWO

June 17, 1993

I don't know why I rolled the window down. Maybe I'd
tired of the long lonely roads between Wisconsin towns. I'd gassed
up, checked the oil, rubbed the bird droppings off the windshield,
unfolded the map, and she suddenly appeared.

She looked wholesome enough. About my height, medium
length stringy blond hair in need of combing. Loose red
windbreaker over a t-shirt, tapered jeans, worn-out Nikes. Your
typical girl next door home from college? An isolated farm girl star-
struck by MTV, anxious to see the world? If she tried selling me
magazines, I might not have been surprised. Nor would it be a shock
if she'd simply broken up with a boyfriend and wanted to leave
town.

"Jeez, I thought no one would ever give me a ride out of
here. Thanks a lot." She put out her hand. "Hey, I'm Janice."

"Hi! I'm Dan. You want to put some of that in the trunk?"

"No," she said. "It'll be fine in the back seat. As long as you
don't care."

I shrugged my shoulders. "Fine with me."

She tossed her backpack into the Toyota. It blended nicely
with the sweatshirts, dirty jeans, and miscellaneous laundry already
there. Threw a small black suitcase farther back into the Camry. I
envisioned her using one while playing hippie, the other when she
went off for some job interview. She jumped into the front seat,
fastened her seatbelt, and turned toward me.

"Okay, guess I'm all set," she announced. "Hey, thanks
again."

I put the car in gear, slung back onto the road, quickly pushed
the speedometer up to fifty-five. "So where are you headed,
anyhow?"

"I'm trying to go to Philadelphia," she said. "But I'd be
thrilled to get past Chicago."

"I can do that," I told her. I'm headed on to Cleveland. That
should be a decent chunk of your trip."

She looked over and smiled. "God, that'll be great.
Anything to be that far in the right direction. You just can't believe

how hard it's been to get a ride. Everybody talks about how friendly Midwesterners are, but no one'll stop for a hitchhiker. I was starting to think about putting up a sign 'will trade sex for ride east'."

"I guess people don't think the world is that safe anymore. In fact, I'm amazed you're hitchhiking such a long distance." I paused. "I doubt offering sex would make it any safer."

"Safety I can worry about later," she replied. "I just wanted a ride."

I focused on the road while calculating the distance to the interstate. From there, south to I-90, then east on to Cleveland. Having some company for a change, if she didn't turn out to be hiding a knife or have some sort of personality disorder, might prove a pleasant diversion.

Janice put her head back and fell asleep. She woke up when I slowed down for the entrance ramp. Just like my dog always used to do.

"So are you from Cleveland?" she asked.

"No, I'm just stopping there for a few days," I replied.

"What's there? Family?"

"No," I said. "Actually I'm going to a couple of baseball games. Might go see the Rock and Roll Hall of Fame while I'm there, too."

"No kidding! The Rock and Roll Hall of Fame's there?" she asked. "Wouldn't you think it'd be in New York? Or San Francisco? Or some other hip place? I mean, Cleveland?"

I laughed. "Wondered the same thing myself. But guess it has to be somewhere. I think a Cleveland disc jockey was important in the early days. And you can be sure money has something to do with it. It always does."

Janice asked if she could turn on the radio. She searched for a rock station, lowered the volume, then reached over the seat for her backpack and pulled out a book. I stole a sideways glance; it was something called *The Sweet Hereafter*.

"What's that about?" I ventured.

"I'm not that far into it," she answered. "It's about a school bus crash in some small mountain town. So far it's been from the perspective of the bus driver, who's a woman, and some lawyer who comes up to see if there's a lawsuit to be had. A friend

[28]

recommended it."

"Any good?" I asked.

"Yeah, so far," she said. "Can you imagine how devastating something like that can be in a small town? In a big city, it might not even make the newspapers. But in some tiny burg, it'd be a front page story for weeks."

That's the way I used to think. Find the personal dimension in any event. Ponder how many others would be impacted by one person's decision or action. Move my brain in and out like an accordion, between individualizing and globalizing the significance of a happening.

When I was married, Mary did the driving. I played navigator and read the maps. It was a perfect job distribution. Driving kept me from looking around and from taking notes. Mary couldn't have figured out how to get from point A to point B even if the route was all interstate.

Janice stretched her arms, let out a sigh. She fiddled in her seat, undid her seat belt and took off the windbreaker, then rebuckled. "You know, why don't you let me pay for gas next time you have to fill up? It's the least I can do for your giving me a ride."

"No," I said "you're not costing me anything. Don't worry about it."

"Well, at least let me buy dinner when we stop."

I wondered again why I'd picked her up. But so far she wasn't a compulsive talker or a serial killer.

We sat in one of six booths at the Highway Diner just outside Valparaiso. She found it quaint that I had chosen a local dive over McDonald's. "How do you know they won't poison you? Some of these places aren't that clean."

"Let me get this straight," I said. "You're thinking about offering sex to the first guy who stops to pick you up on the highway, but you worry about getting salmonella from a hamburger?"

She laughed as she opened the stained, plastic-covered menu. "Okay. But screwing doesn't scare me as much as food poisoning does. At least you can't die from it. "

"Do I take it, then, that you've never heard of AIDS?"

Janice flipped a few strands of hair that had dropped over her eyes. "Do I take it you've never heard of condoms?"

"I see you drink your share of coffee," Janice remarked after we were back in the car.

"Huh?"

"Well, have you seen the floor in back recently?" she asked. "I think from here I can see half a dozen empty cups."

"Bad habit," I said. "Maybe two bad habits. The caffeine and the housekeeping."

After all the time with big crowds in ballparks, it wasn't unpleasant being with one person. Instead of being alone amidst many. I'd established a few things. Her name was Janice. ("Not Jan. Janice.") She came from a rural western New York town I'd never heard of, majored in English at a college in New England, and had no firm strategy for the rest of her life.

We both voted for Bill Clinton over George Bush, agreed we wanted a leader who understood how everyone didn't grow up wealthy, and that poverty couldn't be equated with original sin. She'd worked in a restaurant near her hometown last winter, then went to stay with a friend in Colorado. That didn't turn out as satisfying as she'd hoped, so she was, as she put it, "Back to square one." Lacking any definite plans, she had picked a roundabout route home.

"So what's in Philadelphia?" I asked. "Since it's not your hometown. A job?"

"I'm going to Philadelphia to visit a friend," she answered.

"I'd take you there myself if I were heading straight east." I pushed my memory to recall what came next after the series against the Indians.

My forehead must have wrinkled with the effort to concentrate. She interrupted my train of thought. "What's on your mind?"

"Oh, nothing really," I said. "I was just thinking that if you had something to do in Cleveland for a couple of days, I might be able to take you the rest of the way."

Soon after checking into the Radisson Plaza, I began thinking about Janice. Maybe I missed interpersonal contact more than I admitted. I wondered where she was in Cleveland, or, for that

[30]

matter, whether she had stayed here at all. I'd dropped her at the bus station, promising to pick her up nine o'clock Monday morning. The place looked pretty creepy. I might have bought a ticket for the next bus anywhere, just to get out of there.

First day went by in a blur. I wandered the old harbor. Construction on the Rock and Roll Hall of Fame had started, but it was far from ready. Like Janice; I didn't quite see why Cleveland got to be the place for such a cultural statement. Unless only Cleveland has backers willing to bankroll it.

I suppose rock-and-roll will be my generation's major gift to society. We all expected to change the world, eliminate poverty, bring racial reform. Instead, we'll leave the heritage of the long, loud guitar solo, along with Jimi Hendrix singing "The Star Spangled Banner" at Woodstock, Alvin Lee or Jimmy Page coaxing maximum decibel levels out of their instruments, Paul McCartney saying "I want to hold your hand," and Mick Jagger belting out "you can't always get what you want."

I settled into my seat at the ball park. Upper reserved, not crowded, no corner of the park that I couldn't see decently. Ben McDonald threw well. O's won the first game 4-1.

We got shut out the next afternoon. It was a tough one to lose. Just couldn't get a hit when we needed it. Hard to beat good pitching, though Valenzuela pitched well, too. It felt like the Orioles of the fifties. I could count on stellar defense and good pitching, always keeping a game close. But in the final analysis, you win by scoring runs.

Back within the sterility of the hotel room, a wave of loneliness engulfed me. I felt tired. Not particularly sick. Just empty. Maybe I should have invited Janice to a game.

I rode the elevator down to the lobby. Two men were already in it, dressed casually with black windbreakers and jeans. They looked vaguely familiar.

"You play for the Orioles?" I ventured.

One looked down. Not as though dejected from a loss. Just uninterested in conversation. The other said, "Yeah."

A bit more silence. One forgets how long it takes to descend twenty-two floors.

He put out his hand. "Mike Devereaux."

We shook hands. Once upon a time, I'd have sought an autograph. I didn't refrain out of courtesy. If I thought I might live forever, I'd have asked in an instant.

"Tough one to lose," I offered.

Doors opened to the ground floor just as he replied, "Yeah. All of them are. We'll get 'em back when we get home." A pause. "Nice to meet you."

They exited first. I never got introduced to the other guy.

And it suddenly hit me. The fleet outfielder had certainly been cordial enough, but he didn't show the emotional letdown I felt in losing.

The Orioles toil in the midst of a pennant race. Their ultimate goal is the World Series. The same goal with which every ballplayer at every level begins. A goal for which I might have traded any number of accomplishments in my life.

But I've spent more years of my life waiting– hoping, praying– for the Baltimore uniform to be donned in the postseason than Mike Devereaux has. For me, it's been a lifelong emotional drive. And emotional drain.

To him it's not a matter of survival. Or a challenge to his ability to provide for a family. He's a professional. Even the best teams lose sixty or more times a season. He has to put aside the emotional ups and downs, then get on with the next game. Much the same as a doctor must be prepared, after leaving the room of a dying patient, to go and see the next person.

The realization set in that to them it's simply a job. A business. A livelihood. Not life and death. These players might not even be on the same team next season. They aren't family members with reasons for long service and loyalty. They don't sit up at night worrying about the team year after year like I do. They're entertainers, highly skilled and competitive ones, paid to do a job– to win, but also to entertain, to entertain even when losing. Expected to give their best every day, just as we all are, but no huge obligation beyond that. If the team fails in the pennant race, they can try again next year.

In the final analysis, there's nothing wrong with that. In fact, it's admirable. But I can't count on waking up the next day – or the next season – to try again. Which is my problem, not theirs.

I strolled the lobby, trying to decide whether to eat here or hit

[32]

the streets of Cleveland. Devereaux caught my eye. He gave a quick wave. Nice guy, I thought. Glad he's an Oriole.

O's took two out of three in Cleveland. Valenzuela lost the middle one. McDonald won the first and Moyer the finale, the former throwing as hard as usual, the latter as slowly as humanly possible without letting gravity pull the ball down to the ground. Moyer turned out to be a good pickup. His record was three and three; he hadn't pitched badly in any game.

Heading to meet Janice, I felt like a pilot returning for a camper dropped off at a remote Adirondack lake, wondering if he'll be there at the appointed time. I felt a mix of surprise and pleasure when she appeared at the bus station as planned. She threw her stuff in the back, greeted me as though I was an old friend, then asked if we could take a scenic route instead of the interstate. I pulled out the maps, and we planned our escape from Ohio.

Janice opened the conversation. "So did your team win?"

"Well, two of three." The car had a stale odor. Even though it wasn't hot, I turned on the air conditioner.

"Good games?" she continued.

"Yeah, not bad," I said.

"What makes a good game?" she asked.

Reasonable question. Most fans would say lots of home runs, lots of scoring. I still savor the low-scoring ones. Where the result can turn on every play, every pitch. "I guess having it be close counts a lot," I said. "But in the final analysis, a good game to me is one my team wins."

"So any time they lose, it's a bad game?" Janice concluded.

"To a certain degree, yes. There's something to say for a well-played game, close score, good individual performances. But I can overlook errors and all more easily when they win."

"So when your team isn't very good, do you stop going to games?" she asked.

"Lots of fans sure do." I paused to concentrate on passing a slow moving truck. "But a real fan doesn't. Remember, fan is short for fanatic. That says something about the behavior. There aren't many things I get as caught up in as I do a ball game."

We stopped for lunch in a place called Zoar. Afterwards we walked around. Her legs were long for someone her height; I found it an effort to keep up. We learned Zoar had been some kind of utopian experiment. I must have slept through class the morning they covered that in school. Driving on, we reached Harper's Ferry and learned about John Brown's raid on the armory in 1859, his capture, his subsequent hanging. I surprised Janice with the information his body lies a-moldering in the rural Adirondacks of northern New York.

"Wouldn't you think someone that famous would have ended up buried in some bigger city or something?" Janice observed.

"Maybe back then," I suggested, "they were happy to have him sent back to as remote a place as possible. Anyhow, that's where he was living before he went to Harper's Ferry."

Janice continued, "It makes you wonder where you'll finally end up yourself."

No way she could know the chord she hit. Where would I finally be a-moldering? I might want to begin considering that.

It didn't seem to bother her when I pointed out we'd never make it to Philadelphia that day. "We might have to stay overnight in West Virginia."

"Sure. Okay. Whatever!"

A stranger whom she barely knows announces we're spending the night in an unfamiliar area, and no reaction? I made clear I'd pay for her motel room. Might not be many more opportunities ahead for gallantry. Besides, I couldn't expect her to have extra money to throw away. Wonder what she'd have done if I hadn't so clearly shown my intention to foot the cost.

That night, I pondered the beautiful panorama over the Potomac and Shenandoah Rivers. In contrast, my motel room had frayed chenille bed covers and leaky faucets. Air conditioner was broken. The TV had few channels to choose from; all sent snowy images to the screen. Depressing enough that I found myself thinking about dying. I mulled over jumping from one of the high trestles, just getting the whole thing over with. Then I thought about Zoar and John Brown, and the idealism that both embodied. How some people are driven with such intensity, they're willing to make any sacrifice along the way. More sacrifice than I'd be willing to swallow. Death by hanging couldn't have been a pleasant way to go.

I wondered how it must feel to have such a focused view of life. Then I thought about how much more there was to learn about the world.   How I yearned to see Machu Picchu, the Pyramids, Paris.   Eat kangaroo, cuttlefish, scrapple.   Maybe train a falcon, drive a dogsled.

For the first time since my recurrence, I cried.

I awoke next morning to the sensation of nausea.   Couldn't face greasy eggs and bacon at Denny's, so I held out for a pancake house on a secondary road.   For some reason I figured fake maple syrup would sit gently on my stomach.

The waitress quickly identified us as strangers to the area. "So where you guys from?"

"Oh, I live in Baltimore," I said.

"Hey, I lived there once," she said.   "My father worked for Bethlehem Steel.   Too dirty for me.   Couldn't wait to move out."

"And I'm from nowhere in particular," I heard Janice break in.   "I was hanging around Wisconsin until he picked me up and brought me out here.   It's pretty in these parts."

"Oh, you'll like it if you hang around here, honey," our waitress offered.   "Everyone's friendly, there's lots of fresh air. Only problem, there's not a lot of places to work."

I listened as though I were a spectator on the ceiling. Glanced up and saw the wooden blades of the fan turning in their inexorable circles.   I felt myself squirming.   Nausea coming back. From the motion, or from Janice's sense of timing?

"So why exactly did you have to break in with your story?" I asked when the waitress left to put in our orders.

Her mouth opened wide in surprise.   "What's wrong?   I told her exactly what happened."

"Do you think we could get to Philadelphia without telling the world our whole story?"

"You know," she countered as she put her cup back on the table a little too forcefully, "we don't have that much of a story. When all else fails, it can't hurt to tell the truth."

"Well," I said, "let's hope she's just over there putting butter on the pancakes, and not calling the police to see if anyone's looking for my car."

"Shit, you have a negative attitude," she said.   "She's probably over there marveling at how this old guy managed to pick up such a good-looking young babe."

[35]

Wrinkled gray t-shirt, hair neatly pulled back in a ponytail, some crusting she hadn't washed out of her eyes, lips held tightly together as if working not to smile. Yes, a fashion plate.

"Maybe we could just assume I'm your father bringing you back from college," I suggested. "Can we leave it at that, if anyone asks? There's only one more state line to cross. Do you mind if we manage to avoid suspicion?"

She glared at me. For a moment I thought she might throw something. "So the life lesson I'm going to take from you is that as long as people don't know you, it's all right to lie?"

When the food came, the sweetness of the syrup brought back my nausea.

"By the way," Janice said, looking me straight in the eye, "my father is dead. He died five years ago."

"I'm sorry."

Her eyes blazed as she answered back. "Why are you sorry? You didn't have anything to do with it."

I put down my fork. "Jesus, I'm just trying to be nice about it."

Our bit of drama concluded, Janice ate heartily. I flashed back to simple pleasures of enjoying a meal. Like fresh maple syrup right from a sugar house at the beginning of spring, tasting it moments after it leaves the evaporator. Or bullheads for breakfast after catching them in a stream going by a campsite. The apple squares we picked up at the bakery every Sunday when I was a kid. I guess that's a marker of life turning in a downward direction. You begin to savor all those small happenings you took for granted over the years.

If someone put a sauteed fish in front of me right then, I would have vomited.

While we waited for the bill, I unfolded a map and plotted strategy. "If it's okay with you, I think I'll drop you in Baltimore. Should be a quick ride into Philly for you."

"Fine with me," she said. "If there's not a bus right away, I can always hitch in."

"Do me a favor and don't hitchhike," I said. "You're not in the Midwest anymore. You don't want to get picked up by a stranger outside a big city."

Janice spoke sternly. "And who are you? Since you're not

[36]

my father bringing me home from college for the summer? I don't really think you've earned the right to tell me what to do."

I took a deep breath, inhaling more gas fumes than I'd have liked. "I'm just worried about what could happen. You do have a place to stay in Philadelphia, don't you?"

Now she sounded offended. "Of course I do. It's not me making up the little white lies."

Saying good-bye felt strangely awkward. What do you say to someone you've known for barely a week, of whom you've grown a bit fond, but that you'll likely never see again? I dropped her at the train station. Told her I'd enjoyed meeting and talking to her. Wished her luck in the future. Reminded her to be careful in the big city.

"Hey, I really appreciate the ride," she said. "And the room and the meals. Thanks a lot. Who knows? Maybe we'll cross paths again someday." Just that quickly, she was off.

Only then did it occur to me I'd never asked how she spent the time in Cleveland while I was going to the ball games.

Oriole bullpen worked hard trying to blow the final game of the Detroit series. Mark Williamson may be a nice guy, but I'd lost faith in him as a pitcher. He gave up a run to make it 4-2, and left two more runners on base to face Brad Pennington. Somehow Pennington got the outs, completing a three-game sweep.

It felt reassuring to be back in Baltimore, in my own place, with a familiar doctor to call if things crashed. For all my desire to be on the road, I found more security than ever in being home. Having my team back in the pennant race improved my perspective on life. Nice being fully absorbed with baseball instead of illness.

I went for a checkup early afternoon. Nothing new. White count okay, hemoglobin not low enough to require transfusion. Talked my way out of more CT scans. No matter what they showed, I wouldn't take treatment. Eric had begun to accept he wouldn't change my mind.

I felt good enough for a pre-game dinner with some former colleagues at Chippiarelli's. Though I worried I might have used up my month's quotient of conversation already, Jim and Sid proved their typical irrepressible selves. By the time our matronly waitress had cleared the remains of our garlic-laden salads and brought the

[37]

spaghetti, both were at full throttle.

"You know, it wouldn't hurt you to come in and work a few days," Sid chided. "There's enough people to see. You might even feel good about helping someone."

"No," I said. "I kind of figure I've earned the right to be selfish. Plus, I hate to give out a return appointment knowing it might be me who can't keep his part of the obligation."

"I'm not sure anyone ever earns the right to be selfish," Jim piped up as he cut into a piece of veal. "It's a society. Everyone owes some participation, no matter what else is going on in life."

I sat back and thought out my answer. "I wish I could still be the dreamer and idealist that you are. That I once was. All I really wanted in life was to be a contributor, to avoid being ordinary, to know I'd made a difference for having been in the world." I spun spaghetti onto my fork. "Guess I burned out too fast. I was tired before I was sick. When I made it back from the marrow transplant, I wanted to start fresh. You know, use it as sort of a religious experience. The born-again feeling that zealots have, or at least claim they have. All I did was get tired all over again. Then when Mary and I split, and the fucking cancer came back, I had nothing left."

"There's a lot in life we don't get to choose, that I'll grant you," came Jim's reply. "The deck may get stacked. But you have to play the cards you're dealt. What else can you do?"

Sid supported Jim's reasoning. "I don't have any gripe about your being selfish. You've been through enough. You deserve the right to make your own decisions. But I've known you too long. I know your philosophy. I'd just like to see you feel satisfied. And I know you well enough to realize that when you're selfish, you're not truly satisfied."

Jim poured himself a little more Chianti then cut in. "Want some?" I nodded. He continued, "Remember, it was you who pushed and pushed until we all agreed to put in a few hours every week at a free clinic. And you're the one who said, hey, we should stay open at least one evening a week for the people who can't get off work to go to the doctor."

"As I remember," Sid resumed in his slow Virginia drawl, "you're the one who told us it was time for doctors to do a better job in general of not being selfish. If I recall, it was something to the

[38]

effect that doctors complain as if they're about to go on food stamps, when really we're at the top of society and should always be looking for ways to give back."

Sid would look more imposing if he didn't have a glob of tomato sauce on his chin. Still, these were people I couldn't bullshit. They knew me too well. I put down my fork and tried to put on my most serious demeanor. "Let's suspend logic then. I've had the opposite of a conversion. I don't have that long to live. I want to root for the Orioles. Otherwise I just want to be selfish. Maybe I'm not helping anyone these days, but at least I'm not hurting anyone."

"Well, then," Sid parried, "we just might have to take you out for a pinch hitter."

"So you've been my friend, my rival, my confessor. Now you're my manager?"

"No other way to get through to you sometimes," he countered.

"Bottom line," Jim chuckled, "we know you never like being pulled from the lineup."

The waitress brushed crumbs off the tablecloth, then asked about dessert.

"I pass," I told her.

"Wait!" countered Sid. "You're dying. Why skip the cannoli now? It's people who live forever who need to worry about their weight."

I smiled. Instead of arguing, I saved my energy for the game. As I saw it, my moral obligation was to the team.

Jim had other plans, but Sid came along to the Yankee game. He knew a lot about baseball, so he was always a good companion at the ballpark.

"Remember, Dan, I warned you about the team this year."

"I remember." I chugged down a mouthful of beer. "But you know, Sid, they're really not that bad. I think they can stay in the pennant race."

Sid grinned indulgently. "Not to be overly morbid, but if you continue to refuse treatment, it ought to be a pretty exciting race between the Orioles for the pennant and you heading toward eternity."

"Baseball's a long season," I insisted. "It's too early to know what's going to happen. For either."

[39]

"For your benefit," he said, "I hope it's the longest season ever."

"Hey, Sid, before we get to the seats, wipe the fucking sauce off your chin."

On the field, things could have gone better.

"I guess it's not Valenzuela's night," I remarked.

"Yeah, I probably should go home now before things get any worse," Sid replied.

"So you're a fair weather fan," I said. "This means no more to you than seeing a movie."

Sid parried the jibe. "Hey, look, it's only to you this is life and death. The rest of us have a more balanced existence."

Mills and Frohwirth proved sterling in relief. The O's slowly whittled away the deficit.

"See, aren't you glad you didn't leave?" Mark McLemore had just tripled in the ninth.

"He's only on third base," Sid cautioned. "Don't get ahead of yourself."

As he spoke, a pitch somehow squibbed behind the catcher. McLemore came in to score. I jumped to my feet and shouted, spilling half my beer, then turned to Sid. "How can you stay so calm at a game? Or did you never tell me about the lobotomy you had as a kid?"

The game had a bit of everything. Outfield assists, pickoffs, a botched rundown. And extra innings. Damon Buford doubled in the tenth, then scored the winning run on a bases-loaded walk. That's part of the joy of baseball; no time limit; you always have a chance to win on your last at-bat.

"Well, I apologize for so grossly underestimating this team," Sid conceded. "Guess I'd forgotten you could build a victory on passed balls and walks. Just imagine if these guys could actually hit the ball."

As we left, Sid asked, "So who's this new kid everyone's so excited about?"

"Jeffrey Hammonds?" I asked. The recent Stanford grad got his first two major league hits tonight.

"Yeah!"

"They're pretty high on him," I responded. "Wait and see. If he becomes a star, two hundred thousand people will claim to have seen those hits tonight."

Sid said, "Seems like there's always some young phenom about to become the team's savior. Then it doesn't pan out, and all you serious fans begin stewing again about the future."

"And you call me cynical," I said

Next night, O's rallied from a 6-3 deficit to beat the Yankees again, this time 12-10. Hoiles hit two homers. Hammonds slugged his first major league four-bagger. I went to sleep with my team a mere three games out of first place.

There may be more pleasant ways to spend a sunny summer afternoon than sitting in the Club Section at Camden Yards, but it's hard imagining them. From my upper box seat in Section 372, I couldn't see the crenellated Bromo Seltzer tower, but I had a good view of the long brick B & O railroad warehouse. Carefully mowed stripes decorated the freshly manicured field. The scent of suntan lotion filled the air. Plenty of kids populated the stands, a sure sign the game will continue for future generations. I took it as life-affirming in some vague way. In Club Section seats, I could actually raise my hand and have an attendant bring a hot dog. No fear of nausea was depriving me from the luxury of being waited on at a ball park.

Orioles tenaciously hung on inning after inning. They left lots of runners on base, but got enough clutch hits to make the fans continuing believers. Unfortunately John O'Donoghue wasn't very effective in his major league debut on the mound. Two more hits for Hammonds; by now he must think this major league stuff is easy. Home run for Cal.

I heard a voice calling from below. "Dan!" Wasn't Sid or Jim; they said they couldn't come to the game today. Besides, sounded like a woman. Like I was the only Dan among the thousand people in my section.

"Dan!"

Down below I saw Janice waving up at me. What the hell was she doing here? Feeling foolish, I waved back. She signaled she was coming up. Glancing around, I noted an empty seat two rows behind me. I asked the guy next to it if he'd be willing to switch. Sure, he'd take a front row seat with the best view in the house. I wondered if I should down a quick beer or two.

[41]

Janice reached my row. "Figured if I looked hard enough, I'd eventually find you."

"Sure. Forty thousand people here," I said. "How long can it take to check everyone?"

She had on the same tapered jeans and red windbreaker she wore when I first picked her up. "Yeah." She stopped a second to catch her breath. "I started working my way around the field. Glad you're here in the middle instead of all the way over on the other side."

"Good detective work," I said. "Don't think I'm ignoring you but the inning's about to start. I thought you were in Philadelphia."

"Yeah," she replied, "I spent Friday night, but my friends had plans for the weekend, and I decided to take a bus down. There was a girl in my dorm from Baltimore I always liked but didn't know that well. I took a chance on calling her. She's living in a second-floor apartment in an old house on Roland Avenue. So I'm staying with her a few days."

"Uh-huh." Ground out to second; I scribbled "4-3" on my scorecard.

"So how's the game going?" Janice asked.

I looked back up at her. "Not great. A rookie pitching. Just doesn't have it."

"Well, the Orioles are only losing by two," she said. "Couldn't they still win?"

The naivete of the amateur spectator! "Maybe." I didn't take my eyes off the field.

"So maybe you can teach me a little bit about the game?" she suggested.

My big opportunity to teach Baseball 101. Too bad I wouldn't be around long enough to get tenure. Meanwhile, I couldn't decide if I was happy to see her or not. Supposed it meant something that she made such an effort to find me. But why? I couldn't figure out her motive. Was she trying to escape something? What was in it for her?

In any event, Janice's presence didn't appear to help the team. Orioles teased the fans by staying close. Then Brad Pennington gave up three runs in the ninth, putting the game out of reach. Crowd was pretty classy. They cheered Cal's homer and

Hammonds' two hits, and stood to applaud John O'Donoghue despite his ineffective major league debut. Suppose there's a limit to how much a fan can complain after winning six in a row.

Too beautiful a day for whining, anyhow.

I took Janice to the Inner Harbor. Every city wants to rejuvenate through a mix of historic preservation and shopping. Boston has Quincy Market; this is Baltimore's version. Told her when I visited Baltimore as a kid, no one would let me come down here. Too dangerous, everyone told me. Too many muggers, pickpockets, hookers and assorted ruffians.

We roamed the market complex making meaningless small talk. Finally I had an idea. "I know. Let's go to the aquarium."

"You're not just looking for a way to push me into a tank full of sharks, are you?"

"My sense is, you've already come up against enough sharks that they're more afraid of you than you of them."

Janice stopped short. "That's a mean thing to say!"

Her abruptness surprised me. "I'm sorry. I was just trying to be funny."

"Then it's time to work on your sense of humor."

No place stirs my imagination the way an aquarium does. When I see the incredible variety of form, function, and behavior characterizing undersea creatures, I marvel at what a wonderful world it is. The fantastic colors, the unusual modes of locomotion, the innovative defense mechanisms. A few days in a big aquarium, and anyone should be able to write as fancifully as Jules Verne.

We stopped at length to study octopi, well-camouflaged stonefish, and sea horses. In the simulated tropical rain forest, pastel-colored poison dart frogs from South America caught our attention, as did piranha and alligator-like caiman. Once at the top level, we began a Guggenheim-like spiral downward along the huge central tank. I found fascination with porcupinefish and their inflatable spines, clawless spiny lobsters, and playful spotted eagle rays.

Janice intruded upon my reverie. "So what kind of sea creature would you like to be?"

"I need to think about that one a while," I answered. "Certainly I'd want to be at the top of the food chain rather than the bottom. Guess I'd also want to be one of those fish that goes all over

[43]

the world, not just spend life in one little cranny somewhere."

"I think I'd be a hermit crab," Janice said. "Move around a lot, be sprightly on my feet, be adaptable. Just pick up a new home anywhere I land. Sort of like I'm doing now."

"Actually, that makes me feel a little more comfortable," I said. "It'd worry me a bit if you wanted to be something fierce instead. Like a barracuda."

Janice laughed and sipped on her soda. "Nah, I'm not the nasty type. I can handle myself most of the time, but I don't look for trouble."

We'd known each other barely two weeks. I had friends who had married on the basis of relationships not much longer. I wonder how well they really knew each other.

"Back to your question," I said. "I think I'd want to borrow traits of lots of creatures and make myself some kind of composite organism."

She turned to face me more squarely. "And?"

"Well, first," I said, "I'd like the defensive postures of the squid. You know, squirt out some ink anytime I want to hide myself. Then maybe have the capability of being an electric eel if someone does get too close."

"That's how you deal with relationships?" Janice asked. "First, try to hide, then sting?"

My turn to laugh. "Well, for a start! Now you're beginning to analyze me, like my ex-wife always did. It drove me crazy."

"Good!" she exclaimed. "About time you laughed at one of my lines."

She paused, wrinkled up her face for a few seconds, then continued. "Hey, can I meet you at the stadium tomorrow, maybe watch a whole game with you?"

The nice thing about a home stand was just that, being at home. I'd moved four months ago, after Mary and I split. I wanted to simplify my life. No worries about the lawn, someone available for small repairs, things like that. Gave Mary the Volvo; I kept the well-worn but reliable black Camry, dented fenders, broken cruise control, and all.

My small condo wouldn't be anyone's idea of luxury. Your standard living room, dining room, kitchen, two bedrooms, two baths. I had enough furniture to fill it even after Mary took all she needed. It lacked touches to make it look like a home, like the knickknacks and family pictures. Knowing I wouldn't be here long blunted any desire to remedy that.

Unopened cartons filled one corner of the living room. At this point, suppose I can toss them. The closet looked fairly orderly. I'd put anything I couldn't remember wearing recently into a box for the Salvation Army. Kept a few sweaters in case I survived into the next winter.

Then there were the books. Piles in every room. Those on the floor could go to a library sale. If they hadn't made it to a shelf after lying around this long, hard to argue the necessity of keeping them. I'd always meant to read "War and Peace." Guess I put it off too long.

My neighbor put mail and newspapers inside for me while I was away. Otherwise the place looked no different than when I left. Probably a layer of dust, but I tended not to worry about such things until it was noticeable from a distance. Not for me to run my finger along a table or window sill, picking up germs that could kill me in my current state.

I shopped for bare essentials -- mainly food, but also dish detergent and toilet paper -- at Safeway. My appetite remained good much of the time. For once, I ate whatever I wanted without fear of getting fat. Instead of telling me to drop a few pounds, Eric looked pleased when I put one or two on. That was one positive spin to carrying a cancer around inside.

I had a well-developed routine of reading the accumulated newspapers. Too old a habit to break now. After brewing a pot of coffee, I sat down and learned researchers in the Southwest still hadn't identified the cause of an epidemic on a Navajo reservation. Officials were debating limits on the jacked-up trucks considered among the most dangerous vehicles on the road. Sixth annual Aids Walk scheduled soon in North Baltimore. Important issues that helped put my own illness in perspective. Or that I could mention in casual conversation with fans sitting next to me. Not as critical knowing world news anymore. My presidential vote last November was likely my last. No new tax legislation will impact me by the time it becomes law. I won't be visiting any foreign countries going through political unrest. Doesn't really matter what's happening in the stock market. The funnies aren't as funny.

On page two, I learned that Conway Twitty died. He hadn't been sick; suddenly collapsed from a ruptured aneurysm. Even a country music star isn't spared the statistical probabilities of the population. His family requested donations be sent to the Twitty City Ball Club in lieu of flowers. The Club supports efforts to help needy children learn the game of baseball. That's a legacy I could respect.

Minutiae on the sports pages mattered most. Mary, always pragmatic, called it drivel; I never convinced her of its importance. Read three or four columnists with different takes on the team. Studied players' statistics. Looked up the farm teams in Rochester and Elmira. Sports sections in major league cities devoted little space to opposing teams, so I had to catch up. Thank God for *The Sporting News*. It kept me current on scouting reports, so I'd have an idea who might fill certain positions as players retired or got traded. Along with remembering complex drug regimens, new diagnostic strategies, and the like, I'd have known the full pedigree of any player promoted to the major leagues. I paid bills, tossed junk mail, listened to talk shows, clipped magazine stories to read later on the road. When I wanted to relax in a hotel room, I didn't want long books for fear I'd die without knowing the endings. Short articles– plenty of them– filled the bill. And I headed to the ball park in plenty of time for each game. After being late for everything my whole life, I finally had the leisure to be punctual.

A maid, Sheila, stopped in weekly to clean when I was away, twice a week when the team was home. She washed the dishes, did laundry, vacuumed floors. Perhaps most importantly, freshened the bathroom. My aunt always cleaned her place just before the cleaning woman came-- "I don't want her to think I'm a bad housekeeper." I had no such vanity.

I made a mental note to let Sheila go through my books and take any she wanted before I carted the rest to the library. Every now and then she borrowed a few; maybe she can build up a collection. Let this be part of my legacy, such as it may be.

Next night's game proceeded uneventfully, albeit with the presence of Janice. I tried to teach her a little about baseball. She proved to be an avid listener, which surprised me somewhat. The

[46]

Orioles won. Five games out of first. I found myself dreaming this team can go all the way.

Janice woke me from my reverie. "I don't really have anywhere to stay tonight. Maybe I could stay with you?" In the excitement of victory, I'd almost forgotten she sat so close by. "Most of my things are in Philadelphia. I really don't want to go back to a motel."

Who was this girl, anyhow? I sensed she was intelligent. She certainly was articulate. I felt at ease in conversation with her. Maybe I'd benefit from opening up a bit. Promised myself to spare her excessive tales of woe.

It had been a while since I'd had a roommate, even for a night. Janice stayed in the spare bedroom. Next morning she convinced me to drive her to Philadelphia and pick up her things so she could hang around the rest of the week. In fairness, she tried to be unobtrusive. Helped with the meals. Washed the dishes. Kept her room neater than I kept mine.

On the second morning, she pulled a newspaper out of my hands, moved a cushion out of the way, and sat down next to me on the couch.

"Are you going to trust me a little and tell me what's going on?" she began.

"What do you mean?" I said.

"Well, I run into you traveling across the country, figure you're on some kind of vacation, learn you're a baseball nut or something. Now you're home, and there's still nothing on your mind but baseball." Janice paused to sip her coffee. "Like, do you work or anything?"

I knew this moment would come. Suppose I may as well get it on the table now. "I stopped working a couple of months ago. Sick leave. I've got a kind of cancer, it's called a lymphoma, and it's come back."

A moment of silence filled only by the whirring of the air conditioner. "No! Really?"

"Yes, really," I said.

"I'm sorry," she said. "I didn't know. Are you getting any treatment?"

"Not now," I told her. "I got treated the first time around.

[47]

Thought I might be cured. When it came back, I didn't want to go through it all again."

Janice didn't respond for a moment. I've probably scared her. If anyone had tossed up such a story to me when I was twenty-five, I'd have run away as fast as I could. There I was in gray khakis and an Oriole T-shirt. She had on jeans, a blue top, and a light flannel shirt. We were on the couch with its fading floral pattern. Low oak coffee table in front of us, my old platform rocker to the left, caned Shaker chair to the right, bookcases up against two walls. A mix of old rock concert photos hanging (has she even heard of Otis Redding, or Blood, Sweat, and Tears?) plus a couple of innocuous Frederic Remington prints. Books and newspapers covering more floor area than the scattered rugs did. Not your classic setting for an epiphany.

"Why the baseball stuff?" she asked.

"A promise I made to myself," I said. "That instead of wallowing in self-pity I'd follow my team around the rest of the season."

I saw her swallow hard. "Does that mean you're going to die soon?" she stammered.

"If I'm lucky," I continued, "maybe the cancer will magically go away. More likely, yeah, I'm going to die soon."

"Are you scared?" she asked softly.

"Not really," I said equally quietly. "Everyone has to die sometime. Sure, I didn't plan on dying so young, but we don't always get asked for input on this stuff."

"Is it painful?" Any trace of a smile on her face had dissolved. Her eyes looked down for a moment, giving a sense she had to reorder her thoughts. This was too much. I should have spared her the details.

"Sure it is," I told her. "You have regrets about all the things you wish you still had time to do. It's unnerving to think back to all the time you wasted earlier in your life."

"No, I mean, does it hurt?" Janice clarified. "When my grandfather had cancer, he took pills all the time and still had pain."

"So far, I've been pretty lucky," I said. "Every now and then, I pop some codeine, but not often. My biggest problems are nausea and fatigue. Some days I do great, have lots of energy, can eat anything I want. Other times, the opposite. Like the song said, all you can really do is keep on keeping on. Except that I don't want to drag it out any longer than necessary."

"And baseball keeps your mind off it?"

"Well," I said, "baseball's been an obsession since I was a kid. Now I'm ready to give into it more. I'm not living in the future anymore. And baseball's great if you're living for today." I paused. "Okay, no more questions." I picked the paper up off the floor, folded it to the entertainment page, and resumed reading.

Funny thing. Now that we'd had the talk, everything went on just as before. Janice didn't feel sorry for me, didn't dote on minor complaints, didn't offer to do any more (or less) than before. She behaved as though she'd known me all her life.

However, she did insist on going to all the games.

The team faded, first with a 7-2 loss to Toronto. Two game losing streak, longest in a while. Then McDonald left with a 1-0 lead that would have been bigger had so many scoring opportunities not been squandered. Hoiles had a mental lapse. Pennington couldn't get anyone out. The 1-0 ninth inning lead became a 2-1 defeat. I had to agree with what the radio announcers said through my earphones, that they played like a fourth place team.

Just as I got ready to concede the horsepower wasn't there, O's beat the Blue Jays 6-0 behind Valenzuela. I told Janice how Valenzuela was a sensation when he came up as a rookie for the Dodgers. "He pitched great for several years, then somehow lost his touch. Now he's trying to make a comeback with the Orioles."

"Sort of like you are from the cancer?" Janice queried. I stared at her and bit my tongue.

Last night's collapse notwithstanding, it had been a good month. Orioles only five games out. It was time to think about getting to Chicago.

"I'm coming with you to Chicago," Janice informed me during lunch.

I put on my most stern expression. "Funny, I can't remember inviting you."

"Hey, it's America. Anyone can go to Chicago."

"Can't argue with you on that, Janice," I said. "But the Constitution doesn't say a citizen has to bring along anyone who

[49]

wants to go."

"Well, it'd be cheaper for me to go with you. Won't cost any extra for gas."

This wasn't going anywhere. "Okay, I see what's in it for you," I said. "You get to take a mini-vacation and see a new city. What's the benefit for me?"

She thought a minute. "Chance to have stimulating company?"

I put down my tuna sandwich and faced her squarely. "Look, Janice, this has been a bit strange. From the very minute we met, if you want to call it that. But you don't want to spend your summer following someone like me around the country. I kind of want to be alone, to begin with. And I really don't want to be responsible for someone else."

"I'm twenty-five. I'm independent. You aren't responsible for me. All you're doing-- at most-- is giving me a ride." She paused. "Plus I don't buy all this shit about you wanting to be alone. I think you're dying for someone to talk to."

"Literally," I say.

"What if you get sick?" she went on. "Why not have someone who can take you to a hospital? Or bring in food if you're sweating down a fever. Besides, if you've got someone to share the driving, maybe you'll get there a little more rested."

"Okay, look at it this way," I countered, "even if you do go, how are you going to spend your days? Or is Chicago another place you've got a roommate or dorm buddy or something?"

"Actually, I don't think I know anyone in Chicago," she said. "I'll stay with you."

"Jesus, Janice, I had enough trouble living with someone when I was married. I don't know if I want the hassle again."

"It won't be a hassle," she said. "We don't have to talk to each other. Or eat together. You can always have the bathroom first. Promise." She put her right hand in front of her heart.

"Why do you want to come along?" I asked. "Really?"

She grinned. "Oh, maybe I'll write a book about some dying guy traveling around following his baseball team, all the while hoping to cheat death. I need to gather material."

I glared at her.

"Okay," she said, "maybe I just like you, and think I can

[50]

make your trip easier.   I might even be helpful on occasion. Plus, it's not like I have any other plans right now."

PART THREE

July 1, 1993

Chicago went by quite smoothly, especially considering I only saw the Birds win once.

We missed the best game of the series, Jamie Moyer beating Jack McDowell, 1-0. We'd stopped for the night outside Cincinnati so I could watch the game on television. I'd have seen it so much more clearly on the radio, but I couldn't get an Oriole station in the Ohio River Valley. Made me think of a blind baseball announcer in New Britain whom I'd read about. Next time I'm in New England, need to make a point of tuning him in for a game.

For supper, we picked up take-out chili at Skyline. Four-way Cincinnati-style chili.

"It's got noodles in it," Janice exclaimed.

"Yeah, that's the way they do it here," I informed her.

"Sorry, I think the noodles detract a little bit."

I agreed. "Give me Texas over Ohio any day for chili."

I began to think maybe I should have flown instead of driven. Hated missing a tight pitchers' battle. But naturally we were in plenty of time to catch a 12-1 drubbing the next night.

We did our fair share of sightseeing. Began with a boat ride on the Chicago River. Saw the architecture filling the void left after Mrs. Murphy's cow started the Great Fire. I could have passed the pop quiz on modern, post-modern and all that kind of stuff. The older, more classical Tribune Building made the deepest impression. I think I'm becoming a traditionalist.

Next we went to the Museum of Science. Rode down the "shaft" into the simulated coal mine. Saw the machines that carved out the rock, leaving just pillars for support. Faced the darkness. Enough of an experience to make me happy I'd never had to make my living in the center of the earth. Of course, I'd be headed in that direction soon enough anyhow.

We visited the Field Museum. All I cared about were the dinosaurs. At the Chicago Art Institute, we saw Hopper's "Nighthawks," with its depiction of lonely people late at night. A painting that begs for a story to go along with it.

[53]

"You know that painting, that one you liked so much?" Janice asked. We were in a festive place called Italian Village. Everybody seems to be celebrating something. Everybody else, anyway. "That could be us."

I set down my glass of Chardonnay. "Which one? You mean 'Nighthawks'?"

"Yeah, that's the one." Janice put down her fork, looked straight into my eyes, and offered a challenge. "Think about it. Two people drifting separately, coming into contact at a given place and time, not looking for anything specific, not even sure they should acknowledge each other's presence."

"Please don't go telling me that we're somehow supposed to be characters in an epic of the common man or something," I said.

"I think everybody's a candidate to be a character in an epic of the common man," she went on. "They just don't know it. Maybe they're too preoccupied meeting the needs of day-to-day life; maybe they're too obsessed with money or fame or something; maybe they just don't think about anything anyhow."

Usually I hesitate ordering soft shell crabs if I'm not within walking distance of Chesapeake Bay, but these were terrific. So was Janice's lasagna. The food spurred us to develop philosophies of life based on a stimulus from Edward Hopper. Guess it's good we didn't see an exhibit of Salvadore Dali. Though the eggs that flopped over the side of my plate this morning would have fit smoothly into one of his drawings.

There was no diverting Janice. I picked up the cork and began flicking off small pieces with my fingernail. That habit drove my wife crazy. "All you're saying is that every life has meaning," I said. "Which I desperately want to believe. But I'm just not so sure. Does the world really change, even infinitesimally, from the presence of every man, woman, and child? Would life be different for anyone else if I dropped dead tomorrow as opposed to having dropped dead ten years ago? Truth is, I don't really know. I hope so, but I don't really know."

"But can't you translate that into a will to continue the struggle, rather than giving up?"

"Please don't tell me I'm giving up. I'm just deciding to die my own way. And I don't see anything wrong with that." I squeezed what was left of a lemon wedge over the second crab.

[54]

"There isn't anything wrong with that," she conceded. "But share your thoughts and feelings a little along the way. Maybe you'll make the path smoother for someone else sometime. You don't have to grow a shell like a recently molted lobster just to keep living-- or dying-- your own way."

"Think back to that Hopper painting again," I said. "My interpretation is that the guy and girl aren't talking. They may be thinking about it, but they're not."

"Okay," she laughed, "I surrender. Want to talk about coal mining? And what are you doing to that cork?"

The Orioles came into Independence Day only four games from first.

I focused on baseball to keep my mind off death. Death itself doesn't bother me. It's failure to achieve what I wanted in life that gnaws at me. I think of friends who died young. What dreams they had, what accomplishments they'd hoped for in their lifetimes. All like the guy in Hawthorne's "Ambitious Guest." You'd like your sojourn on earth to add up enough to fill more than a basic home town obituary.

A couple of Cleveland Indian players drowned this spring. Guys who reached heights about which I could only dream. Outside of their families, the only people who will know what they achieved will be those who stumble across their records while looking for someone else's statistics in a baseball registry.

"I can't believe Don Drysdale died." We were on our way to the ballpark. Janice drove so I could read the paper.

"Who's Don Drysdale?" Janice asked.

"He pitched for the Dodgers, then was an announcer," I said. "He's in the Hall of Fame."

"How'd he die?"

I turned the page. "They found him dead in his hotel room in Montreal. Probably a heart attack. He'd just gotten back from the funeral of another Dodger, Roy Campanella."

"I suppose you have a story about him, too," Janice said.

I laughed. "Actually I do. Campanella was a catcher when the Dodgers first won the World Series in 1955. I learned about him from my next door neighbor growing up. He was a big Dodger fan. I used to go over to his house in the afternoons sometimes and listen to games with him. I remember vividly the headline when Campy was paralyzed by an auto accident at the peak of his career. I couldn't have been more than five or six. Mr. Leonard– my neighbor-- was so choked up he couldn't talk about the accident for weeks. That might have been the first time I'd seen anyone emotional about baseball."

Janice stopped short for a stoplight. "And who's the guy again who died yesterday?"

"Don Drysdale," I said. "I have to give someone like him credit. Finished a successful career in baseball, then became determined to do something else of significance."

"Is being an announcer that special?" Janice asked. "I thought lots of players did that."

The traffic was grating on me. "Hey, why don't we park around here?" I said. "We've got plenty of time to walk to the game."

"Sure," she agreed.

"Some players do become announcers, you're right. But only a few," I said. "You've got to be bright, and you have to be articulate. Explain things for the fans, but in such a way that people understand even if they're not wrapped up in baseball."

She took the parking stub, and followed the guy's signals into a spot. "You probably have to do that all the time if you're a doctor."

"Of course," I said. "Although some of my friends have lots of trouble with it."

Janice looked puzzled. "I kind of figured they'd get that point across in medical school."

"They should," I agreed. "But some of it is personality. You've got to want to explain things well."

"Did you?"

"What?" I asked.

"Explain things well," came her reply.

"Yeah, I think so," I said. "At least I hope so."

"So that's something you should be proud of."

"Being able to explain things is just part of the territory," I said. "I took it for granted. No gold stars."

"I think there's merit in doing the things you're supposed to do," Janice asserted. "It's nice to shoot for the moon on occasion,

[56]

but isn't life mostly a matter of taking things as they come and doing a good job?"

By now we'd grabbed our jackets and were ready to walk the last couple of blocks to the park. I threw the newspaper in the back seat, then grabbed an extra pen from the glove compartment just in case my other one ran out of ink.

"Janice, what are you doing, making my case for getting through heaven's doors?"

"No, just killing time," she replied. "if you don't mind the expression, until we get through the turnstiles. After that, I'm sure it'll be all baseball and only baseball on your mind."

We lost to the White Sox 3-1, wasting a good effort from Ben McDonald. Should have left town last night after the sloppy 9-6 victory. By definition, any win is better than a loss.

"So are you pretty wealthy?" Janice had no shortage of questions as we sped toward Kansas City. "I mean, where do you get the money for travel and hotel rooms and everything?"

"No, I'm not wealthy." I'd say no even if I was. No reason to be fodder for an anti-capitalist young student. Or a Bonnie Parker in the making. "But I made a decent living. I saved some. Plus, when you know you're going to die before you reach retirement age, you don't worry about using up some of your pension money."

"You know, I wonder if it'd be worth doing a trip like this when you're young," she suggested. "When you don't care if you run out of money. See how big the country is. Meet a few interesting people. Break out of the narrow sphere you grow up in."

"Sort of like what you're doing now."

"Except I didn't really plan it," she said. "I think I would have enjoyed that part."

I maneuvered back into the right lane. "Yeah, there's value to doing some planning. Finances, for sure. And some general directions for travel. But you wouldn't want to plan too much in detail. You want to leave plenty of room for whatever happens."

Janice leaned over and playfully jabbed my shoulder. "Like running into me, right?"

I laughed. "No, I couldn't have planned that." She did break up the tedium of driving.

Janice unwrapped a stick of gum, popped it in her mouth. "Want one?"

[57]

"No thanks."

"So tell me a little bit about Kansas City," she said. "I've never been there."

I thought a minute. "I don't know it very well. The things that stick in my mind are how clean it always looks, and that it seems to have a lot of fountains."

"Do you think it's clean, just because it's clean in comparison to all those big cities in the east? Any city that doesn't have garbage piled up on the sidewalk seems clean." She paused a second and looked around. "Or maybe it looks clean in comparison to this car."

"Not fair criticizing the car," I said. "It's how it runs that matters, now how it looks. How clean will you be after ninety thousand miles?"

"I thought Kansas City had stockyards," she said. "That can't help keep it clean."

"I don't really know anything about that," I answered. "You may be right. But it's not like stockyards are the same as in the days of Upton Sinclair."

"Who?"

"Shit, Janice, don't they make you kids read anymore in college? Upton Sinclair? Who wrote *The Jungle*? Sort of a muckraking attack on the stockyards in Chicago."

"Is it a good book?" she asked.

Now I had to be a bit sheepish. "I never actually read it."

"So didn't they make you old guys read at all in college?" She tried to hide a smirk.

"Look, at least I learned about it," I told her. "Maybe in a history class."

"So how did Upton Sinclair-- now that we've established neither of us has read him-- make a difference?"

"By bringing attention to working conditions in the stockyards, by bringing up issues of hygiene and contamination of meat." I checked to see if she was paying attention. "Stuff we take for granted. But that someone needed to push before the government would take action."

Janice opened the glove compartment. A bunch of maps fell out; she thumbed through and kept the one for Missouri, crammed the others back where they had been. "I see the glove compartment

[58]

has the same tidy organizational system you use for the rest of the car."

"Enough already," I said. "No fair picking on a defenseless storage bin."

"So I'll see if this map shows anything worth seeing," Janice told me. "After all, you say travel should be enlightening. Maybe Upton Sinclair lived somewhere around here."

"This isn't exactly your trip, Janice. It's mine. And I think Sinclair lived in California."

"Okay, then it should be enlightening for you," she said. "If I get enlightened, it'll be a side benefit."

I shook my head. This could become exasperating. "We'll get to Kansas City, see the first game. Then we can use the next couple of days for sightseeing."

"Let me drive more," she said. "That way we can stay on the road longer, maybe sightsee some tomorrow before the game. Want to grab some fast food and keep going tonight?"

"I'm not really in the mood for an all-nighter," I said. "I gave those up after college."

"Then I'm going to take a nap. And how're you going to stay awake if I'm not jabbering away?" She adjusted the headrest, put the seat back a little, and made good on her promise.

We spent the night somewhere near Columbia. I suggested she could stay there, go to journalism school, get even better at asking questions. Next morning, we lost any time we'd gained by lingering over a late breakfast, an omelet for Janice, blueberry pancakes for me.

"Why'd you leave such a big tip?" Janice asked as she eased the Toyota onto the road.

"What do you mean?"

"What I mean is the bill was fourteen dollars," she said. "You left her five bucks. That's a big tip."

"She was a good waitress. She earned it," I declared. "I try to make sort of a contest of it. Perfunctory service gets ten percent. Some extra effort or enthusiasm gets twenty-five. Maybe a couple dollars extra at breakfast, especially if someone keeps the coffee cup filled. Breakfast servers get a raw deal. They have to keep coming to the table but fifteen percent usually leads to under a buck for the

[59]

effort."

"That's really generous," Janice said. "In Colorado, there were so many times I could work my ass off and not get fifteen percent. I felt sorry for girls who were married with kids and had to live off the tips."

I smiled. "I know what you mean. I had my days waiting tables. I like the idea of rewarding people who do their jobs well. Doesn't happen enough. I also like surprising a few, so they learn you can't predict where the bonuses might come from. I mean, do I look like someone worth extra attention in anticipation of a better payday?"

Janice gave me a look of mock horror. "What, you with your half-combed hair, shirt barely tucked in, one shoe untied? You don't think a waitress could spot you as a generous tipper from a mile away?"

I knew the hair needed more attention, and that weight loss let my shirt fit too loosely. Looked down to check my shoes. She was right. I bent over and re-tied the lace. Maybe I was slipping more than I realized.

As we approached Independence, Janice asked if we could stop at Harry Truman's home.

"My father said Truman brought more common sense to the White House than anyone. He had a newspaper with the headline that Dewey had won the election. Framed it and kept it on the wall in our den."

The house fit my impression of Truman pretty well. A white Victorian adorned with its share of gingerbread, built by Bess Truman's grandfather in the 1860's. Silver maples out front. Wrought iron fence added by the government when he became president. Nice house in a nice neighborhood, nothing more, nothing less. Woodwork largely stained pine; molded plaster; Lincrusta wallpaper. Formal living room and a somewhat austere music room in the front, where dignitaries would be met. Friends came to the 1950's kitchen, complete with can opener and blender sitting on the counter. Or the back porch, with its white table and aluminum folding chairs with woven plastic seats. Neighbors dropped by all the time, just like at my childhood home. I remember my mother loading the refrigerator with beer once a week or so. Never saw either parent take a drink. Ever. But the neighbors went through four or five six-packs a week.

Who can argue with someone who looks up to Harry Truman? Here's a guy who never went to college, never had preparation even remotely of the type needed to lead the most powerful country on earth, then finds himself thrust into a leadership role in the midst of a war that could change civilization forever. How does someone like that mount the fortitude to make a decision on dropping an atomic bomb?

That night, some announcer would describe a batter up with bases loaded, two outs, in the ninth, and call it a life-or-death situation. How do you explain that to a scientist at Los Alamos or a pilot heading for Hiroshima? Or a patient headed for emergency surgery?

We found a downtown hotel in Kansas City. I gambled on living at least three more days and bought two tickets for each game. Janice was still a rookie fan, but her scorekeeping was becoming accurate enough that I could go urinate without worrying about what happened in my absence. That's a big plus.

I've been put on this earth as an Oriole fan perhaps to prove some cosmic truth. Like how one should never assume victory. Tonight, O's brought a 1-0 lead to the bottom of the eighth, only to have Pennington and Williamson surrender seven runs to Kansas City and cheat Fernando Valenzuela (and me) out of a victory. How could this struggling team be just four games out? Even in the face of mediocrity, thou shalt not become overconfident.

We wandered impressive old residential areas. I liked the wide boulevards in Kansas City, with their grassy swaths in the medians. Janice liked the fountains. Could have gone to Hallmark Center, where the ramp collapsed. Or checked out Country Club Plaza, the venerable downtown center that Kansas City claims was America's first planned shopping mall. Apparently it's modeled on Seville. You can pick out Moorish features amidst the usual upscale store names. Anything that delays building of a new mall, with its concrete shells and moat of parking spaces, deserves praise.

Instead, we drove down to Osawatomie, where John Brown killed slave owners during his raids in the 1850's and got his

[61]

reputation for "bloody Kansas."

Once there, we didn't find much to see. It was an attractive place with tree-lined streets and a still vital nineteenth century downtown. John Brown Park on the west edge of town had a statue of the abolitionist in a militant pose with a rifle slung over his back. I suspected more people came for the playgrounds than to remember him. Adair Cabin State Historic Site had a ramshackle cabin, built of hand-hewn logs, standing inside a stone pavilion. Brown lived there briefly in 1858 with his brother-in-law Samuel Adair.

"That place needs some work," Janice said. We sat on a wood bench while Janice studied a brochure on Brown.

"No one can accuse this town of trying to make money off its history," I said.

My stomach was throbbing by the time we got back to the hotel, but I still needed supper. For years I'd read Calvin Trillin's homages to Arthur Bryant's barbecue restaurant in Kansas City. Not bad. Maybe not the best I'd ever eaten, but it did help the throbbing.

"Why baseball?" Janice asked over an early dinner at KC's Masterpiece on our last night in Kansas City. I ate burnt beef and pork ends, onion straws, and barbecued beans. Considered that maybe the combination would be toxic to lymphoma cells.

We'd spent the afternoon roaming the countryside. Pretty farmland, but all I could envision was creeping development. Franchised ice cream parlors where dairy cattle grazed, fried chicken places replacing poultry-populated barnyards, huge supermarkets superseding fields of corn and wheat.

"Well, slavery's already been abolished," I said. "And someone else came up with the atom bomb."

"No, really," Janice insisted. "Why not music, or Scrabble, or something? Why baseball? Because it's a manly thing?"

"I don't know exactly," I said. "I've been this way since childhood. The competitiveness is one aspect. I'd rather have been good enough to compete myself. Being an obsessed fan is about the best I could do."

"Were your parents into baseball?" she asked. "Did they bring you to games?"

"What are you doing, Janice, trying to be psychoanalytical with me? "

"No, I'm just trying to learn something about you."

[62]

"Okay," I answered. "They encouraged me to join Little League. My father played catch with me on weekends. But they never pushed it. In fact, as I look back, I don't think we began talking baseball much until I went to my first major league game."

Janice stopped to ask the waitress for more napkins. Hers was already soaked with barbecue sauce. "Couldn't it have been a different sport? Maybe one you could play yourself?"

"Well," I said, "I played tennis, but there's a limit to what I get out of watching a tennis match. I guess I like the idea baseball has both teamwork and individual achievement, and no team succeeds without both. I love the pace of the game, the strategy, the tradition, the history. Also the fact that time doesn't control it. At this point, lots of my most cherished personal memories revolve somehow around baseball."

"Do you get frustrated with how spoiled some of the players are?" Janice asked. "I mean some of these guys get millions just for being able to hit or throw a ball."

"Yeah," I said. "There's plenty of greediness to go around. Both players and owners. Given time--and fortunately I may not have enough-- that could ruin the sport." I gnawed at what remained of a rib and dropped it on the plate. "You know, I met a player in a hotel in Cleveland. Mike Devereaux. He was a nice guy. Made me realize most of these guys care about what they do. They play hard, they want to win. But over a long season, even the best teams lose sixty games or more. You have to learn how to deal with that. A pennant race isn't life or death, it's a way of making a living. Not much different from the way I had to handle losing a patient. If you let every setback twist you inside out, you're never going to contribute and make a difference."

"While you're sick, why not make a few concessions?" Janice asked. "Stay closer to home, take trains to, say, New York, or Boston. Still see lots of baseball, but get more rest."

"Hey, Janice, what is this?" I raised my voice a little. "An interview of some sort? I can see it. Next up on *Sixty Minutes,* 'Insights Into The Mind of a Dying Baseball Fan.'"

She rolled her eyes. "No, really."

"It's the Orioles who absorb me," I said. "I couldn't enjoy the game without following a specific team. Otherwise the sports pages are just bunches of numbers. Like the stock market reports. I

[63]

mean, I understand my race is one of life and death. At least, like in a baseball game, I don't know for sure in advance when it's going to end. I can go on believing that if the team does get better, does win the pennant, that I can will myself to survive long enough to see it." I swallowed. "Let's change the subject. Think these are as good as Arthur Bryant's?"

"Actually, no," she answered. "The ribs were better there. Of course, it might have been because you told me Arthur Bryant's were the best." She wiped her hands again on an already greasy napkin. "Hey, I know what you could get absorbed in. If you're still going when baseball season ends, you could transfer your obsession to finding the perfect barbecue."

"Too many days when I don't feel like eating," I said. "Then what do I do? Rate the pills that keep me from vomiting?"

"There might be some societal value in that!"

Everyone in Kansas City was friendly. Staff at the Adams Mark Hotel quick with greetings, and to suggest places to visit. "Did you visit Thomas Hart Benton's house?" "You have to see the Nelson-Atkins before you leave. It's as good an art museum as any in the east." Perhaps I'd be less cynical if I'd grown up in a place like this.

Kansas City proved equally affable on the field. Moyer won a shutout 8-0. Mussina cruised to a 6-1 lead after seven and the relievers held it. A return to form by the top starters could keep this erratic Oriole team in the race.   I didn't want to see a trade that mortgages the future.   Let the Birds do what they can in 1993, but build for the years ahead. Shouldn't be greedy. I understood the importance of leaving the world a better place.

I began to value the companionship, if only for the sake of having a relief driver. Plus, most people talk better than they listen. Janice knew how to do both. She let me vent when I needed to, and she knew when to be quiet. Hated to admit it, but these long car trips were becoming increasingly arduous.

"Hey!" Janice yelled. "You're going off the road!"

I jerked my eyes forward, turned the steering wheel to the left. Earlier I'd begun to nod off, but I thought I was back to full alertness. Guess not.

[64]

"Sorry."

Getting harder to stay awake at the wheel. Probably a bad way to expend my remaining energy. But what can an obsessed fan do?

"Want me to drive?" Janice asked.

"No. I think I'm okay," I said. "Must have just nodded a little."

"As long as you're sure you're okay."

"Yeah, I'm fine." I fiddled with the radio, tuned in a new station. "You know, we'll miss the first White Sox game back in Baltimore. Maybe we should take time to see a few sights along the way, get off the road a little."

"Fine with me," Janice said. "It seems like Baltimore plays Chicago a lot anyway."

"It's the way the schedule works out," I said. "You play teams a certain number of times each year. Sometimes there's months in between. Sometimes they come back-to-back."

"Well, you'd think someone would make sure it gets spread out more." Janice was tearing open another of her ubiquitous sticks of gum. Juicy-Fruit, this time.

"I'm sure they try," I said. "At times it may be whether the stadium is free for use."

"Why?" she asked. "What else would be going on?

This is where Janice got frustrating. She simply wouldn't let up on a detail. "Janice, I don't know. Maybe the Rolling Stones are playing. Maybe there's a tractor pull."

"A tractor pull? Hey, could we find one of those to see? I've never seen one."

"Actually, Janice, neither have I. If we come across one, I promise we'll stop."

She glanced over at me, her eyes showing surprise. "You don't have to be nasty."

"I'm sorry," I said. "I guess I still have trouble believing you're traveling around the country with me. And then you hit me with these questions staccato-like. In truth, I still don't know why you want to be doing this. It's not like you care anything about baseball."

"Maybe because I like you and I'm growing to care about you," she said. "Doesn't seem like there's any surplus of people in that department. Maybe you inspire me. Being around you stimulates me to think about things. Maybe I'll accomplish more in life that I otherwise might."

"In contrast to my giving up, you mean?" I tried not to sound argumentative.

"Oh, you take everything all wrong," she said, shaking her head. "If you want me to get lost, just tell me. But it may be that we're good for each other right now."

You always wonder if one event can change your life. I never stop for hitchhikers. What if I hadn't rolled down my window at that gas station in Wisconsin?

A moment of silence passed. "So who does make the baseball schedule?" Janice asked.

"Actually, I don't really know."

"See?" Janice raised a finger in triumph. "That's why you have someone like me around. To make you learn a few more things, too. Even about baseball."

I smiled, then pulled into a rest area to let Janice drive. Within seconds, I fell asleep.

She shook me awake as we neared St Louis. "Did you want to see the arch?"

"I've seen it from the highway before," I said. "Can't believe we're this far already."

"Hey, now that you've got a chauffeur, your travel's a breeze," Janice said.

"I wouldn't call it a breeze," I said. "Sometimes it's more like a tornado. But I'll admit it's nice getting across Missouri so easily."

"So just keep going?" she asked.

"Yeah." I gazed out the window. The arch was just coming into view. "I wish Baltimore was in the same league as the Cardinals. St. Louis is a great baseball town."

"Teams in one league can't play teams in another?" Janice asked.

"No," I responded. "Not unless they meet in the World Series."

"That seems silly," she said. "Wouldn't you think players would like playing different teams once in a while, or that fans

[66]

would want to see the other teams?

"I don't make the rules, Janice. I just follow the schedule that's handed down." We sped over the Mississippi River, ignoring a vile odor emanating from the brown water below.

"Well, what makes St. Louis such a great baseball town?" she asked.

"There you go again," I said. "One question after another."

"You got your nap." She got out another piece of gum and began chewing. "So why?"

"I don't know," I answered. "It's one of those places where people support their team. Win or lose, there are good crowds at the stadium. They've got a long history of good players and colorful players. A reputation for always having good young players on the way up. I think I read that at one time St Louis owned more than half the players in the minor leagues."

"What are the minor leagues?" Janice asked.

"That's where players get their start," I said. "There's several levels. Most players start low, learn the fundamentals, work their way up. Triple A's the highest. That's usually the last step before the majors. And the first step when someone's sent back down."

"Sent down?"

I let out a sigh of exasperation. "You know. When they turn out not to be good enough for the majors. Or they've gotten hurt and need to play themselves back into shape."

"So where are the minor leagues?"

"All over," I said. "Some good-sized cities. Like New Orleans. Buffalo. There's a team in Louisville. Also lots of small places. Burlington, Vermont. Bluefield, West Virginia. Batavia, New York. Places players may not have heard of before being assigned to play there."

"Do many people go to watch minor league games?" Janice asked.

"Sure," I said. "Some places fill their stadiums. But I've also been to minor league games with barely had a few dozen people in the stands."

"Can we maybe go to one?"

Jesus! Here I am looking forward to a home stand in Baltimore. Then a few days for the All-Star break. Suddenly I have

[67]

a hitchhiker– or should I finally be calling her a passenger?– who wants to see minor league games. I should stop for Little League somewhere. She probably wouldn't know the difference. I mean, it's only a little more minor.

After St. Louis, I started counting each mile. I yearned for a buffalo to break up the view, rather than yet another line of cars. Louisville came as a pleasant interruption.

We wandered down by the Ohio River. I enjoy tracing the beginnings of river towns. You look at the oldest buildings by the water and think how they warehoused all the trade. A factory or two gives a sense of the settlement's livelihood. Most, of course, are abandoned now, or tackily made over. One or two have transformed into restaurants. There's a sense of nostalgia until you think about the dreams ruined.

Someday, most river fronts will become gentrified. If the waters were navigable a century ago, that means pleasure boats will set out in the future. The griminess will give way to shiny marinas, beautifying the scene but also setting boundaries against those not wealthy enough to afford them. I wonder if they'd let me dock if I floated in on a raft.

It was disappointing to learn the Louisville Slugger baseball bat factory isn't in the city of its birth any longer. Most famous brand name in baseball (if you don't count the New York Yankees), but the company long ago moved production across the river into Indiana. There ought to be a law about things like that. A Louisville slugger, it ought to be made in Louisville. Just like Philadelphia cream cheese should be made in Philadelphia. Decided not to comment aloud. Didn't want Janice peppering me with questions about bats. Or cream cheese.

"Who do you think Louis was?" she spurted.

I'm sure I once knew. George Rogers Clark, brother of William Clark, who explored the west with Meriwether Lewis, founded the city. Suppose I could have bluffed my way and told Janice it was named after that Lewis. Would she realize the names were spelled differently?

"I don't have any idea," I said. "A French king, maybe?"

"I didn't know the French settled down this far," she said.

Looking over at Janice, I noticed one front tooth was a bit

[68]

jagged. A fall from a bicycle? A fight somewhere along the way?

"Besides," she continued, "wouldn't the name have changed when the British took over, or when the Americans bought the Louisiana Purchase?"

"I think this was American before the Louisiana Purchase," I replied. "Can we stop worrying about history for a minute and find something to eat?" I'll concede Janice has been good for my appetite. Her questions certainly distracted from any nausea I might feel.

"Sure. I'm hungry."

"Well, we're in Kentucky," I said. "We may as well have country ham. No sense worrying about high blood pressure, so no reason to avoid salt. Only other indigenous foods around here are bourbon and fried chicken. Little risk of running into anything healthy to eat."

Janice began getting that look on her face that preceded a disagreement. But this time her pouting dissolved into a smile. "Oh, I get it. You're going to die anyhow, before any other diseases can get you. And you figure if you force feed me enough, I won't live long after you."

I smiled, too. "Sure, then all the transcendent wisdom I'm imparting can be lost without its contaminating the rest of society."

"Well, in that case, can we have ice cream and brownies for dessert?" she asked. "If I'm going to be dying, no need to stay slim."

"Nah, you're in the south," I said. "It's got to be pecan pie instead of brownies."

"Never had it, but I'll defer to age and experience," she said.

"About time you showed some respect."

Louisville offered the chance to show Janice minor league baseball. We waited in a long line at the stadium for Louisville's Redbirds before finally reaching the ticket window.

"Jeez," Janice said, "there's more people here than at the games in Kansas City."

"No kidding!" I agreed. "Maybe it's some kind of state holiday. I'll ask. That is, I'll ask if we ever get up to the window."

Some guy whistled at Janice as he passed. I forget how pretty she is, even when she's not smiling. Women would kill for

[69]

skin that looked so smooth without make-up.

In response to my question, the woman who took my money answered, "Yes, it's really been something this year. Louisville might set a record for attendance if it continues like this. It's so much more fun watching the games when the stadium's full."

Our seats were in the middle of a long row, requiring us to squeeze by a dozen people right after gorging on a classic southern meal. I should have passed on the pecan pie.

Janice said, "Let me fill in the lineups. It's not the sacred Orioles, so it's a good time for me to practice."

"Sure," I replied. "Minor leagues are good places to practice the skills of being a fan."

She rolled up the program and gently hit me with it. "There you go, making fun of me."

"Okay, sorry," I said. "I'll be quiet while they announce the players."

"Good!" She rummaged in her purse. "Hey, give me your pen, will you?"

Triple A combines your greatest hopes and your most bitterly fading dreams. The guys on their way up, dreaming of the big time, putting their hearts into the game while they're still driving old Fords instead of new Cadillacs. The ones on the fringe, who've been to the big leagues briefly and know what they're on the threshold of achieving. The discouraged ones who have been sent down yet again, knowing they may never make it back to the majors. No one grows up wanting to become an experienced Triple A player.

You're a hero in high school, and you get treated as such. No reason not to believe you'll be special all the way through life. Then you find out there's dozens, even hundreds, for every spot at the top. Your dream gets shattered. For some, it becomes a downhill spiral. Others are solidly enough grounded that they pick up the pieces and move in other directions. Maybe if so much attention wasn't lavished on those who made it, more of the others would be prepared for the reality likely ahead. There's something to be said for making it beyond adolescent fantasies.

Somewhere in my apartment sat old programs from games I watched in Elmira, Hagerstown, and other minor league towns. Some are autographed. I should dig them out and find which future stars I've seen. If I luck out with the signature of someone who really made it big, I could trade it for a bigger casket than I'd otherwise get.

"One key part of minor league atmosphere is hucksterism," I said, pointing to the team mascot dancing atop the dugout. "There's always a contest going on, or a drawing for a prize, or something. The players are trying hard to advance, but there's a sense of humor in the stadium."

"Doesn't that distract the players?" Janice was combing her hair back into place after a gust of wind. I noticed a few split ends and realized she hadn't gone for a haircut during the short time I've known her.

"Good question," I said. "I'm not really sure. But those things draw crowds. That's what they want, to play in front of people, not in an empty stadium. Once at a low level minor league game, I saw a guy in the grandstand with a white poodle. I told him I was surprised dogs were allowed in. Turned out he'd bought the dog a season ticket so she'd have her own seat."

I finally timed a trip correctly. We got to Baltimore too late for the loss to Chicago in game one, but we were there in time to see the Orioles cruise to a 15-6 win on the second night. Next day Fernando Valenzuela shut out the White Sox, the highlight of what turned out to be a four-game split. There were full houses at Camden Yards. Fans boisterous. For all their shortcomings, the Orioles sat a mere two games out of first at the All-Star break.

I explained to Janice that as exciting as I found it to watch new young players, it's also a thrill to see a veteran like Valenzuela make a comeback.

"How long do most people play?" she inquired.

"I don't know the average," I said, "but it's pretty unusual to find players over forty."

"Then what do they do?" she asked

"Good question." I thought for a minute. "Some stay in baseball, you know, as scouts, or coaches, or managers. They can work in the minor leagues, too, or at colleges and high schools. A lot go into various businesses. Once you've been a pro ballplayer, there are plenty of places that will hire you just to have you around. Good public relations, and all that."

"Do any go on to back to school, or to totally different

[71]

careers?"

"Some do," I said. "A guy who pitched for Montreal went to medical school along the way, and became a doctor once he was out of baseball. I've read about players who got real estate licenses while they were playing, so they had something to fall back on if baseball didn't work out. I suspect a fair number never adjust well to life after baseball. I mean, these guys have been catered to almost since they were teenagers. Failure hasn't been a big part of their lives."

We stayed up later than usual on a non-game night. Janice intently watched "Casablanca." I'd seen it several times, so I sat skimming the *Sporting News*, looking up just often enough to follow the movie's plot. During a commercial near the end, just after Bogart told Peter Lorre "I think this is going to be a beautiful friendship," I spouted out my new plan.

"Janice, I'm going to spend a few days in the Adirondacks during the All-Star break. Do you want to come, or would you rather stay here?"

She looked up in surprise. "How long have you been planning this?"

"Oh," I said, "the idea hit me while we were driving from Louisville to Baltimore."

"You're sure this isn't your way of getting rid of me?" she asked, sitting forward with what seemed a sense of alarm.

"Well, that's crossed my mind," I kidded. "But no, I just want to spend some time outside of big cities." I went into the kitchen for a Coke. "Want anything while I'm out here?"

"Sure," she said, "bring in that opened bottle of chardonnay. Then maybe you can tell me about the Adirondacks. I've never been there."

I pulled a wine glass off the shelf, then came back into the living room. Janice made a show of clearing space on the couch, then smoothed a cushion. "Here, sit beside me."

"I don't know what there is to tell," I said while I poured her a glass of wine. "It's a mountain region in northern New York, lots of streams and lakes, small waterfalls. When I was a kid, my parents took us there. I worked there summers in college. Lots of places you can hike. There are remote ponds you can have almost to yourself even on a busy summer weekend. Beautiful scenery. It's

[72]

always been one of my favorite places."

"Sounds good to me." Janice repositioned herself with her legs folded under her. "Are we going to camp?"

Campgrounds always brought out the best in me. I enjoy the spectrum of people, from the grandparents to the youngest kids. If I didn't feel like hiking, I could happily lie around with a book, or follow my dog into the water for a swim. My sine wave of emotions always flattened a bit when camping.

"I'd love to," I said, "but I don't think I have the stamina. Maybe we'll rent a cottage. It's midweek, so it shouldn't be hard to get one."

"Okay," she said. "Should I go get hiking boots? They aren't represented in my wardrobe these days. And is there anything else that I'll need?"

"No, Janice, I don't think so. Your sense of humor and your sarcasm should be enough. At least they ought to ward off any bears who come too close."

We reserved a place in the heart of the Adirondacks, at Blue Mountain Lake. On the way, I pulled off the interstate to do a short hike. "Your introduction to the region," I told her.

I chose carefully, but not carefully enough. Severance loomed as more of a mountain than a hill this time. The mere one mile climb took more out of me than I'd expected; Janice pointed out my breathlessness at the top. However, I savored the view of Schroon Lake as much as ever. From this modest height, the water looked as pristine as it must have to Thomas Cole when he painted his canvas a century or so ago. Big resorts once flourished here, as on other Adirondack lakes, but that heyday ended well before my time. With an interstate now going past, it's amazing more developers haven't swooped in to exploit this market.

Once back from our hike, we crossed over on the Blue Ridge Road through Long Lake. Janice insisted on stopping for ice cream at a place called "Custard's Last Stand."

"Oh, come on! How can you resist a name like that?" she asserted.

We finished our cones while driving the last ten miles to Blue Mountain Lake. I was exhausted. One lousy two-mile hike and I was too tired for anything but bed.

[73]

Our cottage smelled a bit musty, but it looked clean enough. Twin beds, the bedspreads pretty worn. A rickety wooden dresser, plus a folding rack to hold the suitcase. Checked the shower; not much water pressure. Towels thin. Paper wrappers on the soap were yellowing. Pretty standard, I guess, for an old place. At least there was a small window air conditioner.

"Hey!" Janice called. "I didn't know they still made black-and-white televisions."

"I wouldn't count on it being new," I said. "Probably doesn't matter. Without cable, I doubt we'll get any stations." Janice tried proving me wrong, but she gave up after getting only a faint picture on Channel 6, nothing anywhere else on the dial.

In the morning we walked across the street to Potter's for breakfast. It's a grand Adirondack log structure, with impossibly clean-cut college kids manning the dining room. I was never that clean-cut. I wonder if Janice ever was.

The place mat doubled as a map of nearby hiking trails. I pointed out a few I'd done in the past, ones with views, like Castle Rock, others with secluded lean-to's, like Cascade Pond.

"You want to hike again today?" Janice asked.

"Yeah," I said. "No sense being all the way up here and staying indoors. I don't think I can do Blue Mountain. Great view, though, with a fire tower on top. I've been up there lots of times. Maybe something shorter."

"Well, I'll do whatever you want," Janice replied. "Just remember you promised me a better dinner than the sandwiches we had last night."

"Damn it, Janice. I told you we could eat wherever you wanted. I would have found something on the menu while you gorged yourself to your heart's content."

She patted my hand. "Don't get so irritable. I'm only kidding. I'm beginning to see how you might have gotten on your wife's nerves."

"Unfair, Janice. You can come for the ride, but no analyzing my past failures."

"Well, shit, you keep telling me you're not going to live long enough for future failures. So why not your past ones?" Janice stifled a yawn.

"Sorry if I'm boring you," I said. "Maybe I should leave you

[74]

here in the mountains. Let you move on to the next phase of your life. So I can die in peace one of these days."

"No way, Dan!" She grinned. "I've got the keys, remember?"

She understood a single argument didn't have to end a relationship, a tolerance that would have put me in good stead earlier in my life. Had I a vestige of religious belief, I might have considered her some kind of divine intervention, to steady me in my final moments.

We decided on Cascade Pond. Janice went to a nearby store to put together a picnic lunch. I walked over toward the beach and rested in a slatted red Adirondack chair.

"Been here before?" a guy asked as he sat down in the yellow chair next to me.

"Yeah," I answered. "Been coming up here off and on since I was a kid."

"So have I," he said. "Always told my wife that when I die, she should bring my ashes up here and sprinkle them around. Can't imagine a better place to spend eternity."

I studied him more carefully. Once I was pretty good at deciphering people's ages, but I lost that ability when I got sick. Aside from a bit of a paunch, he looked to be in reasonable shape. Not much older than I was. I plan to be cremated, too. Maybe I should be thinking about where my ashes will go.

"Didn't work out that way," he continued. "She died of breast cancer two years ago, and I'm still here."

"Hard coming back here without her?" I asked.

"At first it was," he said. "Her family's had a camp up here for generations. They were friends with the guy who started the museum."

"Wow!"

"Yeah," he went on. "Lorrie had been hearing stories of Adirondack history since she was in the cradle. I met her up here one summer when I was working at a hotel in Long Lake. She always talked about both of us trying to find jobs up here. I taught, but she was in finance. So it never happened. Maybe just as well. It was always a place to relax and unwind. If we worked here, maybe it would have become merely another part of the grind."

Janice returned, carrying a large bag and a Styrofoam cooler.

[75]

"Hey, who's your friend?"

He saved me embarrassment, standing to shake her hand, "Hi, I'm Stan Wallett."

We introduced ourselves, and I got up to leave.

Stan began to wave. "Hey, good talking to you. Nice finding someone who understands my attachment to the Adirondacks."

Janice piped up, looking at me, "You mean you're not the only one who's filled up with sentimental Adirondack connections?"

Stan laughed. We crossed the road back over to our cottage. "He told me how he wanted his wife to spread his ashes here when he died," I relayed to Janice. "But then she died first. I suspect he counts on the Adirondacks to keep himself somehow connected to her."

"What'd she die of?" Janice asked. "He doesn't look that old."

"And I do?" I feigned a look of disbelief.

"You know that's not what I mean. How'd she die?"

"Breast cancer," I answered.

"It's sad running across so many stories about death," she said.

"Ultimately we all get one of those stories," I philosophized. "But only one apiece."

"Good thing!"

The hike led past Rock Lake to a lean-to on Cascade Pond. It tired me out, but next morning I wanted to do one more favorite trail, this time with Jack, a friend from college. Janice decided to stay at the cottage. "I can do some reading. If I feel like it, I'll walk up the road to the museum. This way you two can talk about old times without worrying about me. And you won't need to explain who I am and how I happen to be with you. You should appreciate that."

Driving to Newcomb took almost an hour. I turned left toward the long-deserted mining town of Adirondac. A massive stone iron furnace stood on my right. When it was built, I'm sure owners and employees envisioned it would last forever, but it operated barely a few years. It's strong and sturdy a hundred years later, albeit with a tree growing from the top.

I guess I once expected to last forever, too. I certainly didn't

[76]

expect life to end before really coming into bloom. Just when the roots are strongest and the canopy's beginning to maximize, I get cut down and harvested. Merely one tree in a forest plantation. Suppose in time I'd welcome having an oak or a maple marking my presence. Just not this soon. But to whom can you protest that life's unfair?

I'd been one of those people who expected to change the world, make clear that my existence on the planet made a recognizable difference. Once I fantasized about becoming President, but that faded once I understood the nature of politics. In college, I decided on medicine. I figured making a difference would be automatic. Taking care of people who couldn't afford it, maybe opening a clinic in some remote area. The idealism faded in the face of long hours and unlimited demand, but at least I knew I was helping individuals all day, every day. You assume you'll build immunity to all the diseases that can affect everyone else. Then you learn that's not the case.

Jack spent as much time as he could each summer at his Adirondack camp. I thought I wouldn't mind dying in the woods, but at the last minute I developed a fear of going so far into the wilderness alone. Jack's old Toyota pickup was already in the trailhead parking lot.

"This isn't that same old car you were driving last time I saw you, is it?" I asked as we shook hands. "Are there any original parts still left on it?"

"It's kind of like a patient with chronic disease who's always real sick, but that you know is going to outlive you anyway," he laughed.. "I pronounced it a 'do-not-resuscitate' years ago, but you know that doesn't mean 'do not treat'."

Jack practiced internal medicine. He'd enjoyed his work until his first malpractice summons, when he got sued by an alcoholic ne'er do well. The case got thrown out, and the lawyer got censured for bringing a frivolous suit, but for Jack, medicine was never the same again. He limited his practice, sold out to a hospital that couldn't run the practice, ended up on his own again. Said his practice and he were growing old together. He and his patients had been around each other so long they almost knew what each would say in response to a given question or situation. They wouldn't bother him on nights or weekends unless truly necessary. In return he was always there for them spiritually as well as medically. He

[77]

once told me, "I'm fortunate. I can afford to trade money for time, and I do so every chance I get. I'm not saving up all my wild ideas for retirement until someone finds a way to give me a warranty that I'll live that long."

He'd been a Red Sox fan until he decided it was shortening his life. Now he spent a good six weeks each summer, plus a few in the fall and winter, at his camp. Jack didn't hunt, though he did learn fly fishing. He loved Adirondack history, and he would hike on a moment's notice.

It was Jack who first brought me to this trail. He told me the tragic story of David Henderson, co-owner of the ironworks, who was scouting for a dam site in the 1840's when someone threw down a pack with a loaded gun. Henderson was mortally wounded. His thirteen-year-old son was with the group. Henderson called Archie over, told him he was going to die, and for the boy to "give my love to your mother."

The other men carried Henderson's body out on a makeshift stretcher and returned him by train to New Jersey, where he was buried in his hometown. The next winter, family and friends trudged out to this lonely site with a two-ton granite marker. You have to look for it, but once you find it, you're overwhelmed that such a monument can exist out here. Ever since the accident, the water rolling by has been called Calamity Brook.

Not much change in elevation to the trail, but plenty of Adirondack mud. We barely talked except for short interchanges while resting. A swing bridge over a stream brought back fond memories of my first Labrador retriever. Intrepid most of the time, she refused to walk over this vibrating span, choosing instead to cross at water level and rejoin us upstream.

The bridge looked rickety, but the water was too high for wading, so I didn't have much choice. Then again, what if the bridge did collapse? Would only shorten my life a few months, and an accident might stimulate the need for a better span. Maybe they'd name it for me, so people could cross and think, hey, here's a guy who contributed something to the world. Would make Janice proud.

I felt some give in the bridge, an oscillation of sorts, but it only took a dozen steps to get across. Then, just as I put my foot down on the far bank, I slipped. Fell right on my ass.

"Shit!"

[78]

Jack scurried back to see what had happened. He appeared to be suppressing a smile as he looked at me and asked, "Are you okay?"

"Yeah!" I braced my leg and stood back up. There was mud all the way up my left side. I took a few steps and felt no discomfort. Any injury was more to my sense of dignity than to any bones or joints. "Nothing like Adirondack mud to fuck up your day."

"If there wasn't mud," Jack said, "you wouldn't believe you were in the Adirondacks."

"No argument there," I agreed. "After all I've been through this past year, though, it'd be nice to find a more heroic way to meet my end than falling into the mire."

By now, we were fifty feet beyond the crossing. Looked like I would survive the mishap. I'd still have to find another way to die, preferably a less ignominious one. And I'd need to finish the eight-mile round trip.

Jack was upbeat as always. "Well," he offered, "for a guy who's dying, you're holding your own pretty well."

Still, the hike showed my growing limitations. Once I'd have walked this straight through. Now I was happy going half an hour between rest stops. I began considering whether a place like Calamity Brook would be a good spot for my remains– serene, peaceful, surrounded by beauty. I briefly pondered staying in the Adirondacks for the rest of the summer, following in the footsteps of all those TB patients who used to go up there to die. Seeking a cure, of course, but mostly dying. But I'd made my promise. Back to Baltimore and baseball.

Though I was exhausted from the hike, I didn't sleep well. In the morning, we walked back to Potter's for breakfast. I couldn't eat any more than a bowl of corn flakes.

Janice drove the first leg. I tried, generally without success, to nap.

Just south of a place called Glens Falls, she noticed an historical marker about Ulysses S Grant. Exiting, then heading up a hill, Janice found a sign pointing to Grant's Cottage.

It turned out the former President died here of throat cancer. Grant had lost his fortune in a rash of poor financial decisions and desperately needed to finish his memoirs so as to provide for his family. Mark Twain agreed to publish the book. A businessman

[79]

donated use of this cottage so he could write with some peace and quiet, and breathe pure mountain air.

The cancer left him struggling for breath. Lying down cut off his wind, so he slept sitting up in two armchairs facing each other. Managed to finish the memoirs, then died. Sad tale.

I didn't have a memoir project to keep me going.

"Don't you get bored sometimes during a game?" Janice asked. We were at Camden Yards watching the last innings of an Orioles-Twins game.

"No, not really," I said. "There's always something to watch."

"Like what?"

"Sometimes I'll watch a specific player in the field. See if he's doing his job."

Janice showed some impatience in her expression. "Like I said, like what?"

I tried hiding my exasperation by cracking open a couple of peanuts. "Like whether they do what they're supposed to do after the ball is hit. Every player has something he should be doing on every play. Watch, for instance, the next time there's a ground ball. The catcher should be running down behind the first baseman, just in case there's a bad throw."

"Don't give me that sarcastic look," Janice said. "I want to learn something about this."

"Okay, try this," I said. "When there's a runner on first base, watch the second baseman and the shortstop. One has to move toward second base for the throw if the guy tries to steal."

"Which one should it be?

"Depends," I explained. "If it's a right handed batter, he's more likely to hit the ball to the shortstop, so the second baseman would cover. For a left-handed batter, the opposite."

"How long does it take to learn all this?" It was Janice's turn to open some peanuts.

"A long time," I said. "It's not like you learn it from a book. You learn through experience. And through lots of practice. Some plays you repeat so much during spring training that later in the summer you act through muscle memory when there's no time to think, like what to do when there's guys on base with a certain

[80]

number of outs, and the ball comes to you."

"So there must be guys who are good hitters, say, but who can't learn all these other things," Janice observed. "What happens to them?"

"Some of them never make the big time. There's enough competition that you've got to be really good to play at the major league level." I glanced at the scoreboard. Two outs. "Remember, I've never played even close to this level, so there are plenty of situations I can't envision. Sometimes I learn from an announcer, or someone next to me."

"Too complicated for me, I guess," Janice said as she brushed peanut hulls off her shirt.

"Well, let's stop there for now." I smiled at her. "I figure there's a limit to how much baseball you can absorb in one day. Tomorrow we can go on to another lesson."

"Tell you what," she said. "You were pretty patient for a change. I'll go get you a beer. Want a hot dog, too?"

I declined the hot dog but said yes to the beer, then turned my full attention back to the field. By the time Janice came back, Gregg Olson was mopping up a 9-7 win for Mike Mussina. Barring the unforeseen--always a possibility for this crew-- the O's could finish tonight a mere half game out of first.

"You know," said Janice, "I wish my father could have been as fascinated with something as you are with baseball." The Orioles took the field for the top of the ninth inning.

"What do you mean?" I gulped down more beer, spilling some on my scorecard.

"Oh, he worked all the time. It drove my mother crazy." She stopped for a sip of her beer. "She always thought he'd live a lot longer if he had a hobby, something to take his mind off work, something to let him relax. Maybe if he'd been a baseball fan, he'd still be alive."

I pondered the issue a moment. "Well, before you start classifying baseball as a saving grace, let me warn you. My wife certainly didn't see it that way. She used to tell me that some night while I'm tensed up listening to the radio, yelling at the team, throwing a journal against the wall when someone strikes out with the bases loaded, that I'd probably drop dead."

"Well, you're proving her wrong!" Janice exclaimed.

[81]

"Still could turn out to be the case," I laughed. "Just that they'll write lymphoma on the death certificate. If there's no box to check indicating I died because of the Baltimore Orioles."

Olson got the final out. I was ready to go home, have another beer, and crash. Janice wanted to go out for a pizza. What she probably needed to do was go to a bar, pick up some guy, take a break from hanging around a dying baseball fan. Though I didn't want her bringing some stranger home. We compromised. Picked up a pizza, rented a movie, and headed to the condo.

Although I'd become accustomed to having Janice around, I nonetheless developed a mantle of self-consciousness. I was always aware of her presence. When I was reading a newspaper, when I lay around flipping channels on the remote, when I sat in the bathroom taking a shit. Guess I'd forgotten how much privacy you lose when you're no longer living alone. Closing a door was far from enough to preserve a boundary.

In fairness, she did little to invade my space or impede my activity (or lack of such). When I first got married, the early months were an awakening. Mary and I had lived together off and on for two years, but knowing either of us could retreat to our own apartment preserved a certain sense of control. Running into each other all day once legally linked, life began to feel like an existentialist play with no escape. It took us years to get used to each other. Then all that successful adaptation flew out the window when I couldn't handle the stress of the lymphoma.

I felt the same edginess now. But Janice had an instinctive ability not to be in the wrong place at the wrong time. How do you learn that at her age? She had an easy comfort around me. Never expressed any pity, never overly solicitous. Treated me as she would anyone, I suppose, except that I had a disease. To her, it was just another topic of conversation.

I'd become comfortable with her, too. Perhaps too comfortable. She was my primary confidant. I could tell her anything, ask her anything, argue about anything. As long as I was willing to listen in return. Which on occasion involved being judged.

What would Janice be doing if she wasn't with me? Did she truly have no other plans for the summer? Was she looking to latch

[82]

on to someone? Or trying to escape something bad that had happened? She wasn't taking advantage of me. I was spending money on her, but that was my own choosing. Life's not a fairy tale where a supernatural being pops into someone's life. Outside of the chance to travel and see some of the country, what was she getting out of this? I couldn't imagine her trying to rob me. She didn't appear to have a psychiatric issue. Maybe my impending demise made it easier for her. I conjectured she viewed me with the transience of a new boyfriend, but one for whom death was imminent, sparing her the messiness of a breakup.

I figured I should introduce Janice to classic Baltimore cuisine. The hostess at Obrycki's led us through the bar to an almost empty dining room. She seated us in a quiet corner.

"What's good here?" Janice asked.

"You're going to have crabs," I said, "so don't worry about what else they have."

"Well, don't they make crabs different ways?"

"Yes," I said, "but we'll have them steamed, for the classic culinary experience."

"Quite dictatorial, aren't you?" Still, she let me do the ordering when our server came.

Fifteen minutes later, the waitress dropped a dozen steamed crabs on our newspaper covered table.

"Actually, pounding on these poor unsuspecting shells might be a good means of venting right now," I remarked while showing Janice how to crack the claws with a wooden mallet.

I opened up the body as I might open a purse, then rummaged around with pepper covered fingers to urge some meat to the surface. Something elemental about all this. Eons ago crabs might have been eaten similarly. Take them from the fire, pound the shells with a rock, scoop out luscious crabmeat with dirty fingers. My days of dissecting cadavers looked clean and neat by comparison.

"You know," Janice began, "you still haven't really told me why you're such a maniac about baseball."

"How much do you want to hear?"

"I don't know," she said, "how much do you want to tell me?"

[83]

"Oh, like I once told you, it goes back to childhood, I guess." I paused to lick some Old Bay sauce off my fingers. "I tried out for Little League, ended up on a good team. Unfortunately that meant I didn't play a lot. At age nine, I saw my first big-league game. Baltimore won, beating Boston. It was so exciting. After the game, I got a player's autograph. Willie Miranda's. He played shortstop for the Orioles. And he was such a nice guy, talking to me, just a little kid. Then, my parents let me go by train to Baltimore by myself to see a game."

"So it's sentimentalism," she exclaimed. "I didn't know you were sentimental."

"I am about baseball," I conceded. "For years, I looked back at that game as a sentinel event in my life."

"Why?" It was Janice's turn to lick her fingers, then dab her lips with the napkin.

"It was my first trip alone anywhere," I said. "I was barely ten. An uncle had tickets, and I probably threw all sorts of tantrums when my parents couldn't take me. To this day, I wonder if they were just trying to get rid of me for good when they sent me off on my own."

"So what happened?" she asked.

I pounded the claws of another crab then looked at Janice. Her face was a mess, smudges of Old Bay seasoning and tiny bits of shell dotting the usually flawless skin. Doubt I looked any better. "They put me on a bus to New Haven. Got on the train there for New York. I still remember how I had directions written out on a piece of paper. At Grand Central Station, take the shuttle to Penn Station. There, buy a ticket to Baltimore. If you need help, ask at the ticket counter, or find a policeman. Be sure to board the right train so you don't end up in Timbuktu."

"I'm not sure I could have handled all that when I was ten," Janice conceded. First time I'd heard her admit any hint of something she couldn't conquer.

"I doubt I thought about it," I said. "I just followed each step of my instructions. I'd be uncomfortable letting a kid do the same thing today. But you can imagine how exciting it was. The last leg was pretty interesting. A sailor took me under his wing, said he'd help me find my way in Baltimore. Told me about all the places in the world he'd been. How he liked the Navy but looked forward to getting out and starting an auto repair shop. I thought he was the wisest person I'd ever met. Now I realize he was probably barely eighteen or nineteen."

"Now everyone would worry he was a pervert," Janice interjected.

I laughed. "Guess it's good I wouldn't have known what the word meant. He felt the need to keep me occupied so I wouldn't keep getting up and walking up and down the car. Only thing he had to read was a pile of magazines. He gave me one. Turned out to be *Penthouse*. Would give a lot to know now what I was thinking as I turned the pages."

"Look at it this way," she said. "You needed something to make you a little more well rounded if all you cared about was baseball."

I looked up. Janice was even more covered in Old Bay. "Yeah, well rounded would certainly be an apt description."

"So did you assume every woman would have big tits and scanty clothing?" she asked.

I laughed. No one's ever been able to draw me into conversations about sex, not in the dorms, not in the locker room, not anywhere. How could I feel so natural discussing all this in a restaurant with someone I barely know? That elemental quality of eating crabs with no utensils but hands and a mallet must have helped.

"Because I don't have them."

"What?" I gulped some beer then picked up the last crab.

"Big tits," she said. "I don't have them. In case you haven't looked. But it hasn't kept me from having a good time."

"Well, congratulations," I muttered. "I guess!"

"No congratulations needed," Janice said, waving me off. "I get so tired of girls worrying about their tit size. Bad enough the men of the world get so wrought up about it. I figure you get only so many brain cells to use in life. No sense wasting them worrying about your breasts."

"Am I supposed to applaud you for the liberal thinking?" I asked.

"You don't have to be snide."

"I'm sorry, Janice. I still don't know how to take you sometimes."

[85]

"Which is exactly the point," she parried. "If you always know how to take someone, you get bored from the lack of challenge. I'd rather push you a little. Even if it makes you uncomfortable sometimes. As you told me the song says, you can't always get what you want."

I wondered yet again about the forces arranging for me to pick her up that day. I wasn't the type to believe in angels coming to escort you toward death. Best to declare her an accident of fate. Right then I wasn't looking for someone with whom to build an attachment. I'd become like George Washington. I didn't want an entangling alliance.

"Look, no one said you had to follow me," I restated for perhaps the hundredth time. "Remember, you're here on your own."

Janice didn't miss a beat. "Like you can keep on traveling the country alone. You're weak. You almost fall asleep driving. You can't lift a heavy suitcase."

"So when the time comes, I'll fly instead of driving. You'd be surprised how many airports have taxis now to get you into town. I can stay at hotels near ballparks." I smashed a stubborn claw with my wooden mallet.

"And who'll support you when you get faint and lightheaded, and think you might black out? Who'll help clean up the mess when you vomit up the next meal?" She paused to lick more Great Bay seasoning off her fingers. "Which might be this one, by the way."

"I'll only go to sold-out games. The place'll be so thick with people I won't be able to fall down. I'll just drift here and there with the crowd. Janice, I'm merely trying to die peacefully doing something I enjoy. Can't you let it go?"

"Oh stop being so goddamned stubborn," she said. "You like the company, and you know it. You need someone around you so you won't be narcissistic and brood all the time. Or at least all the time you're not at a game. You need someone making sure you don't spend all your time feeling sorry for yourself."

"Meaning?" I stopped to look at her. No smile. Dead serious look on her face.

"You think this team owes you something." Janice put down her mallet and looked directly into my eyes. "That just because you're dying, you deserve to go to another World Series. Like there's not some Yankee or Red Sox fan somewhere dying of a

[86]

terminal disease. They're playing a game out there. It's their job. Just like the waitress dropping the crabs on the table, or the cab driver waiting for you to appear at the airport. Get over it. They don't know you're out there. They're playing to win. They'd play to win even if you weren't there. They'll play to win after you're dead."

"You don't think you can influence what happens around you?" I queried. "You think everything's already predestined?"

"No, I don't. You know I don't." She was speaking more forcefully. "But you're not going to will a team into the World Series just by following it around. It's not like this is the Make-a-wish Foundation or something."

I felt a wave of nausea coming on. Was it the crabs? The conversation? Or the fact that she was right.

I pounded the claw a little too hard. Tiny pieces of crabmeat spewed out onto the table. "So what do you want me to do? Serve food at a soup kitchen? Read Shakespeare? Go to a monastery and repent?"

"I don't know," she said. "Maybe go back in for treatment?"

I slowly put down my mallet and my fork. Tried putting my brain on ten-second delay so I didn't say anything too foolish.

"Look, Janice," I said. "I'm not going back in for treatment. First off, you can't march in and out of chemotherapy like you can if you've gotten your hand stamped at a club. Second, I've been through treatment and you haven't. I know what it's like. Third, I'm a trained professional. I know the data. I know how small the chances are that I'll get better. I decided a long time ago that when the time came to face up to my own death, I'd do it my way. Do what I want. Not what everyone else wants me to do. It's cost me friends. It's cost me my wife. And if it costs me you, that's simply too bad. Like I told you, no one's forcing you to stick around."

"Why are you saying all this?" She looked almost ready to cry. I hoped she wouldn't try rubbing her eyes with Old Bay-covered hands.

"I don't know. Janice, maybe you should move out." I made certain to enunciate each word evenly and calmly. "Being around someone like me right now may not be good for anyone, much less someone who's a chance acquaintance. You're young, you're smart, you're attractive. You have your whole life in front of you. There are better ways to spend your time."

Now she surprised me. I figured she'd storm out or make some vitriolic comment. Like I'd have done. What's in it for her hanging around a frustrated, angry dying guy like me?

She sat quietly. Waiting for my pulse to slow down, perhaps. Then she took my hand. Her touch was warm, and somehow more comforting than I expected.

"Okay," she began. "I haven't known you very long. But I've never felt so close to anyone in my life. You've taught me a lot about living. I suspect you'll teach me a lot about dying. But it's a relationship. And that holds for both of us. That means along with giving it, you're going to have to take it a bit, too."

She picked up her hammer and attacked her crab. After digging out some claw meat, she again looked directly at me. "You're not getting rid of me right now. In fact, I don't know why you'd want to. I may actually be good for you."

We both looked a mess. Old Bay Seasoning all over our hands and faces. Tiny bits of shell stuck to our skin. Our table looked like a tidal pool war zone. "Think I'll go wash some of this crap off me." Janice rose, gave me a quick kiss on the lips, and headed to the bathroom.

I began missing her the moment she was gone.

Janice wanted to sightsee. We'd already seen highlights of the Baltimore Museum of Art– tile floors recovered from the ancient city of Antioch; Impressionist paintings collected by the two spinster Cone sisters, who left them to the museum after they died "if the spirit of appreciation for modern art in Baltimore became improved;" Rodin's sculpture "The Thinker." We had wandered the Johns Hopkins campus, and strolled around the zoo at Druid Hill Park.

She'd never seen any of the Smithsonian, so we headed for Washington. We found a place to park several blocks from the Washington Mall, then walked to the Castle.

No place better encases the history of America. All I could focus on, though, was how many are left out of that history. The millions who have lived in this country over a couple of centuries, versus the few who are memorialized in this national repository of heritage. Political success gets you in. So does the chance

[88]

invention. Or a remarkable natural talent. Only then do future generations get to learn about you, find out who you were, what you did.

I realized how small the chances for enshrinement are.

"There's no Hall of Fame or Hall of History for the average solid person," I said. "The one who works hard and honestly all his or her life, the one who contributes to the community solely by virtue of being steady and reliable, the kind of person without whom the entire enterprise would crumble and those famous people wouldn't even have mattered."

We were eating crab cakes at Capital City Brewing Company for lunch. My beer was a porter with a strong tinge of chocolate. Everyone else had on a coat and tie, or a business suit or dress. They must view us as among the ragamuffins of the world.

"What do you mean?" Janice responded.

"Oh, you know," I said. "The guys who went and fought in World War II; the women who worked in the factories; the nurses who slave through their shifts, managing a smile when it's the only treatment left that'll help a patient; the parents who coach Little League. The Cal Ripkens of everyday life."

She laughed. "I should have known this was going to end up a baseball reference."

We stopped at the National Archives and looked at hallowed documents. It's almost hard to believe the Declaration of Independence is real, that the paper itself still exists. You read it, and its words are just as applicable today as in 1776. Then you see the Constitution. And realize it's only required a couple of dozen changes all these years. I wondered how many times a manager scratches out players' names before coming up with the final batting order for a game.

We still had time to kill by the harbor before Saturday night's game. Janice noticed a sign for the Babe Ruth Home, so we walked in for the tour. She asked why he didn't play for the Orioles since he grew up in Baltimore. I told her because the city didn't have a team yet.

Noticing plaques on the wall, she pointed with her finger and asked, "What are these?"

"Oh," I said. "Each one represents a home run that Babe

Ruth hit."

"How many in all?"

"Seven hundred and fourteen," I told her.

"You know that off the top of your head?"

"Janice, any die-hard baseball fan would know that number."

"So is that such a big deal?"

"Well, let's put it this way," I said. "He hit 714 home runs in his career. Until Willie Mays hit over six hundred, no one had even come close. Then Hank Aaron got to seven hundred, 755 in fact, to become the leader. I think only about ten players have hit five hundred."

"Will anyone ever hit more?"

Her persistence on the topic surprised me. "You'll get lots of opinions on that. No one playing right now, I don't think. I'm a baseball traditionalist. I hope the record stands forever."

She studied the wall up close. "So I see each one is a single home run. What's the name on the plaque?"

"Oh, that's the guy who was pitching, and his home town." I'd scrutinized the plaques myself once upon a time. Disappointed not to find someone from Storrow Springs.

Janice, naturally, has better luck. "Hey, look. Here's a guy from my hometown."

"Well, it's not spoken for," I said. "You should buy it."

"What do you mean?" Janice asked.

"See all those little markers attached to some of the plaques?" I answered. "Those were bought by people who gave a donation to the museum. I'll bet half of them, maybe more, are because the pitcher came from their home town, or the homer was hit on their birthday, or something else like that."

"How much does it cost?"

"Jesus, Janice, I don't know. Hey, we've got a game. Mind if we hurry it up a bit?"

She patted me a couple of times on the shoulder. "Okay, okay, we'll get there for the first pitch. Just let me go buy this."

"If it's been sitting unclaimed this long," I said, "I suspect it'll still be around tomorrow."

"Hey, you should be happy I'm showing some interest in baseball," Janice retorted. "I thought you'd be pleased. Go on to the game. Give me my ticket. I'll meet you there."

[90]

Shit, I thought, I'm having a mundane marital quarrel with some girl I picked up hitchhiking. Sliding into death isn't turning out to be easier than anything else in life.

Janice stood firm, hands on hips, ready to create some kind of scene. "I mean it. Just give me my ticket. I'm going to get this and put my father's name on it."

I handed over the ticket, shook my head, smiled, and walked out.

Orioles lost to Minnesota 4-2.

Janice, who made it to her seat as the first inning started, cared more about her purchase at the museum. "Can't wait to tell Mom. I'll probably have to explain who Babe Ruth is."

"Think you'll have to explain what you're doing in Baltimore?" I asked.

"No," she said. "They're used to me traveling around. It's not like I'm going to say I'm living with some old guy who's dying, and that maybe I'll get his apartment, or something."

"Aren't you the one who doesn't tell little white lies?"

"I'm not mentioning you," she stated. "If she asks, I guess I'll come up with something." A pause. "But she won't."

Day game tomorrow. I needed to get some sleep.

Thornton Wilder wrote, "For what human ill does not dawn seem to be an alleviation?" Camden Yards plays the part of dawn for me. I may have my sweats and fevers. My appetite may go on hiatus after a bout of nausea and vomiting. Pain may become a more constant companion. And there's that always-present sense of foreboding. I don't think you can call it depression or paranoia. There really is something after me. Some fucking disease.

Still, on a sunny summer Sunday afternoon, what better feeling than being amidst forty-six thousand fans at Camden Yards waiting for the Orioles to take the field? We had great seats for this game. High above the plate, I could see which pitches curved and which didn't. From this perspective, every fly ball looked as though it might reach the stands. Rays of false hope at a time I most needed them.

Valenzuela pitched a complete game victory to end the four-game Minnesota series.

[91]

Janice asked, "The Orioles do well against Minnesota. Is Minnesota any good?"

"No," I told her, "but I kind of like playing bad teams. I'm not looking for respect; I'm looking for victories."

"You know, you could lighten up a bit."

Easy for someone to say who's not wrapped up in her last pennant race.

"Actually, Janice, I've been thinking about asking to play Minnesota more often. Think the commissioner's office would honor a dying man's wish?"

The game was over early enough for a drive into the county for dinner. I'd heard about Friendly Farms but had never eaten there. Janice commented the countryside along York Road, with its rolling farmland, white fences, and horse farms, reminded her of where she grew up.

"So where did you grow up exactly?"

She took a sip of iced tea, then looked up. "I grew up in a small town in western New York. You've never heard of it. Place called Warsaw. We lived on the outskirts, where Mom had lots of space for a garden, but I could still walk to school."

She fiddled with her straw before continuing. "Kind of place where everybody knew you. I learned pretty early I couldn't get away with much without my parents finding out. But that was okay. They were pretty strict with my sister and me, but they did let us have fun.

"Sounds like a pretty happy upbringing," I said. "I didn't know you have a sister."

Her smile broadened into a loopy grin. "Oh, that's not all you don't know about me."

"I don't doubt that for a moment, believe me."

Now that she had started, Janice talked more about her early years. Our table filled up with cottage cheese and cole slaw, fresh rolls and apple butter, bowls of beans and corn, not to mention the main dishes– crab cakes for me, fried chicken for Janice. I'm not sure even healthy people can eat this much. It looked like we'd be here a while.

"I guess when I look back," Janice said, "I realize my family was better off than most people in our town. Though you'd never know it by looking around the house. My father was pretty clear

[92]

with us when it came to money. I got my allowance, but never much extra. My friends always bought the latest clothes and had bigger record collections. Their parents always had newer cars than we did, too."

"Was that a problem for you?" I asked.

"No, not really. Except I felt different when I went off to college. I was the only one in my dorm without a credit card and a new stereo. Dad always insisted we earn the money before buying something. I suppose he had credit cards to use for vacations, but we never saw them."

"Well, easy credit is a problem," I said. "Too many students end up with big debts before they have any concept of what's happening."

"Yeah," she said. "I guess some of it came from knowing what his parents went through during the Depression. We'd hear our share of stories of not being able to afford anything but food and necessities. And sometimes not even those." She wiped her mouth with her napkin. "You know, this chicken is really good."

"I heard those stories, too. Anytime I didn't finish everything on my plate, my parents evoked images of kids starving in China. So I kind of learned not to waste anything, either."

"Except now you're wasting something," she said. "Your time."

"Oh, no, not a sermon with my Sunday dinner. The key word, Janice, is 'my.' It's my time. Victimless crime, if you want to call it that. My philosophy is that if I'm not infringing on someone else, or hurting anyone, then there's no immorality or illegality to what I'm doing."

Janice stared a moment. "Don't you think maybe you get put on this earth to contribute something, though?"

Here we go. "Well, actually, I do. I think we all have the responsibility to leave the world a little better than we found it. But I don't think a supreme being keeps a daily scorecard. I mean, I'm willing to concede life isn't exactly like baseball. Even if right now, baseball's the only thing in life for me."

"So you figure you've contributed enough, and now you can slide the rest of the way?"

"Look, Janice. I've got an ultimately fatal disease. Even so, I'm determined not to be a burden on society. Yeah, maybe I'm

[93]

taking advantage of some health insurance, but I'm not wasting scarce resources. I'm a big believer in autonomy. I'm not doing any harm, so I feel I've got the right to die like I want to." Made me think of Leslie Gore– it's my party and I'll cry if I want to. Janice was too young to know the song. I broke into a little smile.

"Shit, don't smirk at me," she retorted. Her facial features tightened. "Maybe I'm not as old and wise as you are, but there's something to what I'm saying."

"Oh, I'm not smirking," I reassured her. "I smiled because I remembered a song from childhood. Had a lyric 'it's my party, and I'll cry if I want to.' That's all. Believe me, I've gotten to know you well enough not to laugh at you."

Her stern look of eased. "Well, I can come up with lyrics, too. Like 'you can't always get what you want.' Which kind of describes your selfishness."

"You know, I resent that," I said. "I'm not a selfish person."

She wasn't about to stop now. "Well, you've got capabilities to help others, and you're not using them. I'd call that selfish."

"God damn it, Janice, I'm dying. I'm not required to work up until my final hour."

"But you're quickening the arrival of that final hour because you won't take treatment."

I tensed with anger. That's an emotion I'd generally learned to channel. If I was going to express rage, I preferred saving it for a tight game when a player took a called third strike with two outs and bases loaded in the ninth. Now that would be something to get angry about.

Keeping my voice even, I continued. "I made a conscious decision to refuse therapy. As was my right. If you're ever unfortunate enough to require chemo yourself, spend your days weak and nauseated or both, you might see my side of it. When there was a chance for a cure, I did everything required of me. But, like I've said, I know the science. There's no cure coming now. Maybe I'm passing my final months living a fantasy, but there's nothing wrong with living a fantasy if it doesn't hurt anyone. I've seen dead people all my life. It never occurred to me I'd end up that way, too. But now that I realize I will, I want a say in how I get there."

No response.

"Don't forget, Janice, no one's forcing you to hang around

with me through the ordeal."

There was no such thing as a clincher in a conversation with Janice. She calmly picked up her fork, snagged a piece of chicken, and remarked almost offhandedly, "What, and miss this rare opportunity to gain insight beyond my years? No way!" And she grinned.

We ate in silence a while, until Janice said, "Don't think I'm planning to skip dessert."

We toured more highlights of Baltimore. The shot tower, where I explained as best I could the process by which molten iron turned into artillery shells on its way down the tall narrow chimney. The Washington Monument in Mount Vernon.

"People here like to brag that this was the first Washington Monument," I said. "Of course, nobody outside of Baltimore has ever heard of it."

"Well," said Janice, "you have to admit the one in Washington does overshadow it a bit. What is it, three times higher?"

I walked over to the sign. "Says this one is 178 feet tall. So I guess you're about right. I like the way this one is so accessible, though, right in the middle of a neighborhood."

"That's the other problem. No parking. People won't go somewhere they can't park."

"That's what's wonderful about America, I guess. If you can't drive to it– and find a place to park– how important can it be?" I pointed down the block. "Hey, c'mon, let me show you one of my favorite places."

We walked over to the Peabody Library. Nothing to distinguish it on the outside, but what an impressive interior.

"Wow! This really is pretty amazing." She gazed around, looking at the six tiers of bookshelves with their cast iron columns and balconies, then up at the ceiling skylight. "Why's it so empty?"

Our whispering seemed to echo above the highly polished floor. "You never see many people here. I don't really know what the rules are for using it. Once upon a time, I thought about what a beautiful place this would be to be buried. Amidst all the books and everything."

"Oh, is this the point?" Janice cut in. "To get back to talking about dying again?"

"Janice, that's enough," I said. "If you don't feel like appreciating beauty for its own sake, let's go get lunch. I'll take you to another venerable Baltimore institution."

Next we headed for Lexington Market.

"I take it you've noticed all the row houses and white steps. They're a Baltimore trademark," I told her.

"Yeah, I have noticed. You can sort of figure out how rich the people living there are by how fancy they are. There's a lot of them made out of one kind of stone."

"Formstone," I confirmed. "Another Baltimore tradition. I don't know much about it, but it's really a form of cement or concrete. I'm not sure I've seen it anywhere else."

"It's really a pretty interesting city to walk around in," Janice said.

"Yeah," I agreed, "at least when you're not looking over your shoulder for the next perpetrator of a violent crime."

We came to the market. Inside we passed by vegetable and fruit stands looking for Faidley's, the seafood place.

"Okay, Janice, I'll buy you your first soft crab sandwich."

"Fine."

The sandwich arrived– a crab plopped between two pieces of white bread, its spindly legs dangling beyond the crusts. I still remembered Mary's scream when I bought her one. Naturally, it didn't faze Janice.

"I suppose you did this to shock me," she said. "But this is really good." It was unusual to see her talking with her mouth full.

"Glad you like it," I said.

"Yeah," she said. "I think the key is making sure you don't start thinking this is some kind of giant insect between the pieces of bread."

"You know, Janice, a comment like that could ruin these for me. Deprive me of yet one more revered pleasure."

"I think I'll try to make myself the last pleasure you have." She wiped her mouth with a paper napkin.

"You argue too much to be the last pleasure I have," I told her.

"You call it arguing," she said. "I call it challenging. Sort of like personal enrichment."

[96]

"Fine. My obituary can say I'm survived by my personal enricher, Janice Browning."

"Hey, I kind of like that!"

That night, Chris Hoiles and Jeffrey Hammonds homered in the opener of a three-game series with the Royals. Jamie Moyer pitched well, at least until the rains come. By the time we found cover, we were both soaked. "Hey," I said. "Finally your hair looks as bad as mine."

"Thanks. So who decides if they cancel the game because of rain?" Janice asked.

"Well, until it starts, it's up to the home team," I said. "Then it's the umpires' call."

"If they stopped playing now," she asked, "would they just continue later?"

"If it's under five innings, the whole thing is cancelled, and the statistics are wiped out."

She looked skeptical. "You mean if a guy hits a home run, it ends up not counting?"

"Exactly," I said

"That's not fair."

I adjusted my hat so the brim would cover my face a little better. "Now why would I expect you to say that?"

"I'm just asking."

"That's the rule," I repeated. "Over five innings, the game's official. Then it all counts."

"So if they stop now, the Orioles win," Janice clarified.

"Yes."

"So if the umpire likes the Orioles," she said, "he should stop it."

I sighed. "The umpire is supposed to be neutral. That's the point of having an umpire."

"You know," she interjected, "I don't want to sit out here in the rain for hours."

"Well, we agree on that, so why don't we stop the discussion right there?" I was beginning to feel a chill. Hoped it was from being wet, and that it didn't represent a fever.

"Deal," she said, "but only if you'll get me another beer."

"Nothing with you comes without a contingency, huh?"

[97]

"Right," she confirmed. "And believe me, a beer is a cheap price for my company."

"Okay, I'll spring for the beer, but you have to go get it," I said. "And bring me something hot, maybe a cup of coffee."

The delay seemed to halt the team's momentum, but the O's held on and won 6-5. Still only a half game out.

Call it a red letter day.

Toronto falls to Chicago, 2-1. Yankees lead 5-0, then lose to Seattle 9-5. Meanwhile at Camden Yards, Ben McDonald crafts a one-hitter. Still striking out Royals in the ninth. A six-run eighth inning blows open a game otherwise slimly preserved by Harold Baines' early homer.

My resurgent Orioles, ten and a half games back on Memorial Day, take the division lead on the ninety-fourth game of the season.

"You think this team is playing over its head?" Janice inquired.

"Actually, they aren't performing as well as I think they should," I answered.

Ripken and Anderson should be hitting better. The relievers have been a shade erratic. Sutcliffe and Mussina are struggling, but McDonald shows signs of maturing as a pitcher. Valenzuela and Moyer offer some stability. Team still needs to hit better in the clutch.

I hope the front office resists temptations to tinker with the team's chemistry. It's pleasing to savor victory by an improving team. Sex has its role, but for now baseball has become a bit more predictable. I'm ready to make my deal with the devil. Let me see one more World Series. Let me enjoy the vicarious satisfaction of urging my team on into October.

"Who knows?" I summarized. "Some days I think this team can beat anyone. Other times I think they'd have trouble against a reasonably good high school squad."

"Does that mean I shouldn't get overly excited?" Janice asked.

"Depends on your point of view. For me, well, why not? It's the main thing I live for."

Life at the top proved transient. The bullpen collapsed in a

[98]

loss to Kansas City, and the team fell back to second. Nonetheless, I enjoyed that one shining moment, when the O's led the division, and all felt right with the world. Now for another trip to Minnesota.

This was when there should be an off day. Leaving late afternoon from rush hour Baltimore, knowing you've got a game the next night in Bloomington, Minnesota; now that's not right. Those people making the schedule should make allowances for deranged fans who think they'll shadow their team's chartered jet via automobile. Sort of like being in the chase car for a hot air balloon, but knowing they've got a day and a half lead on you. And that they'll be waiting not in some rural corn field, but in a luxury hotel, when you finally arrive.

Such thoughts propelled me as I did the brunt of the driving. Once the traffic let up, we managed to put in a solid six hours on the road. When I got hungry, I ate the corned beef sandwich I'd picked up at Attman's. Didn't know how much mustard had dripped onto my shirt until Janice woke up and broke out laughing. Tried to make it past the Indiana state line but settled for Dayton. That meant we needed an early start in the morning.

I figured we had a good six hundred miles still to cover. I started behind the wheel on the premise we'd get in a couple of hours before breakfast. Two cups of coffee in their holders, AM radio blasting through the speakers.

That was another problem when I was married. I liked hearing the local stations. Mary wanted continuous FM music. Fewer commercials, and all. Without local radio I couldn't get a feel for the countryside we were driving through. No, I didn't understand the crop reports, and school calendars could become a bit numbing. The week's lunch menus for senior citizens weren't very interesting, either. Yet there was something reassuring about the big issues being improvements in traffic control, or the rationale for parking meters downtown, rather than the latest murder or corporate scandal. Plus I enjoyed listening to obituaries over the air. In places without a daily newspaper, the radio announcer's words might be the entire encapsulation of a life. I remember one town, I think it was in Kentucky, where in each notice they said the deceased "was taken." John Doe was taken. Jane Smith was taken. Took me a while to grasp they were being taken by the Lord, not by some kidnapping ring in the mountains.

Janice broke the spell of serenity. "Have you thought about the possibility the team will win the championship, but that you might die before they do?"

"Sure, I've thought about it," I answered. "That would be a real bummer!"

"Would you rather have that," she added, "or live longer but see them lose?"

I glanced over to check her expression, determine if she was trying to be combative. "I play to win. Then let the chips fall where they may."

We drove a few miles in silence. Rain fell periodically. Not enough for the wipers to work effectively, so I moved my gaze around the streaks on the windshield.

Janice concentrated on reading *Main Street.* "I want to learn something about Minnesota," she'd said, "and there aren't that many books to choose from."

Soon I started up again. "You know, Janice, I learned early in my career there's a lot doctors can't explain. When I was a med student, I took care of a guy dying of bad lung disease. Something called sarcoid, not something you get from smoking. I got to know him and his family fairly well. It was hard watching him get worse every day. Then one afternoon he told me all he cared about was getting to his daughter's wedding."

I checked to be sure Janice was listening. "It was five weeks away. My resident told me there was no way the guy could make it. Three weeks later, though, he was still alive. So I took up the cause. Did the paperwork for a pass from the hospital, arranged for oxygen, got prescriptions for him. I was going to set up an ambulance but he said, no, he didn't want that. So the family outfitted the back of their station wagon for him. I was there the morning he left, knowing I might never see him again."

I slowed down as some idiot truck driver tried to pass me with his eighteen-wheeler. He sprayed the car, and I put the wipers back on. "As it turned out, everything went well. He enjoyed the wedding, the family enjoyed the time with him. Daughter postponed the honeymoon to stay longer with him. They brought him back to the hospital second morning afterwards, as planned. He died in an hour."

"That's quite a story," Janice spouted out after a few minutes. "Don't forget, though, his disease was incurable. You might have a little better chance than he did if you got treated."

"Okay," I countered, as I slowed for an exit ramp. "That's off limits for you from now on. My life, my decision. Okay?" We were near Lafayette. College town. Picked up more coffee and kept driving. Janice was asleep by the time I'd merged back onto the highway.

I took advantage of a second wind and headed around Chicago. After pulling off at Beloit and finding a pancake house, I woke Janice. It was about eleven o'clock. Time for a late breakfast, then push to do four hundred miles in six hours. Game starting at seven. Will be close, but we should make it. Another tense day in the life of a fan. A dying fan.

Players are spared the tedium of interstates. Teams fly from city to city, probably on charters. As a train rolled along beside us, I thought nostalgically to an era when both players and fans traveled by rail. Like it or not, they'd have to run into each other occasionally. In fact, until the stratospheric salaries of free agency, most players, even quite accomplished ones, had to maintain offseason jobs. Walk the same streets and stalk the same stores as the hoi polloi.

"So have you ever thought about taking up sex again?" Janice asked.

I still wasn't accustomed to having her next to me after all the miles on the road alone. "Come again?"

"You heard me," she said. "You trying to be a monk or something?"

I turned toward her. "In all honesty, I'm not sure that's any of your business."

"Look," she said, her expression deadly serious, "I'm riding around the country with you. I'm staying in your place in Baltimore. I'm staying in hotels everywhere with you. I'm about the only person you talk to outside the ballpark. For all I know, I'm the only friend you have left. There's nothing anymore that's none of my business."

She might be right. "In that case, no, I really haven't thought about it much."

"I mean, if you're worried you can't do it anymore," she continued, "I think I can assure you it's no problem."

I turned toward her again. "And what exactly does that mean?"

Janice grinned sheepishly. "It means that I've checked you in the middle of the night and you're able to get it up okay."

Jesus, what's off limits to this girl? "And you know this how?"

"I know," she said, "because you sleep soundly enough that I've been able to pull the sheets down and see that you've got a hard-on."

"Goddamn it, Janice, aren't I entitled to even a little bit of privacy? I still can't figure out how I let you talk me into letting you come along. Do you not respect any boundary?"

"Hey, I'm just making conversation," she replied. "We talk about death enough. Any reason we can't talk about some life for a change?"

We both stared rigidly straight ahead for a while, working to keep our peripheral visual fields from overlapping. She'd already gotten me to talk about all sorts of subjects I never wanted to broach again. My job frustrations. My marriage failing. My outrage and shame in knowing I'm going to die one of these days. Part therapist, part anonymous traveling companion – the two kinds of people to whom someone is likely to open up.

You expect your life to be one of continuous fireworks. Then you have to settle for a few random sparks. It's disheartening. And here I am playing out the final scenes with a stranger.

"Truce?" she asked.

"Sure," I answered

"So where are we headed again?"

"You know where we're headed, Janice. Minnesota."

"I thought you just played them," she said.

"Yeah," I agreed, "but that was a home series. Now we play them in Minnesota."

Janice persisted. "Why don't you have to play other teams before you play them again?"

And I'm trying to teach this woman the subtleties of the hit-and-run and suicide squeeze? "That's just the way the schedule got

[102]

made. I don't know why. Then we go to Toronto."

"What are you gonna tell them when we cross the border?" she asked. "What if I say I'm being kidnapped?"

"You're really in a talkative mood today, aren't you?" I eased back into the right lane. "There won't be any problem at the border, at least if you keep your mouth shut. If there is, well, I'll tell them I saw 'Lolita' last year and I'm trying the plot out for myself."

"Now there's an idea," she said. "How about we stop to see a movie one of these days?"

"Anything in mind?" I asked.

"No. But not a baseball movie. I'm seeing enough baseball."

Don't know why I pushed so hard to make it in time for the series opener. Rick Sutcliffe, staked to two runs in the top of the first, got clobbered. By the last out in the ninth, sealing a Twins 8-4 win, I was barely paying attention.

I picked up a copy of the *New York Times* and seized upon an article on competitive birdwatching. That's a scenario I'd never envisioned. Annual lists are published of who's seen the most species. People use beepers for signaling short-notice alerts. To think I always assumed bird watchers were laid-back, Type B types. Suddenly my decision to follow the Orioles felt more reasonable. Being obsessed with the fortunes of a baseball team has to be every bit as meritorious as being dedicated to competitive birdwatching.

Driving was taking more out of me. We got to the hotel after midnight, slept till ten. If housekeeping hadn't knocked, I might have laid around until time for tonight's game.

We went down to the university area for a late breakfast in a part of the city nicknamed Dinkytown. If I were a student, I think I'd be insulted if the places I hung out were collectively called Dinkytown. There seemed to be pretty broad consensus among fans we met at the stadium that Al's was *the* place for breakfast in Minneapolis.

It looked the part. The only two empty seats were at the counter, separated by a couple sitting together. My pancakes were great. Off to the side, I could see Janice chowing down an omelet. I enjoyed the respite, which let me study the sports pages without interruption. Right after the waitress poured me another cup of coffee, a familiar voice interrupted my reverie.

"Hey, Mister," I heard Janice exclaim a bit louder than necessary, "you don't happen to be traveling toward Chicago, do you? 'Cause I'd love to have a chance to see Chicago."

She had a flair, I'll give her that. Everyone within earshot turned toward her. I'm sure they're still wondering how she chose me out of the motley assortment available within the diner. I silently shook my head, then answered. "Well, actually I am, Ma'am. If you're the quiet type and don't mind traveling with a stranger, I'll get you there."

"Well, all I've got is this backpack and the clothes on my back," she continued, breaking into a broad smile, "so whenever you finish that cup of coffee, I'll be at the door ready to go."

I asked the girl behind the counter for another cup to take with me, over-tipped her handsomely, and walked out to a smattering of strange looks on patrons' faces.

"You can wipe off that syrup that's stuck below your lip," Janice said.

"Sure," I said, "anything to satisfy a wanton lady who wants a chance to see Chicago."

She laughed, then got out a piece of Kleenex, moistened it, and wiped the syrup off.

We took a quick tour of downtown. Saw the Guthrie Theater. Passed the huge structure where General Mills once made Gold Medal flour. It had closed in the 1960's, then there had been a fire a couple of years ago. Seemed as though I kept running into once stolid places now in varying stages of decay. I looked at each as a symbol of myself.

Janice wanted to see the Mall of America. I passed; I'm in that segment of life when it doesn't do much good to learn how much is out there to consume. After dropping her at a light rail stop, I drove over to the medical school library. I asked the librarian to search for recent literature about lymphoma. She couldn't have been more helpful. It is the Midwest, after all.

I forced myself to read the entries she produced. Always another kind of chemotherapy concoction, always with marginal benefit at best. Magic potions must not make it into the medical literature. Guess I needed to know that while I've been focused on baseball, no one had found out three apricots a day could melt a lymphoma.

You rebel at the idea of cells proliferating wildly within your body. Why's it have to be a cancer that you're condemned to die from? Why not an infection, for which antibiotics might make it a fair fight? Or a heart attack, which you might fix with a balloon catheter and some promises to live better? Maybe some congenital malformation finally coming home to roost, for which there might be some innovative surgery.

No, it's got to be a malignancy. One that occurs for no good reason. For which treatment sometimes works. Unless it doesn't.

Doesn't even sound like a heroic cancer. Lymph nodes. Shit, all most people know about them is that they swell up when you're a kid and you have strep throat or mono. They shouldn't be able to kill you. Lung cancer, everyone know it's a battle. Or the liver. Something affecting a major organ, one that everyone knows if it's destroyed, you're finished. No, it's got to be lymph nodes. You're going to die because of a fucking bunch of swollen glands.

PART FOUR

July 23, 1993

There were reprieves at the ball park. Valenzuela threw a complete game to beat the Twins. Jamie Moyer won the next afternoon. Glad to see both of them win. I viewed Valenzuela as a role model for all those people who worry you only get one chance in life. A symbol for those who have slipped down a ladder, or off the wagon, or whatever, but had the fortitude to give it another try. Moyer's a bit of the same, except he's never been to the top. He doesn't have a blinding fast ball, so he must rely on skill and experience in forging success. A reminder that a dearth of natural talent doesn't consign you to mediocrity if you're willing to put in the hard work. His pitching motion looks so smooth and relaxed, you could imagine him doing this another fifteen or twenty years.

We ate dinner at an old-style supper club. Conversation turned to my professional life.

"If you hated what you were doing so much" Janice asked, "why didn't you quit and try something else?"

"It's not like I hated it," I said. "It was just beginning to get the best of me. It's hard to see the situation when you're right in the middle of it. I mean, I got married. We were thinking about kids. We bought a house so there was a mortgage. My practice load grew. I'd come home late, tired, my mind so full of things to talk about that I didn't say anything at all."

"Did your wife know how frustrated you were?"

I thought a few seconds before answering. "Yes and no, I guess. She had her own career, she was a bookkeeper for a department store. After a while I think we became numb to each other's issues. A bad way to cope, by not talking about things openly when we needed to."

"Why do people clam up when things go bad?" Janice asked. "Seems like it'd be better to just have it out."

"I don't know," I said in reply. "I guess most people want to avoid conflict. And they don't want to give the opportunity to show they might share blame themselves."

"Like any of us are perfect."

[107]

I laughed. "You mean you aren't, either? Then why am I spending time with you?"

She rolled up the newspaper section I'd brought along and gave me a playful swat on the head. "Because even someone who's imperfect will be an improvement for you!"

Back in the room, we packed up for the next day's escape. I had my *Sporting News*. Janice lay in bed reading *The Natural*. She'd asked at the Mall of America for good books about baseball. People recommended Malamud's novel and W. S. Kinsella's *Shoeless Joe*. Guess these will be our topics the next few days. Beats talking about cancer.

The last Oriole win brought them back to only half a game behind. I began looking ahead to the contests coming up in Toronto. We had a day off between series, offering the luxury of two days for the drive from Minneapolis. We'd be going near the place where I first picked Janice up, oh so many weeks ago. I kidded her, suggesting we stop for an anniversary celebration.

"Sure, I'm game. We'll be right near Oshkosh, too. Can we stop there? So I can say I've been to Oshkosh, b'gosh?"

After breakfast at Eau Claire, I took the wheel. We drove secondary roads amidst trim farmhouses and neatly plowed fields. The sweet-sour odor of manure wafted through the open windows. Some farmers call it the "prosperous smell." Janice alternately cruised the radio dial and studied the road map. I chose not to tell her about the dried maple syrup on her T-shirt.

"Janice, I never asked exactly how you happened to be at that gas station in the middle of nowhere in Wisconsin."

"Well, I'd started from Denver, heading to visit a girlfriend in Milwaukee," she began. "Everything went pretty smoothly, until I hit Des Moines. A trucker picked me up. I thought he was going to Milwaukee, but I dozed off and found he was really headed to Minneapolis."

"No fear you were being kidnapped?" I asked.

"No, he was actually a really nice guy," she said. "Married, two young kids, absolutely devoted to his wife. When I told him I thought he'd said Milwaukee, he turned bright red, wanted to know how he could make it up to me. Like it was his fault, not mine, for not listening better." She looked up from the map. "You know it's just like you, thinking the guy knew I was going to Milwaukee and tried to take advantage. Everyone's not intrinsically evil, you know."

"Well, I seem to remember this thing called original sin," I said. "Doesn't that mean everyone's bad till proven good?"

Janice squinted at the map. "Glad I'll never have you on my jury. Anyhow, he bought me lunch in Rochester, then got on his radio to find me a ride. There was a guy heading to LaCrosse, so I said sure, why not? Figured from there I ought to be able to get to Madison or Milwaukee easily enough."

"And?"

Janice put the map aside. "Bad day for traffic to Milwaukee, I guess. I'd made it from Denver to Des Moines in only three rides, then it took me that many just getting from outside of Rochester to that place you picked me up. Hoped I'd find a student heading to Madison or something. All I got were people on vacation. Each ride got me a few miles. Until you drove me all the way to Cleveland. And I guess we've been on the same whirlwind tour ever since."

Neither of us remembered the territory very well. I'd been wandering back roads aimlessly; she hadn't really known where she was. Unfortunately, neither of us remembered the name of the town. We searched for a while but couldn't find the gas station.

"Shit, you know how fast they redevelop land these days," I suggested. "It's probably been torn down and been replaced by a McDonald's already."

"It's not that important," she said. "Let's head toward Oshkosh."

Janice continued studying the map. "Hey, I know what. Let's go up to Green Bay. In college, they taught about some Indian who claimed he was the son of Louis XVI, and how when Louis and Marie Antoinette were beheaded, he was spirited away to America. He lived in Massachusetts a while, then northern New York, I think. Anyhow, somewhere along the way, he ended up in Green Bay. Let's go see if someone there knows anything about it."

"Janice, I think all anyone in Green Bay knows about is the Green Bay Packers. So unless he played for them, I doubt you'll learn very much."

"There you go again," Janice said, raising her voice. "Everything's baseball."

[109]

"No," I corrected. "Actually that's football."

"Whatever."

"Okay, you pick," I said. "Oshkosh or Green Bay. We can't do both. This isn't your trip. It's not your final season."

She chose Oshkosh.

For a change of pace, we took a ferry from Manitowoc, Wisconsin, across Lake Michigan. It gave us a break from driving, plus represented the straightest line from Oshkosh to Toronto, b'gosh. We'd bought sandwiches at a nearby deli for supper. There was only a small crowd aboard, so we staked out spots in the lounge and ate.

One problem of traveling prolonged distances with a single companion is that you talk yourselves out. Less of an issue for Janice, who always has a comment on something, but I was glad for the respite. She skimmed through a company history on Oshkosh clothes. I read *The New Yorker*.

An hour into the ride, Janice got up and walked across the room. When I looked up, I found her petting a golden retriever, apparently a seeing eye dog. The woman with the dog looked closer to my age than Janice's. They sat in animated conversation.

"You should go over and meet that woman," Janice told me upon her return. "Make you feel a little less sorry for yourself."

"Why?" I said. "I'm kind of enjoying the glow of self-pity. Besides, why shouldn't I feel a little sorry for myself every once in a while?"

"She lost her vision to some kind of rare disease when she was in elementary school," Janice told me. "Couldn't do anything with her friends anymore. I can't imagine how bad it would be being a teenager who's blind. All the girls are talking about guys, or clothes, or movies, or whatever, and you can't see any of it." Janice reached down for a soda, popped the top, and took a swallow before continuing.

"Anyhow," she went on, "some blind guy in her town spent time with her, told her not to give up, all that crap, then helped her get a seeing eye dog. She finished high school, got into college. Went to the prom. Think about that. Everyone telling her how pretty she looked and she couldn't look in the mirror and see it."

"Reminds you of how much you take for granted," I

conceded.

"No kidding. So she finished college, moved to Kentucky, and took a job at a place that makes books and tapes for the blind. Ever hear of it?" Janice asked.

"No," I said, "can't say that I have."

"Yeah, she proofreads things that they print in Braille," she took a sip of her Coke. "Amazing, huh? She's blind, can't see a thing, and she's a proofreader."

"Yeah!"

"Don't just say yeah! You'd probably throw yourself off a bridge if you were blind."

"Come on, Janice, you don't really know me well enough to come to that conclusion."

"Well, you're giving up on life, aren't you?" she spouted.

"I don't see it that way," I said. "We each get our time on the planet. I'm just choosing to spend what's left of mine doing something I enjoy."

"Maybe so," she asserted, "but you could still do things for people."

"Someday, Janice, take an ethics course. I'm a big believer in the concept of autonomy. I've told you that before. None of us has the right to do anything that would cause harm to others. As long as you respect that, then you should be able to make your own decisions. I'm choosing to live the final months of my life the way I want. Not only am I not breaking any laws or moral codes, I think more than a few people would envy me the opportunity."

"So let me tell you what else she does," Janice interjected.

"Who?"

"The woman with the dog. She travels around and counsels young people who are blind. Tells them not to give up on life. Or on themselves. She shows how independent she's been and talks about all the jobs you can still do without your sight. Tries to convince them they've got to make some allowances along the way, but that life still can be what you make it."

"You only talked to this person a few minutes, and you got all that?" I was impressed.

"Hey, you've taught me to be a good listener," she said. "Like you've told me, give someone a chance to talk about what they know, and teach you about it, and they'll go as long as you let

[111]

them. You're right about that. But the point is she doesn't give up trying to make a contribution to society. Just like you shouldn't."

"Shit, Janice, I may as well have stayed in organized religion. Here I am trying to die without guilt, and you won't let me do it."

"You can die any way you want. But you can still contribute a little along the way."

"And remind me again just how you're contributing?" I asked.

Janice unwrapped a stick of Wrigley spearmint. "At least I want to contribute."

"I think that's wonderful," I said. "But at this point, I'm not letting good intentions trump a past track record. When you can match what I've accomplished, then we can sit and compare."

"That's not fair," Janice argued. "You know I'm frustrated that I haven't done much with my life. You should encourage me and be glad I'm determined to make something of myself."

"And I am glad," I confirmed. "And I'm happy to be encouraging. But you get on that soapbox every so often, and you know it sets me off. You don't get much chance for experience on how you die, but I think the way I've chosen isn't a bad one."

Janice popped the gum into her mouth. I saw the beginning of a smile. Or was it a smirk? "Okay. Truce? I was just making a point how impressed I am with what that blind woman has been able to do. You know, overcoming what for many would be a big obstacle."

"I'm not disagreeing," I said. "But different people respond to adversity in different ways. There's no one right way."

"Okay already, I get your point." She frowned. "You don't have to be so defensive. I wasn't trying to get on your case."

"Good!" I said. "Now do you have another stick of gum?"

It had been a while since I was so upset about a single ball game.

The evening began pleasantly enough in Toronto. By the time July 27th comes around, I had to expect some muggy days, but the night was a respite. The dome was open. A refreshing breeze reached our seats high above first base.

The Blue Jays' ballpark always fills up so suddenly. Half an hour before a game, the place looks empty. Minutes before the start, everyone magically appears, just in time for the opening pitch. Season ticket holders must have it down to a science.

"How many stadiums have domes?" Janice asked.

The Sky Dome offers a certain fascination. I loved the concept of a retractable dome. A couple of times, I'd hung around in the afternoon to see the thing open. "That's a good question," I replied. "I'm not sure anymore. Houston was the first. And there's one in Montreal."

"Isn't it a little like playing indoors?"

I laughed. "That's what I assumed at first, too. But I guess it's big enough of a space that it doesn't affect the players too much."

"Does it ever open or close during the game?" Janice asked.

"Yeah, once I saw the dome close during a game. Orioles were playing the Blue Jays, and it started to sprinkle. When the rain didn't let up for fifteen minutes or so, the mechanism to close it went into action. It wasn't as exciting as watching groundskeepers race to pull tarps over the field, but every fan sees plenty of that. This is kind of an unusual dome." I put down my beer and pointed upwards. "Each segment has its own motor, so it's sort of like pushing a whole bunch of slices into place to make a whole pie. You could watch through binoculars and see how each tiny engine pushed its segment into place. It took about ten minutes to shut the stadium up tight as a drum."

"Sounds kind of neat to see," she said.

"I was pretty fascinated," I agreed. "I think the Orioles were mesmerized, too. They made a couple of errors while it was happening. Blew what had been a close game till then."

"Sorry!" Janice said, ostentatiously giving me a pat on the shoulder. She got up to walk down to the mezzanine for a hot dog. "Want anything?"

"No." I got out my pen, and juggled my beer and scorecard into place. The pen dropped onto the ground, and I bumped into the woman in the seat next to me.

"Sorry," I said. "Trying to do too many things at once."

"My husband's like that. He gets pretty serious at the ballpark." The man on the other side of her leaned over, put out his hand, "Hi! Jack Turner."

"Dan Jameson. Nice to meet you. Where're you guys

from?"

"Oh, we're from Oshawa," the woman answered. "It's north of Toronto." Her husband added, "We buy tickets to a game against every team. Thirteen games a year. Make a weekend of it each time."

He was retired from work in a steel mill, making parts for automobiles; she'd taught elementary school. Both wore Blue Jay hats. When Janice came back, I introduced everyone around, then got to work filling in the starting lineups on my scorecard.

"You root for Baltimore?" they asked almost in unison. My glee over Harold Baines' home run must have tipped them off. Or maybe it was my groan when Toronto's Paul Molitor hit a matching four-bagger.

We continued our lighthearted banter throughout the game. Toronto fans are nothing if not polite. I'd been to games in their early years when the team languished near the cellar. I've been to games when the pennant hung in the balance. Either way I can root for the Orioles, and the people stay friendly. In New York, I have to keep my mouth shut.

It's 3-2, Toronto. Rick Sutcliffe pitching reasonably well. He's had his good outings and his bad outings. Come to think of it, so have I.

"Sure would be nice to see the Orioles score a few runs here," I murmured after the Orioles put two men on in the eighth.

Toronto manager had gone to the mound and called for a new pitcher. We had a lull while reliever Duane Ward walked in from the bullpen.

"Maybe the guys on base should steal and try to score a run that way," Janice said.

I turned and glared at her. "What are you talking about?"

"TV announcers talk about stealing bases," she said. "Do the Orioles ever do that?"

"First of all, Janice, you generally try to steal only if you have fast runners on the bases. And stealing home is almost impossible. In fact, I don't think I've ever seen it done."

"But if you steal," she said, "you're closer to scoring, aren't you?"

"But if they catch you stealing, you don't score at all. Once you make the third out, the inning's over."

Jack Turner's wife leaned over to get Janice's attention. "You two sound like us. Jack's always telling me how little I know about baseball."

I studied the batter intently, as if to will a run. There was a crack of the bet, and I jumped to my feet. "Holy shit! Janice! Orioles back ahead." Cal Ripken had taken Ward deep for a three-run homer. O's up 5-3. "Good thing you weren't coaching and calling for a steal."

Sutcliffe gave up a one-out single in the bottom of the eighth. Then came the parade.

"I can't believe he's bringing in Mark Williamson," I said.

"Why?"

"I can never figure it out. He looks so good on paper. I mean, he's probably a nice guy, and his statistics look great, but every time I see him pitch, he struggles." I smiled sarcastically. "Sort of the way my blood tests come out so normal while I'm dying with this thing."

"Oh, that's a wonderful metaphor," Janice said

Joe Carter hit a single.

"There," I said. "See what I mean?"

Johnny Oates went back to the mound and signaled for another pitcher, Jim Poole.

"Can't argue that decision," I said. "He's throwing well. Please, just two more outs and let us take a lead into the ninth."

"Want me to get you a beer before you blow a gasket or something?" Janice asked.

John Olerud hit a single.

"Shit, bases loaded."

A few people in the surrounding rows turned around and stared at us.

"Hey," Janice said, "watch your language. There's kids here at the ballpark."

"Janice, if you can't swear about a ball game, what's the use of knowing the words?"

"Gee, Mr. Mature Dying Old Man. You've sure got me there!"

As I stared at this young, sweet, innocent looking girl who wasn't so sweet and innocent, Oates walked out and made yet another pitching change. Gregg Olson's turn on the mound.

"So is this pitcher any good?" she asked.

"Actually, he is," I told her. "I'll think he's better if he gets two outs."

I yelled loudly after Olson struck out Tony Fernandez. "One more, Gregg, just one more."

But Ed Sprague crashed a double. I slammed my half-full beer cup to the ground. Some splashed on the woman in front of me. Her lightheartedness vanished. She turned around and glared. Jack glared at me, too, then raised his beer in a sarcastic toast.

"Sorry" was the best I can manage. Now came Janice's turn to glare.

I was still muttering to myself as Pat Borders hit a slow ground ball and managed to beat the throw to first for a single. "Pat Borders!" I stammered. "A catcher. How can you not throw out a catcher on a ground ball?" Janice gave a frantic signal to keep my voice down.

Olson struck out Turner Ward to end the inning.

"Sure, get a strikeout now, when it doesn't help."

Janice stared at me uncomprehendingly. "Hey! I've never seen you like this. It's a game, for God's sake."

I left my seat without saying a word. Thought about getting another beer, but I was too aggravated. Instead I paced back and forth in front of the concession stand. When I saw play about to resume, I returned to my seat.

"Feel better?" Janice inquired.

I managed a weak smile. "Not much. Yeah, you're right. It's just a game. But in truth, it's never just a game. We had this one won. All these guys needed were a few more outs."

"Well, you know they're trying."

"Janice, enough already. I know they're trying. This is just the way I've always been. I'm out there trying to win. Now more than ever."

"Still, you may want to cool it a little." Her voice dropped to a whisper. "Those people beside us asked if you were okay. I think they heard you talking about dying."

I looked over, but they were gone. For a beer or to use the bathrooms, I hoped. Maybe all this time on the road has made me too insensitive to others around me. Shouldn't let my problems become theirs.

[116]

The game wasn't quite over. Reynolds walked with one out, advanced to third on a Tim Hulett single. Hulett's a gamer. I'm always pleased when he comes through.

Brady Anderson up next. Sacrifice fly? Run-scoring grounder? No, a pop fly to second. "Jesus, why drive in a runner from third when you only make 1.7 million dollars a year? "

Janice looked at me. Didn't bother to say a word. Turned back to the game.

Mark McLemore struck out. Orioles lose 6-5. A wonderful chance to gain ground gone for naught.

I still may die of a heart attack before the cancer can finish eating me up.

I couldn't sleep that night. Too wound up. Most aggravated I'd been with this team since I was in grade school. "I vividly remember coming home from school one afternoon, flopping on the bed, and turning on the radio," I told Janice. "They still played lots of day games back then. The Orioles blew a big lead against the Yankees. Sure, the Yankees were in first place, and Baltimore in last. But this one looked like a sure thing. When they lost, I threw the radio on the floor. Swore I'd never root for Baltimore again. Wouldn't come out of my room for dinner. Refused to look at a baseball score for the rest of the season."

"Glad you've become so much more mature," Janice replied.

Janice had never seen Toronto so I played tour guide. I might have been a mental wreck after last night's game, but physically I felt surprisingly good.

First, we stopped to see dinosaurs at the Royal Ontario Museum. Then we rode the elevator to the top of the CN Tower. You see the soaring steel and glass skyscrapers alongside the more venerable institutional buildings capped by their blue oxidizing copper roofs, then the expanse of Lake Ontario to the east. The commanding life-affirming vista from up there makes it hard to believe you'll shrink down to an insignificant scattering of ashes anytime soon.

Around lunchtime, we strolled over to the St. Lawrence Market, bought pea meal bacon sandwiches, and found a picnic table in a nearby park.

"You know, you seem to pull up such reserves of energy

[117]

when you're traveling," Janice said. "That doesn't make you reconsider going back for treatment?"

"No. No way. I go back for more chemo, I lose these days. Forever. It's not like having pneumonia. You kill the bacteria, you build your strength back up. You're done. Life goes on as before. This thing, it doesn't go away. Best chance for cure is the first time. Odds of getting a prolonged remission the second time around are almost nil. I want to spend my days, however many I've got left, the way I want."

She nibbled on her sandwich. "What if you live longer than you expect? What then?"

"That's a tough one. Not sure I could handle another season following this team. Would probably kill me."

"Jesus," Janice retorted, "you sound like someone out of those Samuel Beckett plays I read in English lit classes."

Janice isn't one for a shoe museum, so we went to the Art Gallery of Ontario for the Henry Moore sculptures, then took a bus out to Casa Loma. It's a spectacularly ostentatious home, built solely because someone could afford to.

Someone needed to tell this guy you can't take it with you. And if you could, well, baseball memories are easier to carry.

It got no easier at the ballpark. Harold Baines homered and doubled for a 4-2 lead.

"We'll get it back," shouted a Blue Jay fan next to us in Section 132. And they did.

Valenzuela surrendered the tying runs. Errors gave the game away in the tenth inning.

"So is it the manager's fault or the pitcher's if he brings in a new pitcher and that guy gives up a bunch of runs?" Janice queried in between shelling peanuts.

"Good question. And not an easy one to answer." I grabbed some peanuts for myself.

"So try me."

"I admit, I don't envy a manager's need to decide who to bring in. Or even when to bring a pitcher in. It's a matter of instinct versus statistics versus what the player wants. Manager becomes a hero or a demon, depending on whether some high-paid relief

[118]

pitcher gets the next guy out. For the salaries they get, you come to expect results. When's the last time you wanted a stock broker who got you a profit 50% of the time, or a surgeon who removed all the tumor on only two-thirds of his operations?" I thought a moment. "Shit, Janice, if my diagnoses had been right only 75% of the time, I would have spent most of my time defending myself in court."

"Then it's unfair to always blame the manager when someone doesn't do well."

"Oh, I don't know," I said. "One privilege you get for being a fan is the right to criticize – and boo – whenever you want. It's amazing the vitriol fans will throw onto the manager and the players, when these guys are among an elite few who can play at that level. Most fans probably lacked the ability to play as far back as Little League."

We'd escaped Toronto's metropolitan area, but traffic hadn't yet thinned out when Janice asked, "So when exactly did you come to the decision to follow your team around like this?"

By now, our conversations had some depth. As if a romance has become established, and the focus was no longer on impressing the other and not making a mistake. This meant some answers required more thought. One-liners and flippant comebacks no longer sufficed.

"I'd seen too many people suffer through long courses of therapy without getting much better. Then I got sick and went through the wringer myself. You know, tests, chemotherapy, infections." I paused while I eased back into the right lane. Why do so many slow drivers insist on staying in the passing lanes? "Once I started vomiting blood, and they thought I was going to die. I wouldn't give up, but I had plenty of days wondering whether the fight was worth it."

How long ago was that? When I thought I might actually be cured. When they told me, with that optimism some doctors feel they have to wear like an ID badge, that the tumor was gone. Before I remembered that "no evidence of disease" really just meant "no evidence of disease right now."

"When I finally did get better, it was great. I mean, there's no describing the sense of burden being lifted. I remember the first time I played tennis afterwards. It felt like a miracle. I began

[119]

appreciating each day for what it was. I knew never to take a minute for granted. But I also thought, okay, I've been through this once, but I'm not so sure I'd ever be willing to go through it again. If the lymphoma came back, I'd have to see what the most current treatment options were, but in general chances of a cure are much smaller the second go-round. And I didn't want to spend my last days lying in a hospital bed tethered to IV lines and feeding tubes."

"So baseball is worth trading your life for?"

I laughed. "Janice, for the first forty years of my life, that's just what I would have done. Traded my life for baseball. I fantasized all the time about playing in the major leagues, but I was nowhere good enough. Second-string high school infielders don't make the pros. I finally learned how to hit halfway decently, but that wasn't enough. I'd need a deal with the devil."

Janice rummaged around in the glove compartment. She began stacking items she pulled out– maps, owner's manual, couple of pens, a bunch of credit card receipts, Reese's wrappers.

"What are you looking for?"

"I stashed a pack of gum in here. Dumb idea. I forgot how hard it would be to find again amidst all your mess." She was still pulling stuff out. "Oh, here it is."

"You going to put everything back?" I asked.

"No, I don't think I am," she said. "Okay, I'll put the owner's book and a couple of pens back. Can't you throw out the rest of this crap? Or, toss it in the back seat and let it blend in with all the other junk."

"You've made your point, Janice, thank you. Someday I'm coming back from the dead to see your house. Or your car. See if you're so perfect a housekeeper."

"Want some gum?" she asked.

"Why is this fucking truck staying in the left lane?" I honked.

I thought Janice was tired of the direction the conversation was taking, so I stayed quiet until she picked up on it again.

"You couldn't coach or something?" she asked. "Or be an announcer or a sports writer?"

"No," I said. "Once I figured out you couldn't go to the want ads and trade souls, and that satanic forces didn't answer those queries you sometimes find in the paper--you know, 'looking for

[120]

long lost devil who passed this way years ago seeking souls of desperate young baseball players'-- I managed to face up to life somewhat realistically. Yeah, I thought about being a sports writer, but I didn't think I could criticize players' skills when they so far exceeded my own. It's one thing to be a Walter Mitty who plays ball; it's another being a journalist telling Cal Ripken or Brady Anderson he ought to be hitting the ball better than he is.

"One night I came home from work and said to my wife, 'you know, if I ever find out I have a terminal disease, I don't think I could go through what I see patients go through all the time in the hospital. I think I'd pick up an Oriole schedule and follow the team around the country instead.' That offhand quip became a mantra, if not an obsession. I didn't follow through when I first got the lymphoma. But I knew I'd do it if the situation came around again."

Janice rarely went so long without interrupting me. I figured she was becoming bored with the topic. But when I glanced over, I thought I saw a tear rolling down one side of her face.

It was at least another full minute before she spoke. "Do you ever regret the decision? I mean, you come so unraveled when the Orioles lose. Do you ever feel betrayed? Do you ever think to yourself, 'hey, it's only a game'?"

"No, I don't spend a whole lot of time on regrets," I said. "I mean, I did at first. But a lot was regret over what I had hoped to accomplish but didn't. I remember thinking it would have been nice to start with spring training. That's the one recurring scene on the planet where hope truly does spring eternal. When basking in optimism is all the ardent fan is asked to do. A sportswriter in Washington said 'life begins on opening day.' There's something to that. But I didn't have the option of waiting for next spring. I took this year's team or none at all. From then on, I decided not to spend a lot of the time I had left on regrets. I wanted to live in the moment. Coming unglued after a bad loss comes with the territory."

I signaled before changing lanes. "Look at it this way. I get to see America. The cities, the broad expanses in between, the roads hopeful youth will travel in the future, maybe some of them playing baseball themselves. Stopping in small towns, learning why people settle in different places, getting a sense of the complex fabric it takes to make a country. If I have any regret at this point, it's that I didn't do something like this earlier, when it might have had more influence on my own direction. Most people never get to appreciate the country this way."

Janice studied the map a bit. "Can we stop while we're going across New York? I want to show you where I grew up."

The request surprised me. Janice had been so guarded about her private life. Maybe I'd finally gain some insight into this girl.

"Sure, Janice, of course we can," I responded

"Hey, let me tell you something," she said. "My father was a doctor in this small New York town called Warsaw."

I turned and stared until Janice pushed my head away. "He was a doctor?" I asked. "I can't believe you waited this long to tell me."

"I thought I did tell you," she said. "Yeah, he was a general practitioner who really cared about his patients. If people couldn't pay, he'd still treat them. He couldn't imagine saying no. He used to tell me everyone was part of the town together, and if some are less well off, well, you can't just let them go without food or shelter or medical care.

"Funny thing is," she continued, "most people wanted to pay him, even the poorest ones. Nobody wanted free care. So he bartered a lot. All the vegetables we'd need in the summer. Venison. Sometimes bear meat. He'd drive a car until it was ready to rust away, knowing he could always trade for mechanical work. One guy did the plowing all winter in return for Dad taking care of his family. Even after my father died, the guy kept showing up whenever it snowed. Another guy brought manure for Mom's gardens every spring and fall. He said he never felt so good about being a doctor as when he got paid in trade rather than getting a check from the government or an insurance company."

I began to speak but Janice stopped me.

"So I guess that's what I am. A barterer. I don't really have a lot of skills. And it's a bit unwieldy carrying manure around the country to unload. Back in high school, my girlfriends and I stood in awe of this girl who was a year older. My parents didn't want me to hang around her. They told me she was 'too fast.' That was all I needed, I guess, to get fascinated by sex. In college I found out how little most guys knew about sex, except that they wanted it. You'd let them do a few pushups on you, and they were happy. I didn't worry too much about the emotional involvement. So I guess I decided it

[122]

was a good trade item. Sex is pretty portable."

"Portable. Now there's a description I haven't heard applied to sex," I muttered.

"There are probably lots of 'descriptions'" – she raised to hands to demonstrate quotation marks– "you haven't thought about in relation to sex. Like, maybe, 'fun'"

"You know," I said, "there are times when you're impossible."

"I'm not convinced it's a bad thing to be impossible at times," she parried.

"So, Janice, do you think trading sex for rides is what your father hoped to stimulate when he did all that bartering in his practice?"

She laughed. "You know, I kind of knew you'd say something like that. And it doesn't deserve an answer. But I will say this. I think he'd be proud that I learned to be confident and self-sufficient, and that I could take care of myself after a setback."

"You mean, like leaving Colorado and heading back east?" I asked.

"Yeah, like that."

As we approached the border I began feeling a little apprehensive. How would I explain Janice's presence if questions were asked? Plus, there were the painkillers. I should have carried medical records, or copies of prescriptions. I had to assume we don't fit whatever profile they use to select people for full-scale searches.

Naturally, we sailed through uneventfully. Border officer asked only where we lived and where we were born. Why do I get so tense about things that end up not mattering? I mean, more suspicious-looking people than Janice and I must cross over to Niagara Falls every day.

Once at our destination, we played typical tourist, walking around for views of the American and Canadian falls, then taking a ride on the Maid of the Mist. People might have thought we were honeymooners if Janice didn't look young enough to be my daughter.

Such awesome power in the Niagara River's flow. Power

that would surge over that ledge indefinitely. As close to an image of immortality as I think I've seen. I've sat by tiny cascades in the mountains for hours mesmerized by the continuous flow. Amazed that somehow the water kept pouring and pouring, yet more would always be coming. Somehow there are enough springs and rivulets to ensure broad walls of water will drop over the Niagara Escarpment eternally. Now that's a miracle.

"Why do so many people go to Niagara Falls for their honeymoons?" Janice wondered aloud as we walked the path on Goat Island, heading toward the Canadian falls.

"I don't really know. Maybe people see waterfalls as romantic," I said.

"I think going over the falls in a barrel would be more romantic than hanging around some of those honky-tonk places on a honeymoon."

I smiled. "Guess they're glad most people don't think like you do. Except maybe for the barrel makers. They might be able to mount some kind of comeback."

"Where'd you go on your honeymoon?"

"Oh, we went to a resort in the Smoky Mountains. Pretty nice place. Had a good time."

"You ever going to tell me what happened to your marriage?" Janice asked.

I spoke a little more softly. "You don't want to hear about stuff like that."

"Why not?" she said. "I may as well know everything I can about you."

"Okay," I warned. "You asked for it. We broke up after my remission. It's not a whole lot of fun being around someone who's that sick. Cleaning up after I vomited. Cooking nice meals only to have me not be hungry. Waking up with me when I had a fever at night. I'm not sure I was that easy to live with when I was healthy. I certainly wasn't a treat when I was sick and at my worst. Shit, I'm not much of a treat to be around now, you may have noticed."

"Yeah, I'd agree with that," Janice nodded as she spoke, "but isn't that what marriage is all about? You stick by each other. You sacrifice for each other when you need to?"

I sighed. "Janice, you're living a century too late. Once upon a time that might have been the case. People seem to split up

[124]

these days if they can't agree on where to go for dinner. But Mary wasn't like that. I couldn't have married anyone any better. We had so much fun our first years together, in fact, our first dozen years. Then I just became too much. For anyone."

"Was she a difficult person?"

"No, not really. At least no more than anyone else." I paused a second to wipe some of the spray from the falls off my glasses. "Certainly no more difficult a person than I am. She worked hard, had lots of interests. Took good care of herself. I don't think I ever saw anyone who dressed and looked better on a day-to-day basis."

"She spend lots of money on clothes?"

"No," I said. "She just had a great sense of what looked good on her. Until she got too busy, she made a lot of her own clothes."

"You never had any kids?" Janice interjected.

"No," I answered. "At first we planned to. Then she had a miscarriage. After that it just never happened. Somehow we'd always manage to talk around the issue. Looking back, it's hard to know whether kids would have been a good idea or not."

"So was it tough breaking up?"

"Sure it was tough," I said. "And tougher when I had the relapse. I called to tell her. It was the first time we'd talked in months. She tried to be empathetic and supportive. I resisted her offers to come over, cook some meals, all of that." I thought back to our last conversation. "I knew she was sincere and really wanted to help me. But I couldn't handle dealing with her feelings along with my own. I guess I decided I wouldn't let her get any closer."

"So she knew you were following through on this?" Janice asked. "Traveling around and watching baseball until you died?"

"Yeah, she knew," I said. "In fact, she even offered to make some of the trips with me."

"Did you think about any other options?"

"Sure," I answered. "For a while, I thought about committing suicide. But I figured why waste the effort? I'd be dying soon enough anyway."

Janice exhaled loudly. "I never know whether to take you seriously or not."

"Don't sweat it, Janice. Neither do I anymore."

[125]

"So how do you want people to deal with you?

I had to think a bit. "I guess I want them to treat me as a person, not as a patient. Don't handle me gently as though you think I'm about to break. Don't tell me to rest or take it easy. I'm not into rationing my final days."

We left Niagara Falls, but Janice decided she didn't want to visit her hometown after all.

"No, Dan," she said. "Dad's gone. Mom doesn't live there anymore. I don't have any close friends there. I don't want to run into people I knew casually and have to explain what I'm doing now. And I don't want to drive around and look at a bunch of buildings I used to know."

"Come on, Janice, why not?" I urged. "It's your home town. It might bring back some good memories."

She felt no need for further explanation. "You know, I'm not really one for nostalgia. Couldn't the two of us work on making new memories instead?"

Though I'd become curious by now, I couldn't change her mind. Instead we continued wandering secondary roads to the east. We began seeing unusual houses built with tiny cobblestones. When we stopped at a church that's a cobblestone museum, we learned that most cobblestone houses in the country are right around here.

One belonged to Horace Greeley. He said, "Go West, young man." I guess that's why the Dodgers and Giants eventually moved to California. Forcing an entire generation to stay up late for ball scores from the west coast. If God wanted there to be baseball in the Pacific time zone you would think He'd have invented it out there.

We arrived at Rochester in time to tour George Eastman House. There was a guy with an idea. Load cameras with film, let people buy them, then send them back for processing and reloading. He conjured up the name Kodak out of thin air. Talk about a monopoly. That company will be around forever. You do something like that--or you win the Triple Crown, or hit sixty home runs, or something-- and people remember your name.

Wish there'd been a minor league game that night, but no such luck. We had dinner at a place called Nick Tahou's. I got the garbage plate, an intimidating conglomeration of hot dogs, onions, home fries, baked beans, macaroni salad, chili sauce, and a couple of pieces of bread. Think of it as everything you've ever eaten in a diner, all on one plate.

"I can't believe you ordered that," Janice said. "If you finish it and don't get sick, I may stop believing you really have a fatal disease."

The spread did look imposing. "One good thing about knowing you'll die of cancer, you don't worry about cholesterol. I've heard about this place for years. Had to try it at least once."

"Does it ever seem unfair?" Janice asked. "You know, trying to eat halfway decently, getting exercise, working to keep your weight down. And then you come down with something bad anyway?"

"I guess life is always kind of a crap shoot," I said. "Probably wouldn't be good to know how you're going to die. Shit, if you know you're going to get something like lymphoma, should you smoke all the cigarettes you want, drink yourself into oblivion every night, and all that?"

After dinner, Janice wanted to drive. I told her to stop someplace for the night near Cooperstown. From there, it would be only a few hours along the Susquehanna River back to Baltimore. Boston tomorrow night. Three and a half out. If this team is going to make a serious run, might be about time to start.

We stopped for gas just outside Geneva. Janice felt the urge to clean the inside of the car, so I pumped gas and cleaned the windshield. She was still tossing paper cups and receipts when I came back from going inside to pay.

"This really is a rolling landfill," she remarked as she got into the driver's side.

I thanked her a bit too sarcastically for her efforts. "Someday you'll have your chance to be on your death bed and see why I don't make cleaning up a priority."

"Hey, your emergency brake doesn't work," Janice said, as she adjusted the seat and prepared to turn on the ignition.

"Yeah, I know. That happens sometimes."

"Well, want to stop and get it fixed?" She began rolling the car down toward the road.

"Why? It's been broken for a while. You just haven't noticed it."

"Figure you're not going to live long enough to make fixing

[127]

it worthwhile?" she asked.

"Actually, Janice, the thought did cross my mind. Besides, I can't remember ever using the emergency brake in an emergency situation."

"Might come in handy if the regular brakes fail," she said.

"I tend to be law-abiding," I retorted, "so I do get the car inspected. The regular brakes are fine."

"It's not just you riding in this car these days, you know," she countered.

"Janice, if you have an accident, and you think the brakes would have saved you, then you can sue me."

Janice stopped the car beside a phone booth at the edge of the gas station lot. She swiveled in her seat and looked straight at me. "You don't have to be an asshole. There's no reason not to take what I'm saying seriously."

I snapped back, "I refuse to have an argument with you late at night on a back road in upstate New York."

"Well, you are."

"Janice, enough. You're here with me voluntarily. I can drop you off anywhere you like. Back in the town you grew up, near an airport or bus station, whatever you say. But I'm not continuing this discussion."

"Jesus," she said, "you're just like my last boyfriend. One thing goes wrong, and the relationship's over. Why are guys like that?"

"Janice, what do you mean, relationship? We've barely known each other a few weeks."

"Hey! We're living together, we're traveling together, we're learning each other's lives."

I undid my seat belt and got out of the car. I walked around to the driver's side, opened the door, and asked Janice for the keys.

"Why?" she asked.

"Because I'm going to drive."

"I don't see why you're in such a snit."

"I'm not," I said. "I just want to drive."

"Okay, be that way." She got out, stood across from me, and put her hands on her hips. "I don't know what you want me to do. I'm not going to break down and cry, if that's what you're expecting."

"I don't want you to cry," I said. "I just want to get back on the fucking road and find a place to stay tonight. Then tomorrow, if you want, I'll take you wherever you say so you can move forward with the rest of your life."

"You know, this all started just because I noticed your emergency brake was broken," Janice reminded me. "Then you spiraled out of control. Maybe you're putting too much stress on yourself with this baseball thing."

I took a deep breath and reminded myself how ludicrous this situation was. "Janice. Dying probably is stressful. Very few people wake up in the morning hoping they can begin the process that day. But my coping mechanisms are okay. For me, at least. I don't understand why you want to come along. I mean, I'm happy to have a companion and the stimulation. But I'm not going to spend more time having arguments that I don't need to have."

Janice still had the keys in her hand. I started to grab for them, but she intercepted and gave me a hug. "Sorry, you're not getting rid of me that easily. I apologize for my part of the argument. I didn't expect you to get so bent out of shape. Can we go on and be civil again?"

"You know, you've got grease all down the front of your T-shirt. Do I need to teach you table manners, too, along with all the other life lessons I'm sharing?" She looked down, felt the cotton, then laughed.

"And your apology," I continued, "is a pretty weak one. But instead of standing on the side of the road waiting to be hit by a car, maybe it is time to drive."

She began opening the driver side door.

"Oh, no," I interrupted. "Keys, please. I'll drive."

"Good," Janice yelled a little louder than necessary. "I can take a nap."

I started the Toyota and eased it back onto the road. I was drained from the argument. No way I could let Janice know that. One of those times I simply had to soldier on.

We spent our morning in Cooperstown, home of the Baseball Hall of Fame. A village built on baseball, beer, and sewing machines. Pleasant and bucolic, a nice contrast to our stormy outbursts the night before. Gives a sense of innocence to baseball,

[129]

thinking it began here. It probably didn't, of course. But the myth of Abner Doubleday has lived as long as some religions, and I like the idea that a pretty rural town rules as the Mecca which every true baseball fan must visit someday.

"I assume you've been here before," Janice said.

"Oh, yeah, many times."

"The place every fan has to see, huh?"

"You got that right," I told her. "I could spend hours, maybe days, studying every obscure fact and statistic here."

"You don't get tired of seeing the same museum again and again?" she asked.

"Not when it's about baseball. Plus there's more than just seeing the museum," I reflected. "I came here years ago to see Frank Robinson inducted into the Hall of Fame. He was the guy who led the Orioles to their first world championship back in 1966. It was thrilling to hear him say how as a poor kid growing up in Oakland, you didn't dare think about something as marvelous as making it into baseball's sacred shrine."

That's part of what I missed. That sense you might be playing stickball in the streets of the city, or throwing balls against the barn somewhere out on the farm, and you could dream of being in the big leagues. I grew up in between, in a classic American small town, with a backyard from which I could reach the next lot when I hit, and room to field the high pop flies I bounced off the garage roof. Dreams of a life in baseball were somehow rational when so many players had come from similarly humble circumstances.

We sat in green slatted seats for the overview movie at the Grandstand Theater. I figured Janice wouldn't tolerate much memorabilia, but I did make her spend enough time on the history floor to learn about the Black Sox scandal and go through the Babe Ruth section. She enjoyed Abbott and Costello's "Who's on First?" routine.

Then we went to the shrine itself. Rows of engraved plaques summarizing the achievements of the best ever to play the sport. I was ready to linger and read every word. "I don't see anything honoring the greatest fans of all time," Janice observed as we studied plaques of players, managers, writers, announcers, and team executives in the Hall of Fame. Fans do get short shrift. Players make enough money to forget it's fans that support the enterprise.

Plenty of behavior ignores the fact fans even exist.

I doubt many players understand there are fans who'll die for their team.

The home stand opened July 30th with a 8-7 loss to the Red Sox. A Red Sox team we needed to beat. Orioles in fourth place, four games out. Only took eleven days to drop from first down to fourth. Still, the team's situation is better than I could have imagined back in April.

Janice tells me I'm getting too self-absorbed. Like she has a right to tell me anything, after attaching herself to my life almost like a postscript to a letter. She irritates me with her ability to be so nonjudgmental. So that I'm immediately disarmed and unlikely to be defensive.

"Can't you figure out some way to spend a few of your hours doing something besides sleeping, eating, and for all I know pissing baseball?" she asked.

I wasn't in a self-justifying mood. "Look, I'm tired. Let me relax and read a little."

"It's not like you're reading *War and Peace* or the Bible," she countered. "You're just poring over more fucking box scores. You're rereading columns in the *Sporting News*."

"What's so evil or subversive about that? I'm obeying the dictum, first do no harm."

"Okay, do no harm," Janice said. "Maybe I'll find an alternative to the ballpark tonight."

"Why are you in such a mood?" I finally asked.

"I don't know," she went on. "Shit, maybe it's because I wish I could do some good for somebody. Like my father did. But I can't. I've got a fucking degree in English and I can't do anything with it. I can't even teach without going back and getting certified. I've broken up with my boyfriend. I had a big argument with my mom and my best friend when I moved to Colorado with him in the first place. I feel like I've wasted most of my life. Now I run into you. Don't get me wrong, this has been great. But you've had all these chances to make a difference, to benefit society, and now you're quitting. I know it's not your fault you got sick. But I just feel empty."

I didn't know quite how to respond. I'd never seen her so

[131]

intense.

"Janice, relax a little. It almost sounds as if you want me to solve society's ills just so you can take part vicariously. You'll have plenty of time to find your way and make a difference. It's not like something you write on your to-do list so you can cross it off later."

While I pondered what to say next, she got up, walked out the front door, and slammed it behind her.

Next morning's newspaper had more on the trial of that Anne Arundel County teacher who had affairs with at least eight students. It turns out his wife was one of those students-- the first one. Gives the gossip mongers something to discuss besides baseball.

I also learned that the bankruptcy auction for the Orioles was set for this week in New York City. Means I might get an idea of what the team is really worth. My worst fear? Having the Orioles bought by a conglomerate of Yankee fans and then dismantled.

I wasn't feeling too bad, but I was losing ground. Belt tightened another notch. Pants that were snug a year ago felt like bloomers, the way they ballooned out below the waist. You don't want to buy a new wardrobe when you know you're not going to be wearing it very long. I even resented the money for a shroud.

Janice was in a better mood; she wanted to go for brunch. "Hey, tomorrow's August first. Let's celebrate the beginning of each new month. It's a mark of survival. You say you've learned to appreciate every day now, so let's make some of them into occasions."

We settled on Obrycki's for our celebrating.

"Let's say you'd found out in October about your relapse, instead of in May," Janice asked, "Would you have taken therapy in hopes of being around the next season?"

"I ask myself that same question a lot," I told her. "And I don't have a good answer. No way I was going back to chemotherapy. The idea of beginning with spring training has appeal. Would be much more pleasant spending February and March in Florida, than up north. Those early months are more forgiving. If things are going bad, you can still imagine your team is going to improve. If I died early in the season, I could go to my grave believing they had a shot of making the World Series, no matter how good or bad they really are."

[132]

The waitress poured Janice a cup of coffee. She held it up to her lips for a minute, then continued, "Seems like it's the same situation now, isn't it?"

"I'm lucky that's the case," I admitted. "Far from the best Oriole team I've ever seen, but one good week could move them back into the race. I'm sentimental enough to believe that I'll live longer if they can stay in it, that I'll mount the emotional reserve to see the season out. Just like that patient I told you about who survived until his daughter's wedding." I paused a minute. "Plus I'm still convinced that being at the game makes a difference. Call it analogous to gravity, how two bodies each have an impact on the other, regardless of relative size and all. I think the outcome of a game will be different depending on the size and makeup of a crowd. After I listen to a loss on the radio, I always wonder what the outcome would have been if I'd been there."

Janice smiled. "I guess you're not much of a believer in predestination."

"Bingo!" I said. "If everything was predetermined, I don't think there'd be any cosmic significance in our being here."

"So you don't believe in a God who has a plan?"

"I just don't believe in a God who wants to interfere that much," I said. "I think of His power, His omnipotence, as coming from omniscience. That's what power is to me, the knowledge of everything that's going to happen, not the ability to micromanage it."

"Well," Janice asked, "doesn't that assume a bit of predetermination?"

"Not to me," I said. "I don't see God necessarily knowing who the manager is going to bring in when he needs a reliever, I just figure he knows what's likely to happen for each choice."

"So do you figure He knew that you'd give me a ride in Wisconsin?"

"Janice, I'm not sure if any greater being could have accounted for you."

And then it happened.

We finished the crabs, plus perhaps a beer or two more than we should have. Considered getting a cab, but it was daylight and we wanted the exercise. So what if there was razor wire atop the fences and guys loitering along the street.

[133]

"You know, I washed my hands twice," Janice said, "but I don't think I'll ever get out the smell of crabmeat and —what's that stuff they put in it?"

"Old Bay seasoning," I reminded her.

"Yeah, Old Bay. It stings a little where I scratched myself with a shell. You don't think I'll get gangrene or anything, do you?"

"I don't have any research to back it up," I said, "but I don't remember any epidemics of people dying of Old Bay seasoning infection. I don't think you have to worry."

"That's good," Janice said, "because you're right, the crabs really are good, even if they're a mess."

"But like I've told you, they're only that good right here. In Baltimore. I've pretty much given up ordering them anywhere else."

Suddenly a man was in front of us hollering. "Okay, give me your wallet!"

I tried not to panic. "I don't have one."

"Then pull out your money."

I reached into each front pocket. There was a twenty in one, a loosely wadded clump of money in the other. I leaned over and dropped them on the ground. Only now did I pay attention to what he looked like. Black, average height, clean shaven, young. Gray sweatshirt, ripped jeans, scuffed white running shoes. I didn't feel comfortable staring him in the face.

He turned to Janice. "Okay, you. Drop that purse."

"No way!"

He pulled out a gun, pointed it first at me, then at Janice.

"I said drop it!"

"No!"

"Janice, give him the fucking purse, will you?" I couldn't believe her stubbornness.

"Bullshit! I'm not letting some punk rob me."

"Hey, lady. I'm telling you. Drop that purse."

I noticed people on nearby porches. Wondered if they knew this guy. Wondered if anyone would call the police.

Wondered if Janice would drop the purse.

I heard the shot almost as I heard the siren. Janice fell to the ground, yelling, "Asshole!"

He took a quick look around, saw a police car turning the corner toward us. I heard him say "Shit!" as he began to run. He

[134]

tripped on the curb, broke the fall with his hands, lost the gun, picked himself up, beat it down Pratt Street.

I ran to Janice. Blood soaked her t-shirt. She was breathing fine but had both hands on her abdomen. That damned purse still dangled around her arm.

"How bad does it hurt?" I stammered.

"Not that bad," she murmured. "I guess he got me in the stomach. Felt first like a truck hit me, but now it's not too bad."

An ambulance rolled up. Techs began asking Janice questions, taking her blood pressure, checking a wound on the left side of her abdomen. Her vital signs were good.

A cop picked up the gun with a handkerchief. He came over and asked us both questions. I told him what I remembered. Janice told him he was dark black in color, had an elongated oval face, wide flattened nose. "Anything else distinctive about him?"

"Yeah," she added. "He had a gold tooth."

"Which side?" the policeman asked.

"Let's see, my right, his left. On top. And there was a tooth missing next to it."

I was pretty impressed. I couldn't have described a single facial feature, and I'm not the one who got shot.

EMT's began lifting her onto a stretcher. As they moved her, she stiffened with pain and started vomiting. "Blood pressure still okay," one guy shouted. "Let's get her moving."

"Where you taking her?" I questioned.

"Maryland Trauma. You can meet her there."

I talked to the cops-- there were two now-- a few more minutes, told them what little more I remembered. They gave me a ride to the hospital. Told me Baltimore was safer now than it used to be, but that it'll never be a crime-free city. Even in daylight, always a risk.

As I arrived at the emergency room, I began feeling nauseated. Before checking on Janice, I found the nearest bathroom. Went in and puked. Crab meat and Old Bay taste miserable coming back up. Hoped this wouldn't ruin my affection for the stuff.

Janice looked fairly comfortable in the emergency room. Nurses told me vital signs were stable, and that blood work was still pending. She'd be going off for CT scans in a couple of minutes. As I looked over, I saw her break into a tense smile. "At least I've

[135]

still got my purse," she whispered weakly. "Want some money so you can get a cab home?"

When the orderlies whisked her off, I walked outside to ponder the situation. Here I am responsible for this girl I barely know. She'll be in the hospital in what for her is a strange city. What in the world am I going to tell her family? How am I going to introduce myself over the phone? Do they even have a clue she's in this part of the country? Would I be thought selfish if I wanted her to stay and recuperate here with me? Questions began rolling through my mind like the waves of a storm-ridden surf.

I went to see Janice as soon as they had her situated in a room. She smiled and put her finger over her mouth, signaling me not to say anything until the nurses left. One told me Janice had been lucky. A small nick of bowel had to be sewn up, otherwise no significant damage.

A surgeon walked in. He looked vaguely familiar. Told me the same things the nurse had, but in more detail. No organ damage, no vessels hit, should recover uneventfully, figure on a couple of days before eating, maybe a week in the hospital.

He glanced back over at me. "Hey, aren't you Dan Jameson?"

"Yeah," I said. "Do we know each other?"

"Sure." He led me out to the hallway. "You were a resident at Baker when I was doing my first clinical rotation. You helped me do a spinal tap." He stuck his hand out. "Jim Whalen."

"Nice to meet you. Or, I guess, nice to see you again." I said as we shook.

"I couldn't get the damned needle in the right place," he said. "You had to do it. You reassured me it's a matter of practice and experience, that I'd master it when the time came. Let me tell you, no one was that understanding during my surgery program! Is she your daughter?"

I smiled. "No, she's a friend. Haven't known her very long. She's visiting. Wanted to see Baltimore. She's seen the Orioles play. She's been to the Harbor. Now I can tell her she's experienced one of the best hospitals in the state."

"*The* best hospital," he grinned. "At least the best one if you come in with a gunshot wound. Lousy memory for her to take back home."

"Hey," I told him, "as long as she goes home fully healed, it's a memory she can handle."

"Well, better run," Jimmy said. "Nice to see you after all this time. Let me know if there's any way I can help while she's here."

Janice appeared to be dozing but woke right up when I re-entered the room. She smiled as she uttered a greeting. "Hey! Good to see you! I guess it's good to see anybody."

"Guess the bullet didn't rupture your sense of humor," I said.

"That might be what gets me through all this," she replied.

"Well, the doctors say you're going to escape with minimal damage. No major injuries to any organs, just had to patch up your bowel a little."

She sighed. "Yeah, that's what they told me, too. Guess I'm lucky. I might only have to be in the hospital for a few days."

"You'll need some rest afterwards, too," I added. "Figure you'll head home for a while?"

She tried to sit up but couldn't. "Bullshit! I'm staying here with you. This is where I'm living right now. Or did you set this up to get rid of me?"

I wasn't in the mood for an argument. "We can talk about all this later. Right now I just want to see you get better."

"Later, nothing," Janice insisted. "I'm staying in Baltimore. You've got me wrapped up in all this baseball shit, and I'm staying to see what happens. If you don't want me around, say so, and I'll get my own apartment."

Her vehemence surprised me. "Janice, this is not the time and place for a fight. I'm not kicking you out. If you want to stay, you can. Besides, you're not working, you can't have that much money left from Colorado, and you're going to need some help while you recover."

"Okay, then." She smiled. "I feel better already. See what a healing influence you are?"

"Think I'll go get something to eat," I said. "I'll come by first thing in the morning."

"Don't worry!" she chirped. "I'll be here."

As I reached the door, she called me back. "Hey! Aren't you going to kiss me good-bye?"

[137]

I walked back over to the bed and gave her a little peck on the cheek.

"Well, that was a pretty weenie kiss. You scared of me or something?"

"Actually, I might be. At least a little." I went back and kissed her on the lips. "Have a quiet night. Don't cause any trouble. See you in the morning."

I took a cab home. After warming up some soup, I sifted through mail then read part of the paper. Janice's absence in the apartment was palpable. Pulled out two bowls for soup, then caught myself. For months I've slowly prepared to die, trying to distract myself along the way. Now here I am missing somebody.

I slowly sipped my liquid dinner. The television offered background noise. I listed reasons to get Janice back to her world and out of mine. They all felt wooden and insincere.

My hands still smelled of Old Bay.

When I arrived at the hospital next morning, Janice was up in the solarium. Tethered to an IV pole and dressed in a patient gown, she looked older and somehow dependent. That's the first rule of being sick. Be certain there's a loss of control. I guess I'd expected Janice to be exempt.

She sat talking to a gentleman in a suit and tie. He stood and introduced himself. "Hi! Detective Joseph Jenkins. Please feel free to call me Joe."

We shook hands. He explained that fingerprints on the gun had been tentatively identified. Janice was being asked if she felt comfortable going to a lineup at the police precinct.

"Sure, I am! I want this scumbag locked up for as long as possible. When do we do it?"

He rubbed his chin, looked at me and then at Janice. "It can wait until you're out of the hospital. And then at some point, you may have to testify at a trial."

"No problem," she said.

"Well, I guess that's all I have for today," Detective Jenkins concluded. "I appreciate your cooperation. I have to say your ability to be so detailed in describing the guy proved very helpful. Not everyone can be so exact in such a stressful situation." He stood, shook hands with us both, and walked out.

I gave her a brief hug, then sat where Detective Jenkins had been. "You know, I was pretty amazed myself hearing you describe that guy so well."

Janice grinned. "When I was in college we talked all the time about how we'd react if we were raped. Everyone always talked about how they'd scream as loud as possible, hoping to scare the guy away. That'd be fine if there were other people around. I always worried I'd be alone in some dark alley or some cellar or somewhere."

"Always the optimist," I interjected.

"Sure, why not?" came her retort. "Then I'd try to imagine going along with it, not fighting, just accepting it as lousy sex, in hopes he'd go away, and that I'd get to tell the story."

"Probably a sensible approach," I said. "That is, if you can control yourself that well."

"Well," she went on. "I'd try to remember that controlling myself might save my life. But I'd want the asshole caught and strung up. I'm not much of a bleeding heart when it comes to rape. I told myself I should concentrate on every detail. So that when the police asked questions, I could do better than those women who can barely remember if the guy was black or white, tall or short, young or old." Janice toyed a little with the IV needle. "I'd practice. With the one-night stands, or the guys you thought would be fun to go out with, but then they weren't. In bed with them, I'd focus on shape of the face, slant of the eyes, thickness of the nose and lips, whether they had a scar, or an earring, or a ring on their finger. I'd try to identify the soap or cologne they used. I never got very good at that." She laughed. "Though I could pick up Ivory soap and Canoe. I couldn't believe so many guys splashed on Canoe."

My turn to smile. "I confess I used it myself in high school. But by college, I'd decided it was a waste of time and money. Figured if I needed that to get a girl to like me, couldn't be much of a relationship anyhow."

"Guess I can put that in your column of positive qualities," said Janice.

"I have to admit I can't imagine being so disciplined in that kind of situation," I said. "Maybe I underestimate you sometimes."

"Well, my mind wanders during sex anyhow. Doesn't

yours?" Janice stopped and winked. "So I just use the time to become a better observer."

I forced myself to keep a straight face. "I'm still impressed you had the presence of mind to focus on so much detail while you were being shot."

"Remember, he did tell me to drop the purse a few times," she said. "That's what I'm not good at, by the way, trying to describe someone's voice. I never took my eyes off him. Though I tried to avoid looking him right in the eye. I worried that would irritate him and make him more angry. But I swear, while I was falling, I kept looking at him, making sure I had the face right. And I noticed the gold ring on his left hand, and that he was missing the end of one finger."

"You didn't mention all that yesterday," I said.

"They really didn't give me much time to think. Mostly, they wheeled me here and there, and got me ready for surgery. I told the detective today, though." She stopped, looked at me, continued. "Hey, here's the good news. That surgeon you know came by this morning, told me I was doing great, that I might be able to go in just three or four days. He said since I had someone to take care of me, no reason to hang around a hospital any longer than necessary."

"Dare I ask what you told him about us?" I asked.

"You can ask anything you want," she said. "Do you want to know the answer?"

My response wouldn't matter, so I kept quiet.

"I told him I'd known you a few months," Janice continued, "that you'd helped me when I was having some personal issues. Then you'd offered to show me around Baltimore and Washington before I started a job search. Told him I was staying with you for a couple of weeks. And that we weren't having sex. Though that was a unilateral decision on your part, not mine."

I tried again not to react.

Janice flashed her grin. "Hey, don't be so quiet. I thought you'd like that answer. A little bit of truth, so I could feel honest. A little bit of exaggeration, like you seem to expect, so as not to get you into any trouble."

"Janice, it's not like I can tell you what to say. Guess that description's as good as any. I didn't know you were about to begin looking for a job."

[140]

"Well, I'm going to need a job some time. Can't count on you to take care of me forever. Though I think you owe me."

"For what?" I asked.

"Think about it. For two days, you haven't had any time to feel sorry for yourself, or to think about dying." That sly smile again. "And all because of me."

At Janice's insistence I went to the game that afternoon instead of staying at the hospital.

Ben McDonald had beaten the Red Sox and Roger Clemens 5-0 last night, when I had more important things on my mind. Today Rick Sutcliffe pitched well, but got no run support. Boston prevailed, 2-1. Just like that, five games back again.

Not that I could keep my mind on the game.

Janice's shooting led me to focus more clearly on my own upcoming moment of death. If I'm lucky, I'll get some notice, sort of like the two-minute warning near the end of a football game. So I can call an extra time-out or two and finish up a few final tasks. Wonder if I should draw up a list of what I'd do if I got notified I had only forty-eight hours to go.

Orioles won three straight against Milwaukee. Cleveland came to town, and Sutcliffe came alive to pitch an 8-1 win. Toronto lost a few. The O's back to two games behind.

Janice was right. I hadn't thought about my illness for a few days. Baseball again provided the escape I needed– baseball, and Janice. I felt an eerie sense of gratitude for both.

I went for my check-up. Eric introduced the young oncology fellow working with him, then went on to his usual questioning. He appeared skeptical when I told him my appetite was better, that the nausea seemed under control, and that I wasn't using much pain medicine.

"You know, your CT scans don't show much progression. No reason we still couldn't give chemotherapy a shot," he reported. "Would be some toxicity, but who knows, it might give you a whole new season to follow."

He'd gotten over the rational approach. Now he framed my possibilities in terms of baseball. Fans love to point out baseball's the one game where you don't have to worry about the clock. Until the last out in the bottom of the ninth, the home team always has a chance.

"No, Eric, I don't think so," I said. "You'd be proud of me. In Minneapolis, I went to the med school library and read up on treatment again. Figured I should be current with the data. No salvage therapy looks that good. I may as well just keep following my team."

Eric addressed the fellow, a quiet woman who didn't look much older than Janice. "Doctors are often the worst patients, Jennie. They think they know everything, of course, plus they have enough knowledge and experience to argue about anything you try to tell them." Jennie looked quizzical. As well she should. Early August, so she must have started her fellowship only a month ago. Too soon for dealing with a patient like me.

"Been a while since you had a transfusion," Eric resumed. "But your counts are holding up. When do you travel again?"

"I'm on the road next week," I said. "I leave Sunday for Detroit, then New York and Seattle. Back here around the twentieth."

"Then why don't we hold off for now?" he said. "Maybe you could get blood drawn before you go to Seattle. I assume you'd fly if you go there."

"Yeah," I agreed. "I don't have the stamina to drive all the way cross-country, just to see three games. I'm not quite as irrational as you assume."

"No one's accusing you of being irrational, Dan," Eric continued as his mouth opened into a broad smile. "Maybe a bit loony, certainly stubborn, but I wouldn't call you irrational."

"You wouldn't mind putting that in writing for me, would you?" I said. "Maybe on your letterhead. So if I need to go to an ER, they won't bring down the social workers and shrinks to convince me why I should be treated. Wish I could carry blood in a cooler, then transfuse myself in a hotel room instead of facing the stares when I explain that all I want is the blood, no chemo, thank you, no high-pressure oncologist trying to change my mind."

Eric laughed. "Dan, the American dream is to live forever. And as with anything else in America, if you go against the dream, people wonder about you. Actually, I thought you'd enjoy the mental sparring with someone new and smart who challenges your

[142]

world view."

"Actually, Eric, my world view has narrowed a bit. I've got a pennant race on my hands. I can force everything else from my mind to concentrate on it. No diversions, no post-call fatigue, no guilt from watching the games instead of reading this week's journals. Most focused I've been on anything in years."

Eric laughed again. "You know, you might be in for a big letdown after the season ends. You've held up better than I expected. Than any of us expected. How're you going to handle it if you're still alive and kicking over the winter?"

"You've got me there." I guess I'd always assumed the emotional letdown would be so dramatic that it would kill me. A few months ago, they told me I'd be lucky to have a few months to live. Could I handle the irony of surviving the season, then going forward without anything to distract me? Prospect of a cold winter holed up in my condo depressed the hell out of me. Idea of going someplace warm, where I didn't know anyone, repulsed me even more.

Suddenly I wondered if I should be more scared of survival than I was of death.

Janice was indeed out of the hospital on the fifth day. I stopped by Safeway and bought fresh vegetables for a pasta primavera to celebrate her return

While she napped afterwards, I perused medical journals. An abstract in one described a study showing a high fat diet increases the risk for prostate cancer. I congratulated myself on the healthy dinner that will help stave off such an affliction. I should have cancelled those subscriptions. Must make a note to let them lapse.

Janice agreed to skip the Cleveland opener but refused to stay home after that. Told me that after her own bout with death, she's not wasting any more days of her life.

Orioles won. Mills got the victory in relief of Valenzuela, Olsen with a save. Ripken hit two homers. McLemore went four-for-four plus a walk. Hulett made a terrific diving catch of a line drive in the ninth.

Bobby Ojeda pitched two innings, his first effort since being in that boat accident during spring training that killed two other players. That gives a little perspective. Reminds you that life

[143]

doesn't exist solely between the foul lines of a stadium. Maybe baseball isn't life-and-death after all. I mean, baseball only kills you figuratively. It still takes some accident, or a heart attack– or cancer– to finally remove you from the planet altogether.

Toronto lost; O's only one game out. 110 games down, 52 to go, my team still in the race.

The car was already packed. No sense arguing for Janice to stay home and recuperate. At her insistence, I put the Camry through a car wash. Told her I'd miss the patina of accumulated dirt, and, besides, a clean car would be just as dirty again after a couple of days driving the interstates. Within an hour of getting back from Camden Yards, we took off for Detroit. We needed a good jump on Sunday to make a game on Monday night.

Janice got us well into Ohio Sunday night. She pulled into a nondescript chain motel somewhere near Akron, then woke me up so I could go in and fall back asleep. We had time for a more leisurely pace on Monday.

We ate breakfast outside Elyria. "Look how dirty this water glass is," she said, holding it up for inspection. "You don't think we'll catch anything by eating here?"

"It's probably no more dirty than the glasses we use at my condo," I said.

"Yes," she conceded, "but there at least I know they're getting rinsed with hot water. So most of the bugs are probably gone."

"Well, I guess you have two choices."

"Go ahead," she ordered.

"You can sit here and watch me eat, or you can eat along with me," I said. "Because I'm having my pancakes whether you join me or not. And we're not stopping again in an hour for you to have your own separate breakfast."

Janice made a mock bow. "Okay, exalted ruler of the diner. I hope they only have fake maple syrup." The rest of the meal proceeded uneventfully. It cost me fifty cents extra but I did get genuine syrup. Within an hour we were back on the road.

Janice was into stopping at spots with interesting names. That's why we'd picked Elyria for breakfast. Now Ypsilanti, in Michigan, caught her attention.

"What do you suppose it means?"

"Probably an old Indian name," I offered. "Maybe it translates something like 'place where the automobile will be made'."

"Oh, you're such a fountain of information."

She insisted on stopping. At the local historical society, we learned Ypsilanti was an early health spa. And a producer of under garments.

"Get a look at this," Janice said. "The Ypsilanti Health Underwear factory–'the perfect underwear for progressive people

> Never rip and never tear,
> Ypsilanti underwear!'

Don't you feel a little guilty now for wearing Fruit of the Loom?"

Surprisingly, Ypsilanti wasn't some Native American word. "Get this, Janice! Here's the scoop on the city's name. Demetrius Ypsilantis was a Greek general who helped defeat the Turks in the1820's, just about the time the town was coming into being. Who'd have thunk?"

Confident we were among the small minority in America aware of this important nugget of information, we headed on to Detroit.

Substitutes helped carry the team as the Orioles won their eighth in a row. Only half a game out of first place. We celebrated with a long lunch in Greek Town. I wavered but decided on the moussaka. No reason not to indulge while I'm feeling okay and the team is winning. The retsina had probably taken hold. Who ever thought of making a wine that tastes like pine resin?

"So what are you going to do with yourself once the traveling bug wears off?" I asked.

Janice swallowed another aliquot of wine. "Truth is, I have lots of things I'd like to do. But I'll have to go back to school for any of them. I wouldn't mind teaching, but I tense up at the thought of standing in front of a room of students. I don't want to just lecture. That's what school was like for me. I sat there bored all the time. I want kids to be excited about learning."

"I don't think there's a law requiring you to lecture every minute," I offered.

"Yeah, but how else do you keep thirty kids occupied all the

[145]

time?" she said.

"Bring in a TV and have them watch ball games," I said. "Spin in a bit of history with it, have them read those books you bought in Minnesota. Require they learn some statistics. For a bit of vocational training, you could teach them to keep score."

Her audible groan caught the attention of the next table. "See, there you go again. You don't take anything I say seriously."

"Jesus, Janice, maybe sometimes it's you who's too serious. I shouldn't have to be the one who lightens up the conversation. But, really, think about it. Use baseball to get the kids interested. Talk about Abner Doubleday at Fort Sumter, and why the game grew after the Civil War. Study how the game adapted to the World Wars, remind them Ted Williams was a war hero as well as a home run hitter. Make them study the free agency issue, and learn how the courts works. There's plenty of math. Let them learn fractions by calculating batting averages."

She fiddled unwrapping a piece of gum. "So I should teach at a boys' school."

"Not necessarily," I said. "Find things to engage the girls. Show how sex stereotypes developed; show ways they get broken down. Tell them there was once a pro girls' league."

To my astonishment, Janice showed interest. "You know, that might be worth trying. Couldn't be any more boring than memorizing dates of battles in the French and Indian War, or what gets mined in Bolivia. How about you teaching it with me?"

"First of all, this is summer," I said. "I never think about school in the summer. Secondly, I'm not a good long term candidate for the job. Even if you did find a school silly enough to pay for two teachers when one would do."

"Do it without pay," she said. "You're not exactly making oodles of cash right now. In fact, you still need to enlighten me on how you afford all this traveling around."

We finished off the retsina. I'd begun to feel a bit lightheaded. "Tell you what. If miraculously I'm alive a year from now, I'll teach with you. Meanwhile, I'll help you outline a course. It can become the Dan Jameson Memorial Baseball in Life Curriculum."

"Sounds good to me. Deal?"

"Deal!"

[146]

Orioles don't subtly end a winning streak. They do it with a bang. Three losses to the Tigers.

15-1.

15-5.

17-11.

We slept in both days, ate late breakfasts, then went out for some history and culture.

One afternoon got devoted to the Henry Ford Museum. I suggested Janice could teach the roles of industrialization and urbanization as factors in baseball's rapid growth. "Let's face it, you're not going to fill ballparks with thousands of people if everyone still lives on isolated farms." Next day we toured Greenfield Village. Ford sought out houses belonging to people he admired, and then transported them here.

Janice began, "Do you mind if I ask you a question?"

We were going through another carwash. God knows the Camry needed it again. I worried they might charge double because of all the caked-on dirt.

"Of course not," I said. "I didn't think you thought you needed permission."

Janice chuckled. "Why do you still want to sightsee and go to museums and all that? For that matter, why do you still read so much? You know, if you're expecting to die so soon?"

I grinned. "Besides the need to entertain you, you mean?

"No. Really."

I noticed soapsuds running down the inside of the rear driver's side window. Guess I hadn't fully closed it. Probably the interior glass needed cleaning, anyhow.

"I don't know," I answered. "Maybe it's habit by now, trying to learn all I can about a new place. It distracts me. Beats staying fixated on hospital beds and cremation. I guess in the final analysis, I'm still trying to understand the world, figure out how and why it's put together."

"So did seeing the car in which Kennedy was shot help you understand the world better?"

"Sure," I said. "It reminded me of lost dreams. Parents should make us write down what we want to do in life, starting around age ten, then make us review it every few years. That way

[147]

we'll have a better idea of whether life measured up to our expectations. Plus, Kennedy's assassination is a good reminder how it's not such a tragedy if I don't live forever, either."

"I can always count on you for gloominess," Janice broke in.

We had passed the gauntlet of huge rotating brushes. The final rinse began. Janice looked lost in thought. "How about that Airstream? You could get one of those for the rest of the trip. Or the rest of the season. Or the rest of your life. Or whatever you want to call it."

"You laugh," I said. "I thought about that before starting out this spring. Years ago, I told Mary we should do that when we retire. Get a big RV, go and discover America for ourselves. See the scenery, meet people all across the country, get a handle on the complexity of it all."

"And?"

"She thought it was a silly idea. Like I've told you, she was too practical. Would have calculated how much it cost, then how much a year of hotels would cost, and on and on until I'd ditch the thought. At this point, what's the sense in making such a big purchase? Couldn't take it with me." I sighed before continuing. "Though it'd make a terrific casket, wouldn't it?"

"You know, Dan, your gloominess is marking new depths."

"That's one of the great things about gloominess," I said. "No limits."

The hot blasts of drying air ceased, and we edged the car back out into daylight. Our moods had felt dark enough that the bright sunshine took me by surprise.

I woke up in the middle of the night. Couldn't figure out where I was at first. Another of those motel rooms without identifying features. The place looked sterile. Blinked to be sure I wasn't in a hospital. Seeing Janice in the other bed helped orient me. Red numerals on the clock radio provided the only light, as if I were developing film in a darkroom and had to be protected from incandescent rays.

A wave of nausea rose in my throat. I stumbled to the bathroom. Couldn't find the light switch. Plumbing fixtures glowed with an otherworldly phosphorescence. For all I knew, the toilet emitted its own deadly radiation. A rebuke, perhaps, for the therapy I'd refused months ago.

I vomited, then sat still a while. The cooling of skin felt pleasant as the sweat evaporated. Don't let this be the end, I thought. I didn't want to take an ambulance to some strange hospital in an alien city. Especially Detroit, a place already inhospitable with the Tigers beating the Orioles so badly three games in a row. Maybe that's why I was throwing up. Being trounced three times would make any fan sick to his stomach.

Lights came on in the bedroom. Janice knocked on the bathroom door. "Can I come in?"

"Sure," I answered. "If you feel like seeing a dying person at his worst."

She moistened a washcloth and came over to dab my forehead. "Feeling any better?"

"A little," I said. "Sorry for waking you up."

"As if you need to apologize," she replied. "Can I get anything for you?"

"No. Maybe it was those hot dogs at the ballpark. Think they try to poison Oriole fans?"

"Oh, they probably try to poison people rooting for any opposing teams, not just yours."

"Thanks for the reassurance," I managed to say.

I hadn't flushed the toilet, so I stood up and did so now. There was vomitus on the rim of the bowl; I took the washcloth and cleaned it off. In the mirror, I saw flecks on my face, too.

Janice smiled weakly. "Well, finally I get to be a nurse. That should solidify the need for me to be with you on these trips."

"I'm sorry. I know this part of things isn't pleasant."

"Oh, stop worrying," she said. "It'll take more than a bout of vomiting to scare me off."

The last game was an afternoon one. We had a brief argument about whether I was in shape to go. Despite the way Detroit was treating the Orioles, I still hated skipping a game. I managed to sleep a few hours. We packed the car, but opted for a cab to Tiger Stadium.

Our driver was preoccupied with his headphones, so Janice and I whiled away time looking through dirty windows at the cityscape. Empty buildings, abandoned cars, lots of graffiti. Hadn't noticed it all before. Night may make an illness feel more intense,

[149]

but it's good for masking urban blight. "It doesn't take a sociologist to sense Detroit has seen better days," I told Janice. "It's every bit as debilitated as a body riddled by cancer."

"Now that's a pleasing analogy," she responded.

That night the Orioles lost again. I was ready to move on.

En route to New York, we both felt a bit subdued. Janice began, "You know, you could save a lot of time and trouble by flying more places instead of driving."

"Sure, Janice, plus I'd have a better chance to get to know America. If Steinbeck had left his dog home and flown everywhere, his book would have described the country as patches of Tarmac surrounded by highways, each ending in a McDonald's, Dairy Queen, and Holiday Inn."

"You've got an answer for everything, don't you?" she asked.

"Well," I said, "I do have lots of time to think these days. Besides, I hate airports."

She turned to a logistical approach. "I've looked at those schedules you keep around the room. Want to tell me how you're going from New York to a game at Seattle the next day?"

I wondered that myself. I'd lost stamina. No longer could I expect to see every game, even if I flew. I'd already considered skipping the West Coast swing. For a couple of days, I'd been toying with sending Janice in my stead. I equated it with using a proxy vote. If she went as my official representative, the journey still counted as my trip.

Of course, that assumed she'd want to go.

"Janice, I'll make you a deal. You can be my surrogate in Seattle. It'll give you a chance to wean yourself from this relationship, or attachment, or whatever it is. You've got to keep a scorecard, though."

She betrayed a hint of surprise. No response for a full minute. "Like you won't be scoring the game yourself while you're watching it on the tube."

"So?" I said. "We'll compare notes when you get back. I can give you constructive feedback, which you'll need to get used to if you ever plan to accomplish anything anyway."

Janice nodded. "Okay, but you have to promise you won't

[150]

die while I'm away."

"That's not an easy promise to make, you know."

It's sobering to think about how you'll die.

Number one on the list is infection. Any one of those dread fevers, those terrible chills, those awful sweats could herald the end. As long as the season goes on, I can go and get treated, try to get out of the hospital as soon as I can, sneak in a few more games on the borrowed time.

Bleeding would be a bad way to go. Vomiting blood would be a mess. For me, and for everyone else. Bleeding inside the head wouldn't be bad if it were quick. I could do without "the worst headache in my life," as the textbooks like to describe it. Would be best to bleed massively, quickly, and well away from help. So I don't end my days tethered to some machine.

Then there's starving. I've been lucky in some ways. Not much pain, quite often a decent appetite. Controlling nausea goes well enough most of the time, though the spasms of retching after eating are entirely unpredictable. My weight keeps falling. But on days I feel like eating, I'm able to tolerate whatever I want. Don't feel like I have to pick out my last meal yet, but when the time comes, I hope I can tolerate a lobster.

Suicide. Always a consideration. I've saved up the pills. Some have probably expired, but they'll still work. My apartment's not high enough for jumping. I kept my promise to Mary not to have a gun in the house, and I would never put myself through the discomfort of hanging. Then again, there's no reason to kill myself if my team still has a chance of making the World Series. Besides, pondering suicide at this point makes me feel too much like a character in a Beckett play. *Endgame.* "If I don't kill that rat, he'll die," or something like that. Plus I'm not sure I could put Janice through the shock of a suicide.

Janice broke into my reverie of demise. "So how about while I'm in Seattle, maybe you can find something useful to do with your time."

"You mean instead of reading, watching the games, getting ready to die in peace?"

No response, merely a glare.

"Okay," I said. "Ideas?"

"Yeah," she said. "Do something for someone younger than

[151]

you. Talk to some kids. Go to a hospital and help some sick kid who doesn't think he's going to get better. My father always said there was nothing sadder than a terminally ill child. Someone who hadn't lived long enough to screw up a life, but who got dealt an unfair hand. Bring a little hope into the world. If you don't want any hope for yourself, give it to some kid."

"Just what I----"

Janice put her index finger up to my lips. "Be quiet a minute. I listen to you. I pay attention to what you say. So listen to me for once. I respect what you're doing. We all have to make up our own minds on something like this. You give me all this crap about contributing in life. But somehow you feel you're exempt now that you're sick. I don't think that's fair."

"I'm not so sure that what a sick kid needs is to have me around," I replied.

She smiled. The smile that made me pick her up that day in the first place. "That's okay. You didn't know that you needed someone like me around."

I still remembered the excitement of our annual family trips to New York. Basketball games, plays, restaurants. I loved the glitz of the big city. My parents tried to instill a bit of culture, too, taking us to museums like the Metropolitan and the Whitney. They could have saved the money. But dinosaurs at the Museum of Natural History, sky shows at the Hayden Planetarium. Those were great. Ironically, an exhibition of baseball cards is running right now at the Metropolitan. That's culture I would have jumped at as a kid.

I couldn't mount the effort for a Broadway show, but I did convince Janice to see one. She got a ticket to "The Sisters Rosenzweig" with Madeline Kahn, on Saturday night. For drama, I didn't need much more than the subway rides back and forth to Yankee Stadium. I envisioned getting lost in the South Bronx, getting knifed on the street. Enjoyed perversely imagining some career criminal going to prison for life, for killing a guy who was just about to die anyway. In its own twisted way, my last good deed, getting the guy off the street. Janice could be proud.

The New York Times was gloating even before Baltimore first took the field. Writer Claire Smith pointed out O's were outscored

47-17 in Detroit, "an onslaught of record proportions."

We settled into seats on the main level, down the left field line, beyond the Oriole dugout.

I told Janice about the glories of Yankee Stadium, all the legendary people who played there. "See those monuments out in center field? They're for Babe Ruth, Lou Gehrig, and Miller Huggins. Lots of people say that without Babe Ruth hitting all his home runs, baseball never would have developed its hold on the American psyche. Lou Gehrig played 2,130 games in a row. That's the record Cal Ripken's trying to break."

"Do any other stadiums have monuments like these?" she asked.

"No," I told her. "Yankee Stadium is somehow larger-than-life. Visiting teams come to realize if they can't win here, they can't expect to win championships."

"The view's a little disappointing," Janice said. "I mean, it's New York, you'd expect to see the Statue of Liberty, or maybe the Empire State Building."

I was digging through my box of Cracker Jacks, looking for the prize. "They're too far away. When the New York Giants played they had a stadium in Manhattan. By the time the Yankees built, there must have been space only up here in the Bronx."

"The New York Giants?"

"Yeah," I said. "Once New York had three baseball teams, the Yankees, the Giants, and the Brooklyn Dodgers. Each with their own stadium."

"Why aren't there three now?"

"Well," I answered, "in the 1950's the owners of the Giants and Dodgers moved them to the west coast. Fans were pretty angry, but to the owners it was just business. All about the money. Greed isn't something that's new. Eventually an expansion team got put here, the Mets, with a stadium in Queens."

The public address announcer began giving the starting lineups. My hands were sticky from the caramel popcorn coating, but I nonetheless began writing names onto the scorecard.

Once the line-ups were completed, I turned back to Janice. "You know, Janice, I remember one moment here when I first felt the Orioles might finally reach the top. It was 1966. The Orioles had traded for a star player on Cincinnati named Frank Robinson.

He brought not only talent, but also an intensity and passion that wouldn't tolerate losing. First super star in the team's history. Someone who would help make stars of the others around him.

"It was the ninth inning of a game in June. Orioles up a couple of runs, Yankees with two men on base and Roy White at the plate. Our seats were behind first base, right where I could see the power in his swing. He swung, the ball took off, soaring to its destination. Game on the line.

"Frank drifted back in right field. Deep, to the wall, looking up at a tremendous blast that threatened to give the game to the Yankees. I remember him getting to the wall, leaping up, not coming down but instead disappearing into the stands. Other fielders drifted down the foul line to see what was happening. Players crept out of both dugouts. An umpire raced to the scene.

"And Frank finally came up to the surface with the ball in his glove. An umpire raised his right hand high in the 'out' sign. The Orioles won the game. And I knew– not just sensed, but knew-- my years of patience and loyalty were about to be rewarded. My team was ready to elevate to a new level. I made a mental note to block off time in October. And I saw my first World Series that year."

"You have no idea the way you glowed when you tell that story," Janice said.

"It was a pretty big deal at the time."

She responded, "It looks to me like it's a pretty big deal now."

That was then, and this was now. Oriole pitchers gave up a mere nine runs in three games against the Yankees, but the bats went dormant. Three runs for the entire series. Ben McDonald gave up a single run-- a homer by Don Mattingly-- and lost the final one, 1-0. He deserved better.

So, of course, did I. The O's had lost six in a row. We came into town two games behind Toronto, New York, and Boston. Now we're as far back as we were a month ago.

Somehow I managed to eat half of a corned beef on rye at Carnegie Deli, washing it down with a couple of cream sodas. Didn't I deserve a last classic New York meal? Back at the hotel, I vomited it up. Housecleaning staff won't be happy we got granted a late check-out. Janice had planned on a cab to LaGuardia while I drove back to Baltimore. Now she insisted on getting me home herself. I felt sick the whole way. Would never have told her, but glad I wasn't alone.

Orioles went to the coast. Janice flew to Seattle to be my eyes and ears on the O's. I considered it sort of an advance scouting report to have on hand in case, up in heaven, I get called upon to assemble a team.

In the newspaper, I read about a New York businessman kidnapped and held prisoner in an underground vault. He used his Marine training to avoid panic, allowing him to survive until the hiding place was found. How real each day of life must feel after such a threat. Maybe we all need a scare so that we learn to live life to the fullest.

I used the time for another checkup.

Housewives have their sale coupons, stockbrokers have their quotes, baseball junkies have their box scores. Patients? We have our blood counts and our x-ray reports. Over which we have no more control than over a lottery drawing. What will it be this morning? More risk for infection? The need for transfusion? Maybe my day to bleed?

Sometimes I wish Eric would be less gracious. I don't deserve such attentive care as I refuse most of what he has to offer.

"Just dragged out, that's all," I open. "All I can do to walk the next block, go up the next flight of stairs. Sometimes I wish for a couple of men who could carry me around the stadium in one of those old sedan chairs."

"Fatigue is understandable," Eric said. "No fevers, no chills? Nausea? Pain issues?" He doodled on a pad of paper as we talked.

"Yeah," I said, "I feel sick to my stomach occasionally, but nothing terrible. Most of my pain comes from headaches induced by the Orioles."

"Appetite okay?"

I told Eric I was still eating pretty well. "In New York, I vomited up a corned beef sandwich. Funny thing is that on my good days, I can handle anything-- Thai food, sauerkraut on hot dogs, soft shell crabs, the works. Not that it's keeping me from losing weight." I'd lost another dozen pounds. Not sure I've weighed this little since junior high.

"Well, your counts are down," he said. "It's probably a good idea to transfuse you again. At least your platelets are staying up."

"Good, I'd just as soon not bleed to death."

"I don't know, Dan. Bleeding has the advantage of proceeding relatively rapidly. All those years of jogging have given you a good heart, so I don't expect you to have a sudden painless exit. And since you tell me you won't come into the hospital no matter what, an untreated infection may be a pretty tough way to go."

"Thanks for the encouragement. Look, Eric, if I want to feel worse about life, all I have to do is pick up a list of team statistics to study."

He chuckled. "Well, next time you're doing that, check out the lowest average on the list. Because even that's a bit better than the chances you and I are going to be talking next year if you don't take any treatment."

Eric didn't try to make me feel guilty anymore. He's accepted my decisions, if not my philosophy. I need his occasional infusions of reality. "Death be not proud", read the John Donne poem I memorized in school, and my years since have confirmed it. People don't want to die in pain, and they don't want to die alone. Medicine can handle the former. I'd always convinced myself I could steel myself against the latter.

Until I had Janice in my life.

PART FIVE

August 17, 1993

I don't know why I woke feeling so euphoric. I had slept soundly. Janice was in Seattle. Orioles lost the first one out on the coast, their seventh loss in a row. Barely a week ago they'd been a mere half-game out of first. Hope they're not in the midst of a terminal free fall. Maybe I just felt good being home in Baltimore. It couldn't be because of baseball.

I needed groceries, dishwashing detergent, and a few other things, so I drove over to Safeway. There I ran into Debbi Madison. I met her when I was in med school. She'd been a pediatric oncology nurse at Maryland as long as I could remember.

Debbi had the perfect attitude for the job. Always upbeat, consistently optimistic view toward life, never met a person she didn't like. She'd find any excuse for a party to divert the kids, then come dressed as a clown, ready to be the star of the show. One of those stars, though, who makes sure all the attention goes to the audience. She saw herself as a facilitator, never the principal player. I'd seen the tears, of course. It's hard to survive the stresses of watching kids die. But no child or parent left her charge without some sense of hope. She had been good friends with Mary, and visited me a lot during my initial chemotherapy.

We went over to a small place near Cross Keys for an early lunch.

"So you're going to Oriole games every day?" Debbi asked. "Even when they're away?"

"Yeah," I said, "one of those snap decisions that I'd actually thought about for a long time. It's a great distraction. I didn't want to just sit around and feel sorry for myself. Plus I didn't think it'd be too smart going on a safari or backpacking in Europe right now."

She flipped a few strands of hair away from her eyes. "Spending any time with Mary?"

I drew in a deep breath. "No, not really. I told her about the relapse, and about my plans. We've spoken only a handful of times since then."

"So most of the time you're alone?"

"Of course not, Debbi. Tens of thousands of people with me at every game."

Her face reflected exasperation. "Just like you to say. So, hey, want to come over for dinner sometime? I mean, you still eat, don't you?"

I smiled. "Sure, I'd love to."

As she picked up the last bit of her sandwich, I decided to confide a little. "I really should tell you, for a month now, there's been a woman going on the trips with me."

Debbi grinned. "So who is she?"

I swallowed hard. "She's a young woman I met traveling. For some reason, we hit it off. For a month, she's been staying with me in Baltimore. She knows about the lymphoma."

Debbi put her sandwich back down and looked at me studiously. "She a gold digger?"

"I don't think so," I said. "To tell you the truth, I'm not sure why she's interested in me.'

"You don't think your charming personality is enough?" She popped the last morsel of bread into her mouth.

As she got up to leave, Debbi looked directly at me. "Why don't you come over to the ward? The kids love visitors. Playing a game, talking baseball, anything at all, they light up. You'd be great at it. Just don't lie to them, or talk down to them. They can always pick up on it."

"I don't know, Deb. I'm not the best spirit to have around right now."

"Hey," she said. "If you don't want to do it for the kids, do it for yourself. You may be surprised how much you learn from some of them."

We talked back and forth a little. Finally, I agreed. "Okay, I'll come over tomorrow."

"Great. I work three to eleven. I'll go in early to make sure I'm on top of anything new that might have happened. Come to the children's wing, and have the clerk buzz me on the ward." She leaned over, gave me a kiss, and sped to the door.

Time at the hospital flew by. I played gin rummy with the older kids, held my own in Chutes and Ladders with the younger ones, excelled at Monopoly with both. Mainly we talked baseball.

Their eyes lit up when they talked about the game. All were Oriole fans, even a fourteen-year-old who'd moved to Salisbury from Boston last year. When I told them how many games I'd seen this year, you'd have thought from the reaction that I was a player myself.

"Does Cal look tired with the streak?"

"Why isn't Devereaux hitting like he used to?"

"Do you think Moose's arm is okay? Looks like he's straining."

"How come they can't beat the Yankees?"

My knowledge of the Orioles was the key to passing "go" and getting my two hundred dollars. Talking to them, I saw anew why I hadn't outgrown my enthusiasm. Almost before realizing it, I committed myself to a quick return.

"Hey, guys," I said. "The Orioles play Seattle Wednesday afternoon. How about I come by and watch the game with you?'

It was like I'd given each a birthday present. Mothers smiled appreciatively. A couple of nurses pumped their fists. And all I'd done was promise to come over and watch a little TV. We so often fail to realize how much satisfaction we can deliver with a very modest effort.

Two units of blood later (Eric had arranged for me to get transfused at the end of the day), I went out and caught a cab. Good thing about games on the coast, I didn't have to worry about being home in time to watch. After seeing them lose one game already in Seattle, I ruminated on whether to stay up late again. I do, of course. They lose again. Of course.

I was tired but I'd made a promise. So I arrived at the children's unit, sacks of peanuts in hand, plus a case of sodas. Nurses brought us a blackboard. We agreed to keep score. Each kid did half an inning. That would give everyone a chance.

Game began at three-thirty. Debbi arranged for hot dogs and hamburgers around five, at least for those who could eat them. From the noise we generated, you'd have thought we were actually at the ball park, not just in front of the TV. The kids are great fans. They hang on every pitch. Complain about the calls. Cheer for the hits. Swear at the questionable called strikes. As if nothing could be more important at the moment.

Which, I would agree, was the case.

Thank God for Jamie Moyer. The win doesn't put the O's back in the pennant race, but at least the losing streak ends at eight. And I don't have to kick the television or break down in tears in front of the kids.

"Jesus, if you're feeling well before you fly, a day hanging around airports will certainly make you sick enough." Janice hadn't even put her suitcase down before she began her litany of complaints.

"Oh, not bad, thanks," I said. "And how've you been doing?"

She stopped. And smiled. "Okay, sorry. I just get so tired of waiting, getting lied to about delays, eating airport food."

"Must be almost as bad as being in a hospital, huh?"

The smile wouldn't quit. "Yeah, I think that's a good comparison. But in a hospital sometimes you die and it ends. In an airport, you worry life will go on like this forever."

Janice had taken the red-eye home. Her clothes were wrinkled from eight hours in an uncomfortable airplane seat. Her face was smeared, her hair was matted, yet she appeared to have all the energy in the world. Once I could work all night, still concentrate on tasks the next day, then go out and party. Now each hour I strive to get through the next sixty minutes. Only during a game can I forget life's deadlines. If there's enough extra innings, the contest never ends.

"You might want to take a nap," I said. "At least if you're planning to go to a game later."

"Damned straight I'm going to a game later," she snapped. "I didn't fly all night just to sit in an apartment while you go out and have all the fun."

"Janice, I'll have to admit, it's nice to have you back."

I rarely saw her taken aback. After a few moments, she spoke. "Hey, we've become a bit of a partnership by now. It's not just your pennant race anymore. They're playing baseball for those of us who plan to live a few more years, too."

She took her suitcase to the other room. I was beginning to think of it as "her room." "Anything decent to eat? Or can we go out and get something?"

[160]

I'd bought steaks to have on hand for a victory dinner. Instead of lugging out the grill and buying charcoal, I sliced one up and made beef stroganoff. Guess I'd tired of her comments about how little men do around the house, how without a woman such simple tasks as making meals and doing the laundry never get done. Decided what the hell, I've got free time when there's a night game. I'll show her a man on his deathbed can still handle things.

"I figured you'd be tired and not in the mood to go out. So I made dinner."

"Oh, Jesus, Dan," she said, "not another one of your tuna melts?"

"Be quiet," I said. "Sit down, relax. Grab a beer. Things'll be set in about an hour."

Janice came in, gave me a funny look. She poured a glass of chardonnay from a half-finished bottle in the refrigerator, then sat down and turned on the news.

"I'm impressed," she conceded as I set the meal on the table. "But, shit, Brussels sprouts? I hate Brussels sprouts."

"Okay, bad guess," I said.

"I thought everybody hated Brussels sprout," she argued.

"People in Belgium love them," I quipped. "I'll eat yours."

She liked the stroganoff. All the times I've made it over the years, I'd never seasoned it this perfectly. I should be grateful that for all the other lymphoma-related problems, I still can enjoy food so often, and not just force it down as necessary fuel.

Janice put down her fork and looked over at me. "So tell me about your week, honey!"

How did this girl come to have such a well honed sense of sarcasm at her young age?

"The usual," I said. "Stayed up late watching my team lose. Got a few units of blood. Did the laundry. Rewrote my will."

"Pretty exciting stuff."

"Oh," I added, "I also went over to the children's cancer unit at Hopkins a couple of times. I watched yesterday afternoon's game with them. Turned out to be a lot of fun."

She had begun to pick up her wine glass, but she stopped and stared at me. Her eyes lit up. Her facial muscles crept into a smile of deep approval. You'd think I'd made the honor roll.

[161]

I broke the brief silence. "Got a few extra tickets for Saturday. You're the advance scout. Think the team is good enough to win a couple in a row?"

Up the road in Philadelphia, surgeons separated two seven-week-old Siamese twins joined at the heart. One died, but the other has a chance at a normal life.

I read part of the story to Janice. "Now there's something medicine can be proud of. Sorry I won't be around in a few years to see how the survivor did."

"Yeah, but I bet there's already a bunch of people out there who are alive because of something you did for them once upon a time," Janice said. "You look for drama too much. Bet if you could add up all the smaller things you've done along the way, it would leave separating a couple of Siamese twins in the dust."

"You know, Janice, even if the lymphoma magically melted away, I still wouldn't live long enough to figure you out. If there's one thing I think would be worth staying alive for, it would be to see how your life turns out."

Janice laughed. "Well, please feel free to try."

We had a night off from baseball, so we relaxed by seeing "The Searchers" at the Senator. John Wayne. He'd have kicked the ass out of my lymphoma.

"Why didn't you bring me to that theater sooner?" Janice asked after the movie.

"What do you mean?" I responded.

"It's such a neat place." The 1939 theater had a rotunda-style lobby, brass chandeliers, a curtain to pull before the show starts. "It's cool how that guy comes out to introduce the movie."

"Yeah," I said, "but it's still just seeing a movie."

"No. It's a real evening out, not just another race to the mall," she added. "This was fun."

"I guess it never occurred to me that it's so unique," I went on. "I must be slipping."

"You must be," she agreed. "Maybe your sense of style is dying faster than you are."

"That's a nice sentiment, Janice. Thanks." She was right, however. I'm the one who wanted to savor every experience, now

[162]

that the potential for them has lessened. It boosted my spirits that she enjoyed the Senator.

"So who do we play next?" Janice asked.

"I like that. 'We.' About time you declared your allegiance."

"Okay, cut the shit, Dan. Who?"

"The Texas Rangers," I told her.

"And how good are they?" she asked.

"Good enough," I said. "But I'll try to be optimistic. I'd like to see us sweep this series."

As I fell off to sleep I read about the centennial of Johns Hopkins' medical school. An article described development of prostate surgery in 1902. It replaced castration in the treatment of bladder symptoms in men. No man will argue about that being an advance.

I woke with a terrible rigor next morning. Took my temperature. A hundred and two. It wasn't fair. I'd been feeling so good. Couldn't the disease lie low just another six weeks? Let me finish the goddamned season in peace?

I decided to play this one straight. Called Eric. Janice drove me to get a chest x-ray then over to meet him in his office. Pneumonia. My blood counts weren't bad. He agreed to set me up for IV antibiotics that day, and again the next morning. If I held my own, we'd continue treatment as an outpatient. All three of us knew I wouldn't come into the hospital even if he recommended it.

"And take a night off from the Orioles!" Eric insisted.

"Sure, ruin all my fun," I said. "Tell me I've got pneumonia, remind me that in my condition it might kill me, then take away the one pleasure I've got left."

"Save the dramatics," Eric replied. "No game tonight."

"Yes, sir!" I gave him a mock salute.

Had Janice not come along, I could have lied and headed for the ballpark. No chance for that now. At least the Orioles provided a 'get well' present of sorts, creaming the Rangers, 10-5.

Saturday morning I got my infusion of antibiotics. Plenty of time to rest up afterwards for a night game. Though I needed more energy for the argument than I did for the game.

"Look, Janice," I said, "Eric said no game last night. I'm

[163]

better today, so I'm going. Feel free to stay home if you want."

"Jesus Christ," Janice began. "You'd think you'd want to rest up so you can still go to Texas and California next week. Isn't that enough reason to stay home a few days? You go to Camden Yards all the time. Don't you want a last chance to see them play out west?"

"I think I'll keep taking it one day at a time," I answered. "If I feel good enough to go to the game, I'm going. It's not going to make the pneumonia worse. It won't change the odds of feeling good next week. Remember. It's my life, it's my death. I get to do it any way I like."

I did take one more game off. Between the paroxysms of coughing and the bouts of nausea, I wouldn't have made fit company for anyone around me in the stands. Who knew the human body could produce such a steady outflow of greenish-yellow mucus? If I'm grossing myself out, how much worse would it be for someone sitting next to me?

"Can't you just cough that crap up until it's done?" Janice asked.

Sparing her a discourse on inflammation and infection, I replied, "Hey, it's pneumonia. You cough up this stuff. Only thing worse would be not coughing it up and letting it sit there."

"Well, I don't know how to make chicken soup. Anything you want from the store?"

"Not really," I answered. "I don't feel like eating. Maybe some ice cream at the game."

We'd settled into this humdrum household existence, like a couple living together long enough to wonder if it'll work out long term. We talked late into most evenings. I'd come home wound up from a game, unable to fall asleep. Janice was always ready for conversation. I think she could talk twenty-four hours a day. Any time she wasn't talking, she was out jogging, or sitting somewhere reading a book.

I'd come to appreciate, indeed rely on, her presence. I gotten so weak, I no longer knew if I'd make it there alone. Her instincts remained good. No pity, no fear, no fawning. She was disarming in her straightforwardness. Her arguments could be emotional at times, yet she never saw them as duels. She asked questions, made me feel my responses were worthwhile. Almost as if she planned to protect my legacy.

Whatever that legacy was, I had twenty-four fewer hours to create it.

When Jack Voigt crossed the plate to give the Orioles a win in the twelfth inning, I was so tired I headed straight to bed. No talking to Janice. No replaying the game in my mind. No thinking about tomorrow's pitcher. Is this how it'll all end? The sap of life slowly draining. No explosion of death, not even a bare whimper. Hard to accept your life force may be no more than that.

We made our way downtown for Sunday afternoon's game. Janice suggested we go early, have brunch, avoid the hassle of driving when the traffic mounts. My coughing was less, but the nausea continued. It was that gnawing feeling of sickness mixed with vague hunger, so that you don't know if eating will help or make you throw up. The aroma of her coffee sickened me. The mere thought of eggs brought a bitter taste to the back of my throat. I needed something sweet.

Pancakes, perhaps. Like Jim Palmer always had for his pre-game meal.

"I mean, can you really taste the difference between real and fake syrup?" Janice asked.

"Put it this way," I answered. "Can you tell the difference between Pepsi and Coke?"

"Of course I can," she said.

"Syrup's sort of the same way," I continued. "Once you've had the real thing, you don't want any artificial substitute."

"Sort of like sex with a vibrator!"

I coughed. Must have caught some orange juice in my throat. "Well," I conceded, "I've never used a vibrator, but probably, yes, like that. I'll give you credit. Sexual imagery for pancakes. Maybe you should become a writer. That kind of thought process sells."

"Nah, writing's an ordeal for me," she said. "For term papers, I loved going to the library and doing the research, putting it all down on three by five cards. But back in my room, trying to put it all in order on paper, that was so hard. I hated it."

[165]

"I'm not so sure all writers find their way so easily," I said. "I suspect many of them struggle on every page. They've got the ideas they want to express. Then they're driven to keep going until they get them out."

"Sort of like how you're driven to get to every ball game," Janice noted.

"Yeah, maybe."

After signaling the waitress for more coffee, Janice resumed speaking. "So remind me what you're going to do if you magically survive, if you're still alive when the season ends."

"That in itself might be enough to kill me," I said. "There are moments when I'm able to think about death so dispassionately, that I worry I've become emotionally crippled. I guess there'll be a letdown. How big a one I'm not sure."

"Well, you might want to start thinking about it." Janice stirred more sugar into her coffee. "I mean, you've bounced back from the pneumonia so quickly, I'm beginning to think you've got more strength than anyone would have figured."

"Thank God for little things," I said. "Yesterday I wondered whether I'd ever see another game. Just going to the park today signals a victory of sorts."

The only victory of the day, it turned out. Texas had no trouble against Arthur Rhodes and the relievers who followed. An 11-4 loss keeps Baltimore five behind Toronto. Suffered the ignominy of the first inside-the-park home run at Camden Yards. Mike Devereaux lost the ball in the sun; it hit him on the arm. Then the relay throw hit the batter in the head.

More of the same Monday. 13 to 6. You can't give up that many runs and expect to win.

Wondered if my illness might be bringing the team down. As though there was a direct link between my clinical deterioration and the team's losing streak. Maybe it is time to die.

My horoscope reads "Make clear your way is best for you and you intend to follow it."

Disappointment from the Texas series dissipated in the face of Jamie Moyer's 1-0 shutout of California. Cal Ripken drove in the sole run, his gift back to the fans on his thirty-third birthday.

[166]

Fittingly, the heroics came on Cal Ripken Junior Oriole Night. Team still five games out, and I'm looking for an omen. Maybe this is it.

Over breakfast next morning, Janice asked why the fans pay so much attention to Ripken.

"He was kind of born to the Orioles. His father was an Oriole coach. Cal used to hang around the ballpark as a little kid. When the team drafted him, it seemed part of a divine plan."

Her eyes showed confusion. "What do you mean, drafted?"

"Every year they have a day when the teams get to choose from the amateur prospects."

"In other words," she asked, "a team has to pick you before you can play?"

"Yeah," I answered. "In so many words."

"What if they don't want to play for the teams that pick them?

"Well, they can not sign," I said. "Then see if anyone picks them the next year."

"Isn't that sort of like slavery?"

I laughed. "Now you sound like the union leaders."

"Well, isn't it?"

"There are pros and cons." I walked over to pour another cup of coffee. "Want any?" She shook her head. "If there wasn't a draft, the teams with the most money would always end up with the best players."

"So tell me more about Ripken," Janice said.

"Baltimore drafted him. He came up to the majors in 1982 and was Rookie of the Year. Next year the Orioles won the World Series, and Ripken was the league's Most Valuable Player."

"Was that the last time the Orioles have been to the World Series?"

"Yeah," I said. "And ten years feels like a lifetime to a fan. Anyhow, Ripken never wanted to sit out a game. After a while, people realized he hadn't missed a game in years. And now he has a chance to break the record for most consecutive games played."

"What's the big deal about playing a lot of games in a row?" Janice asked. "Don't they all do that? I mean, you told me they get paid well enough."

"No," I said. "They get injured, they get sick, they need a

[167]

day to rest. The record is by Lou Gehrig, 2130 consecutive games. But's there's a big drop-off after him."

"You mean the Lou Gehrig Disease guy?"

"Yeah," I said. "Ripken has to play every game for two more years to break the record."

"Wouldn't you like to see it? I'd expect you to be first in line at the stadium that day."

From childhood, baseball's been the common thread to my sequence of life experiences. It's been the fulcrum around which my personal gyroscope periodically rebalanced. I've survived long enough to see my favorite game become a bastion of selfishness, erratic play, and obsession with money. Ripken's the last embodiment of the steadiness our national pastime once provided.

"Sure, I'd love to be there when he breaks the record. But looks like I won't be. So I at least want the streak to still be going when I die."

Every city has a home where Edgar Allan Poe lived or wrote, or, probably, drank. Janice wanted to see the one in Baltimore. Baltimore merits an asterisk. He died here, apparently after being found sick on the street. Hopefully not what happens to me when the time comes. If I'm going to be alone for my last breaths, I'd prefer being home listening to a game, or at the ballpark.

It wasn't easy finding the Poe Home. Once there, we found it closed. Not for the day. Perhaps forever. Let me rephrase. Want to visit Poe's last home? Quoth the raven, nevermore.

"Would you settle for Flag House?" I offered.

"What's that?" Janice asked.

"I don't know that much about it," I pre-empted, "but it's where the lady lived who sewed the flag that became the Star-Spangled Banner."

"Huh?" she blurted.

"The flag on the ship Frances Scott Key was on during the British attack on Baltimore when he wrote the 'Star-Spangled Banner.'"

"Sure," she said. "I'm game."

Flag House was a compact brick home near the harbor. A guide showed us around.

"Who ever thought flag making would have been a good

business two hundred years ago?" Janice whispered as we moved through the dining room to the parlor.

"What amazes me," I whispered back, "is that they've still got a copy of the receipt for it. When I do my taxes, I'm lucky I can find receipts from a month ago. Plus, four hundred bucks must have been a fortune back then." The bill had come to $405.90 for what became the Star Spangled Banner plus one additional flag.

"These mannequins show Mary Pickersgill, her mother, and her daughter," Kathy, our guide, told the group of six. "When complete, the flag was thirty feet by forty-two feet in dimension. Each stripe was two feet, and each star, tip to tip, was also two feet."

"Wow!" Janice exclaimed. "How long did it take to make?"

"About six weeks," Kathy replied. "Look closely; you'll notice eight stitches to the inch."

"You know what bothers me?" I began, as we left Flag House. "Here's a woman who sewed maybe the most important symbol in the history of the United States, and she's been completely forgotten."

"Yeah," agreed Janice. "I mean, look, she supported a family at a time when women didn't have many opportunities. Plus, how about the way she established a home for domestic violence victims? This lady was way ahead of her time."

"Makes you wonder how long anyone will be remembered after they die." I paused. "Makes me glad I'm devoting my time to baseball. If I'm going to be forgotten quickly, may as well be doing something I enjoy."

"Oh, cut this 'nobody remembers' crap," she said. "People will remember you. Some, of course, will remember you only for this baseball stuff. I'll remember you. If you want, I'll come down to your grave every now and then and talk to you there. You'll never get rid of me."

"I feel better already," I laughed. "Want to catch dinner before the game?"

We drove to Angelina's, one of those places the locals know but that tourists rarely find. It's a boisterous family Italian restaurant in a northeast Baltimore row-house neighborhood.

"Get the crab cakes," I told Janice. "They always win the award for the best in town."

That night's game was a killer. Mussina lost to California, 2-1. Being on the wrong end of a pitcher's duel is heartbreaking. A great performance, yet you fall another game behind in the standings. Makes one think the powers up there are against you. And against the Orioles.

"Stop moaning already," Janice admonished after patiently enduring an hour of post-game rumination. "It's just a game. Remember?"

"Shit, Janice, can't you remember anything you wanted more than anything else in the world? Some part in a play, some guy to ask you to the prom, some job offer right out of college? Something you'd be ready to kill for, or to die for? Well, that's how I feel right now."

"Yeah, I know," she said.

"No, you don't."

"Don't interrupt, damn it."

Her stridency took me aback, but I let her continue. "I do know. But for you it's year after year, game after game. There's got to be a limit on how many things you can die for. There's certainly a limit on how many things you can kill for. Hey, half the teams that played today lost. Like they do every day. So this wasn't one of your days. Live with it."

"Okay," I agreed, "as long as you don't interfere with my right to feel the same way tomorrow." If I argued any more, I'd boost adrenaline levels and lie awake all night. Then fall asleep in the fourth or fifth inning tomorrow out at Camden Yards. I needed the rest.

Next game proved worth staying awake for. The bats operated on overdrive. Nine runs. Always good to close a home stand with an impressive win. Wished they'd scored a few of them yesterday for Mussina. Would still have been enough left to win this one comfortably.

"Hey, I told the kids I'd bring pizza for them tonight," I said. "Want to come along?"

Janice, clearly surprised, approved. "When'd you set that up? Thought all you'd been doing was crying in your beer, or whatever it is you're drinking these days."

"Oh, I told them last week I'd come over after the day game."

[170]

"And the promise didn't get lost in your bad mood last night?" she asked.

"No, Janice, it didn't. Promises never get lost on me. I told them I was coming. So I am. All I asked is whether you want to join me or not."

"Sure, I'll come," she said. "Can I have pepperoni on mine?"

I called Debbi. She told me the kids were still expecting me. The ones who were eating refused to order any supper because of it. Talk about pressure.

I brought along a video of "Field of Dreams." After the movie, one boy exhorted, "Boy, can you imagine baseball ever being that important to someone?"

"Ask Dan," Janice ventured. "It is to him."

I glared at her for an instant, then I addressed the waiting faces.

"You have dreams in life," I began. "I wanted to be a pro baseball player from the first moment I knew anything about the game. We read a story in school. About a deal you could make with the devil. You'd promise him your soul, and in return he'd grant you any desire you had. I figured the chance to be a major leaguer was worth giving up a soul later on." I picked up another slice of pizza. "It helped, of course, that I really didn't have any idea what a soul was."

"You can't give up your soul!" Marie exclaimed. She was about fifteen, had lost her leg to an osteosarcoma. I'd been told how religious she was, and how I better not swear with her in the room. "If you do, you spend eternity in hell."

"I'm smarter now than I was back then, Marie," I told her. "I finally realized anything worth accomplishing took a lot of hard work, not just a prayer or a deal with the devil."

"But you didn't become a baseball player," Johnny countered.

"No. I tried, but I wasn't good enough. Everybody can't do exactly what they want in life." I suddenly felt selfish and inconsequential. Here I am talking platitudes to a bunch of kids with cancer, who have had so many opportunities taken away from them so early. "I found other things I could do well. But that didn't mean I couldn't still love baseball."

"That's why you go to so many games?" asked Jessica.

[171]

"I guess so," I weakly replied. "For me, the best substitute was to learn all I could about the game, and all I could about my team. Hoping that if I became a great fan, it might help the team do better than it otherwise might."

"Do you think it makes a difference?" Johnny again.

"Yeah, I do," I said. "I think everything we do makes a difference. I'm sure there were a few games where I cheered harder and it inspired a few players to work a little harder to win."

"And what happens if you cheer harder and your team loses?" Jessica interjected.

"You go back and try harder next time," I said. "It's a long season. You bounce back."

"Now you sound like the doctors when something goes wrong or treatment doesn't work," Ann asserted. She wasn't much of a baseball fan, but I'd noticed how closely she listened to everything I said. Nurses told me she spent most of her time reading. She once said if she got through all this she would become a doctor herself and find out the cause of cancer. Frequently she told the staff she got tired of hearing doctors saying they didn't know what caused the disease. "If they don't know what causes it, how can they figure out how to treat it?" she'd argue.

"Yeah, I guess so. We don't get guarantees of how things are going to go for us," I went on. "But we do get the chance to keep fighting in hopes that next time things will go better."

I noticed Janice's broad smile. A smile implying, okay, you've said it, now live up to it. I bit into my pizza and promised myself not to be drawn into further argument on the subject.

Back home, we sat on the couch fruitlessly flipping channels in search of something worth watching. I'd changed into a pair of jeans. Janice wore an Orioles t-shirt and shorts. While I manned the remote, she began, "I loved that comment about how your being a great fan would make the team better."

"Well, why not?" I said.

"I don't know," Janice replied. "It just sounded so idealistic for you. Being so positive."

Janice hadn't shaved her legs recently, I noticed. That helped to reassure me she wasn't perfect. I raised my voice more than I'd planned. "Janice, I meant what I said. I knew early on I wouldn't be a great baseball player. But baseball could still be a big part of my life."

"You make it sound like some kind of sudden enlightenment. You know, one of those things that James Joyce's stories had. An epiphany."

"In some ways it may have been like that," I said.

"What do you mean?" she asked.

"Hey, Janice, if I tell you a story, a long one, will you shut up and listen?"

"I listen to everything you say."

"No, really," I said.

She scrunched up on the couch with her legs bent underneath her. "Okay, shoot!"

"I'll never forget the feeling of my first home run. It was sophomore year in high school. We were ahead by seven runs over Rocky Falls in the eighth inning, so Coach Krane felt comfortable putting in a bunch of us second-stringers.

"I hadn't played much that season, and I'd come to terms with the fact I'd never have the arm to realize my dream of being a shortstop. When the team took the field, I headed out to second base. There was a gentle breeze, and a smell of pine and balsam in the air. Some pollen still stuck to the bag at second.

"With two outs, a sharp ground ball came my way. I so much wanted to field it cleanly. Quickly went two steps to my left. The ball bounced off my glove but I kept it in front of me. Slow runner, so I had no trouble throwing him out. Not pretty but I made the play.

"I led off in the bottom of the inning. I don't remember who was pitching, but he had good control and threw hard. I always took a first strike, a habit so well engrained that I'm sure every pitcher within a hundred miles knew it. I spent so much of my life hoping I'd get on via a walk, then take advantage of my speed to move around the bases, that I virtually assured myself of getting behind in the count.

"First pitch came in belt high and over the plate. Strike one. A sour taste came into my throat. I started to reach for the next offering but let it go outside. My coach at third yelled 'Good eye!' He gave a bunch of signals but none for anything specific. I was still

[173]

on my own.

"The next pitch was a fastball. It seemed to float and enlarge, much as a harvest moon throws off such an oversized image. When the bat made contact, I felt the ball compress and fly off. I had never hit a pitch so squarely.

"I pushed off my back foot and started toward first, but not before hesitating just a second to follow the flight of the ball. When I saw it soar on a line over the right fielder's head, I enjoyed a moment of jubilation matched only a few times in my life. I ran as fast as I could to first, rounded the bag, headed toward second.

"My thoughts registered so clearly. I felt in full control. Watch the coaches, I told myself. The first base coach waved me on. I looked toward third to be sure he didn't stop me. And he was telling me to come on. I saw the dejection on the pitcher's face, the shortstop tossing down his glove in disgust. My teammates sprung out of the dugout. The third base coach kept windmilling his arms.

"By then I began realizing I should have slowed down a bit and enjoyed the sensation. But speed added to the moment's intensity. I wanted the experience to be an uncompromised one.

"All I ever wanted was to be a baseball player.

"By the next day, reality set in. Guys who can't hit eighty mile an hour fast balls don't play pro ball. Nor do those unable to make the throw from deep short. My ability to draw walks and then steal bases would not be enough to get me to the major leagues.

"I decided the best I could do was bring that same intensity to being a fan."

Janice sat there without saying a word.

"You still awake?" I asked.

She finally talked. "That was about the most impassioned story I've heard from you. Maybe from anyone."

"I don't need the false praise, thank you."

"No. Really." She slid a little closer to me. "Watching you and listening to you tell that gives me a whole new sense of who you are. And why you're doing what you're doing."

Summer heat wasn't letting up. And it's not just me dragging out there.

I learned the Baltimore Housing Authority wilts in the hot

[174]

weather, too. If it's 90 degrees and 55% humidity at noon, everyone gets the afternoon off with pay. Now there's a union with clout. Seventeen times so far this year, the rule has gone into effect. Taxpayers might never have known about their largesse, but yesterday the workers were let out when it was only eighty-nine. So there's a stink about it in the papers.

I'd missed enough games already this year. I wanted to make the trip to Texas. My pneumonia was better. I could walk a couple of blocks --slowly-- without getting too short of breath. Three days of packing won't require too heavy a suitcase. Taxis can get me anywhere I need to go once I'm there.

Janice had decided to visit her mother for a few days, so I'd be on my own. I knew my limits. I'd hit the three games in Texas then decide whether to go on to California. If I felt too tired, I could fly to San Francisco and wait until the O's came to Oakland. Watch the California series on TV. My memories of that first trip to Los Angeles weren't very fond anyway.

Traffic conspired against me. We were still stuck behind cars on the Beltway. An accident up ahead, the cab driver told me. I began to feel weak. And sick to my stomach. More troopers pulled up by the median. Lights flashed. Suddenly it felt like all those beams were heading for me. Oscillating blues, vibrating reds, harsh yellows. It began to resemble a psychedelic party from my college days. I vaguely remember hearing the driver. "Hey, you all right, man? You look kind of sick."

I woke up on a ventilator. A fucking ventilator. Why didn't somebody stop them? Doesn't anybody look at medical records anymore?

White coats blended together, as if a breeze was blowing clothes dry on a line. Low murmurs swirled around me. I heard a man's voice say "we have a couple of interesting cases in here today." Wonderful. I knew the code. Something interesting to doctors never meant something good for the patient. Maybe I'll die of a disease I never heard of.

A nurse noticed me struggling to get up. "Mr. Jameson," she began. "You're in the intensive care unit of Maryland General Hospital. You were brought in after blacking out in a cab. Do you remember any of this?"

[175]

I nodded.

"You have pneumonia. You're on antibiotics."

I pointed to the tubing connecting me to the rhythmic machine. "The tube? You weren't breathing when you got to the emergency room. The doctors put a tube into your lungs to be sure you got enough oxygen into your body."

I made enough of a motion toward my throat that she got the drift. "You want this out. Actually, on rounds this morning, the doctors commented on how well you were doing. I expect it can come out within a day or two."

I forcefully shook my head no. She smiled. "Try to relax a little. I know this is all scary. But everything is going to be okay."

No, it isn't. It's never going to be okay.

A bit frantic, I motioned for something to write on. She brought me a pad of yellow paper and took a pen out of her jacket pocket. In shaky letters, I asked her to contact Eric.

Forget Texas. Probably California, too.

No sense fighting it. In a hospital, they always have the upper hand. If I pull the tube out, they'll restrain me, tie my arms to the bed. Then push some medicine into the IV tube and sedate me. Consider me a difficult patient, as a judge might deem someone a hostile witness. Better to just bide my time until I can talk -- make that write-- to someone with the authority to give orders. Orders to get me off this fucking machine.

John Franklin, the physician in charge, extubated me early in the evening, then stayed around to talk. "You're doing pretty well. Turns out the pneumonia we see on x-ray isn't any more prominent that it had been a week ago. You probably passed out from a combination of fatigue and anemia."

A unit of blood dripped slowly through a catheter into my arm. My throat hurt; I assumed that was from the endotracheal tube.

"Anyhow, I called Eric Bell. We've known each other since med school at Hopkins. He filled us in on the lymphoma. And on this wild plan of yours to see every game the Orioles play." His face betrayed a bit of disbelief.

I smiled. I'd long since given up defending the concept. It wasn't anyone's business but my own.

"I checked the schedule," the doctor continued. "Three

[176]

games coming up in Texas, counting tonight's, then a bunch on the coast. I wouldn't plan to be at any of them. With a little luck, though, you should be ready for the home stand come Monday next."

"Thanks," I managed. "I appreciate it."

"There's something I feel I should say."

"Okay."

"You know there might be chemotherapy regimens that would still help you," he asserted. "I realize chances of response are lower after having treatment failure. But still there might be a shot of giving you more seasons to watch."

"I know," I blurted out in my most resigned tone of voice. "But chances are slim enough that I decided to see the games now. While I can. You know, bird in the hand, and all that."

"Especially if the bird's an Oriole, huh?" He managed a grim smile. "It's your call. We'll certainly respect it."

Dr. Franklin began walking away, then came back. "In the spirit of full disclosure, I should tell you I'm a Toronto fan. I grew up in Buffalo, and that was my team. So don't take it personally if I'm rooting against you the rest of the summer."

"I guess that's your right," I told him. "Just don't root too hard when our teams play each other. Winning them could mean a few extra for me to watch."

"I can understand that. If it's your final season, you'd like it to go on as long as possible."

In an attempt to keep boredom at bay, I perused the newspapers.

Government declares every cigarette shortens one's life an average of seven minutes. Wonder if, near the end, I can cash in on that knowledge and assure early relief to any suffering.

Housing Authority policy on heat leave gets suspended. Wonder what the union will seek in return during the next negotiations.

Father of those Siamese twins separated in Philadelphia gets arrested for drugs. Turns out he was on probation after a recent knife fight. And he's been stealing donations for his own use. He deserves capital punishment in my opinion.

The name "Ravens" gets selected for Baltimore's new

[177]

football team. People strive their entire lives to be remembered. Poe merely dies in Baltimore and gets memorialized.

Too drowsy to read much more, I content myself with the pressure of an Oriole game. While I battle for life, or at least what's left of it, the Orioles struggle, too. I'd counted on pitching to propel them to a pennant, but no such luck. Only Jamie Moyer manages to win in Texas. I should apologize for my skepticism when he was first called up.

Orioles manage to float about five games out. I feel like I'm floating right along with them. Nurses insist they're not giving me any sedation, so it must be the illness impairing my concentration. Dr. Franklin convinced me to take some transfusions and stay a couple more days. No way I'm flying to the coast now, anyway, so I didn't put up my usual resistance.

I suggested to Janice she go as my stand-in again.

"Like I'm flying to California knowing you're in the hospital and might die. Right!" Instead, she joined me in the ritual of watching late night baseball on television.

Out in Anaheim, the Orioles began winning again. They continued doing so in Oakland. Mussina won with his third straight solid performance. Ben McDonald and Arthur Rhodes pitched well. One game went thirteen innings. I dozed off around the eighth or ninth, but I woke up in time for the ending. Then Moyer and Mussina won the last two games of the road trip. Errorless ball in the field. Each night someone different in the cast of characters played hero.

I turned the volume down on the television so I could listen instead to WBAL. Janice never understood why I appreciated the game more on the radio. How a good announcer could give vivid details, then let me finish the painting in my own mind. Imagine the catcher backing up first on a ground ball, or the pitcher scuffing up the mound just before staring in for the sign, or the runner brushing dirt off his pants after sliding in for a double.

Newspapers continued offering their unintended diet of tragi-comic relief.

The Maryland Court of Appeals strikes down a ban on racially-motivated cross burnings. Calls it a "form of free speech." Checked the dateline to be sure I had a paper from August 1993, not

[178]

August 1893.

There's the suicide of a priest facing charges of child abuse ten years previously. Troopers find that cars slow down when they pass a police cruiser with a mannequin at the wheel. I believe it. Now here's a ploy that might really save money and lives. Though not mine.

It's the centennial of the Ferris wheel. The better anniversary is one in Chattanooga, where a guy does a 176-foot bungee jump to celebrate his ninetieth birthday.

Thermometer hits a hundred for the twelfth time this summer.

Orioles came back to Baltimore on a seven-game winning streak. I had my own streak. Four days without fever. Four days with an appetite. For food and for victory.

We celebrated Labor Day back out at the ball park. Beautiful day, sunny, in the eighties. I briefly muttered a prayer of thanks for another fall evening watching a game in Camden Yards. I knew that last stretch on a ventilator could have meant the end. Of everything. In celebration, I started on the beer early. Peanuts tasted fresher than usual. Hot dog perfectly steamed. Just as in those sentimental stories, life's so much more savored after a close brush with death.

"Those stadiums on TV were half-empty," Janice observed. "Baltimore is always full."

"Yeah," I said. "I hope it lasts. A lot of it is having the new stadium. Let the team have a few bad years and see how many turn out night after night."

She really has gotten caught up in the team. "It's easy to see how great a pitcher Mussina is, but Moyer throws so slow and easy," she said. "I don't understand it. If the ball comes in slow, why isn't it easy to hit? I mean, I can see why it's hard when the ball's a blur."

I looked up from my scorecard. "There's more to it than speed. Otherwise the team with the fastest pitchers would always win. You look at each pitch as a test of nerves with the batter. You throw it at different speeds, you change how high or low you aim, you throw a curve when you think the batter expects a fast ball. You remember what each batter's strengths and weaknesses are. Moyer's knows he can't blow hitters away. So he must be a smart pitcher.

[179]

He might be able to do this another ten years or more."

"Sounds like my psychology classes," Janice suggested. "Observe how people react to certain situations, and let that determine your response."

"Yeah, sort of," I agreed.

"You think baseball players are that thoughtful about it all?" she asked.

"The good ones are," I said. "I mean, all these guys are stars in Little League and high school. Once you get to the top, everyone's that good. Being stronger or pitching faster doesn't cut it anymore. The ones who want to make it have to show they can learn along the way."

"So if a guy can't hit a curve ball, or whatever, can't he practice until he gets better?"

I laughed. "You're catching on. But if the pitcher's smart, he'll foul the batter up some other way."

"Like what?"

"Maybe hide a whiffle ball in his pocket and throw that instead of the real ball."

"You never take me seriously," she said.

"Oh, I take you seriously enough."

Ben McDonald overpowered Seattle. Crowd gave him a standing ovation when he left in the eighth. Hoiles and Anderson homered.

Twenty-five games to go. My team's had plenty of chances to collapse, and they haven't. If they didn't roll over after last month's losing streak, maybe they won't roll over at all. I'd like to believe I have some kind of cosmic deal. As long as the team keeps winning, I get to stay alive and enjoy it.

A foul ball came near us, and a flock of kids were suddenly in somewhat of a melee. We heard a few shouted recriminations, but one boy raised his hand high with his trophy. I yelled over that he should get it autographed.

"Do you think Cal would sign it?" the kid shouts. "He hit it, and he's my favorite player."

No sense separating truth from fiction now. "Sure," I reassured him, "he signed one that I caught last year. Someday you'll look back at him as one of the great players in baseball. It'll

[180]

be neat that you've got an autographed ball."

He goes off running. I hear his trailing voice. "...and I'm going to get Cal to sign it for me. This guy up there told me he signed one for him last year!" Janice is right. It feels so good knowing you made someone's day a little brighter. Would that I could bottle my attitude at such times, then drink of it on demand.

Once home, Janice wanted to see the ball that Cal signed. I told her it was packed away.

Next night brought more false hopes.

We'd gone to Little Italy for an early dinner at Sabatini's. Janice pointed to a sign advertising the outdoor movies shown down the block during the summer. "How come we never did that? That would have been fun."

"It is fun," I answered. "Sort of an old-fashioned neighborhood picnic, right in the middle of the city. Guess most nights there were Oriole games, and otherwise we were on the road."

"Well if you live into next summer," Janice said, her hands on her hips in her most authoritarian pose, "we're going to the first one."

"You know what, you're on. If I'm still around in a year, we'll do it." I hesitated before adding, "So let me ask. Does that mean if I'm around until next summer, you'll be around, too?"

"Well, right now I don't have other plans," she said. "That's as far as I'll go. But no matter what I'm doing, I'll meet you for that first outdoor movie of the season. Good enough?"

"I don't turn down any offers these days," I admitted, "though I do hesitate making long-range plans."

"Okay, then short-range plans. Time for the game?"

I mopped up some more tomato sauce with a piece of garlic bread. "No time for cannoli. This'll serve as dessert!"

I paid the check. We arrived at Camden Yards just in time to hear the starting lineups.

The game stayed tight through the opening innings. Arthur Rhodes hadn't yet yielded a hit in a 0-0 pitching duel. Then, just like that, he lost his no-hitter in the seventh, gave up two homers, Orioles behind 3-0. Cal struck out to end a bottom-of-the-ninth rally. We lost 3-2.

Toronto and New York lost, too. It's September, and the

[181]

team managed to be within two games of first place. I couldn't complain.

I visited the kids again. Janice came along. We talked about the game. They second-guess the manager even more than I do. I reminded them the guys are trying as hard as they can. Every day can't be a good day. Working to convince myself as much as to persuade them.

Patterns were developing. Kids with pneumonia talked about getting home and going to the ballpark themselves. The chronic ones behaved as though the hospital had become home, the place they feel secure and comfortable. None talked about their illnesses. Some endured rather than enjoyed visits from family members. As if each was equivalent to one more lab test or x-ray that had to be done that day.

Two had leukemia. Bitter coincidence was that both were adopted, each the only kid in the family. Must be terrible waiting so long to have a child, then have your lifetime of hopes dissolved by deadly illness. You saw the forced smiles on the parents' faces. I had fifty years to screw up my life. These kids hadn't had a chance.

Janice called for attention. "Listen up, guys. Your doctors said we can have a picnic tomorrow. Maybe we'll do it outside. If it rains, they'll close off a cafeteria section for us."

She talks and immediately they're energized. It's a gift.

"What're we gonna have?"

"I want hot dogs. I never get hot dogs in here."

"Hey, my Mom makes the best potato salad. I'll get her to make some."

"So what? Wait'll you taste my mother's cookies."

Here came some organizational skill. "Okay, tell you what," Janice said. "We'll have Jamie's mother bring those famous cookies. Bobby, tell your mother it needs to be potato salad for twenty-four. I'm bringing the hot dogs and hamburgers. Teresa's dad told me he'll get special rolls from the bakery where he works. Dan here will bring a dessert."

I took my cue. "Yeah, I'll bring a great cheesecake from this place I know in Pikeville. It's got chocolate cake for the crust instead of graham cracker crumbs. You'll all love it."

"If you guys don't mind," Janice continued, "I'd like to bring

[182]

a couple of my friends, too. I think you'll like meeting them."

"Sure," the ensemble responded. "Why not?"

On the way home, I commented, "Hey, I thought you didn't know anyone in Baltimore."

"Well, I don't, really. But I managed to meet a couple of guys who might bring some life to the party." She looked over at me. "Want to hear who's coming?"

"Sure!"

"Well, one's Mike Devereaux."

I was momentarily speechless. "Want to tell me how you managed that?"

She smiled. "Well, you've told me he's supposed to be a good guy, and I've heard that story ten times of how you met him on the elevator. So I called him – he doesn't remember the elevator incident, by the way – and told him about you. How you're following the Orioles around the country, but that you've been doing other things, too. Like visiting sick kids in the hospital. You know, enough to make him curious. We picked tomorrow because it's an off day and he won't have to rush to the ballpark."

"And how long have you been working on this?" I asked.

"Oh, a while, though really it's none of your business. Besides, it's for the kids, not for you. Not that you won't have a good time, too."

We strolled the Inner Harbor before the game. Crab harvest had been good this summer, so I wanted to work up an appetite. Walking took more out of me these days, but the breeze felt therapeutic. For a while we sat watching a juggler perform on one of the brick plazas.

"Does it mean anything to you that I don't want you to die?" Janice asked. "That I missed you when I was out west? That it felt good to be scoring the game for you, to have a purpose in being there?"

"It feels great to hear you say all that," I said, "but I don't think it's going to keep me from dying. Unless you have some incredible medical insight that's eluded researchers all this time."

"Can't you be serious once?" she implored. "I mean it. I've never felt this way before."

[183]

We sat down on an empty bench. I watched a haggard man in a tattered brown coat throw bread scraps at the pigeons. Behind him, a water taxi discharged its riders.

"I'm not sure what I'm supposed to say, Janice. I mean, I missed you, too, while you were gone. You've made these past few months so much better. I probably would have croaked in the middle of a losing streak if you hadn't been here. But you only get to beat the odds for so long."

"I watch you," she said. "I see you losing weight. I see you puffing harder while we walk. But your spirit stays strong. Your mind's sharp. You don't occasionally second guess yourself about refusing treatment?"

"My spirit's holding up because the team keeps winning," I pointed out. "Or at least winning enough. Once my body fails a little more, it won't mean shit if my mind stays sharp."

"But if you got treated—"

I stopped her. "Remember! No more on that subject."

"You know, sometimes I admire your passion so much," Janice conceded. "Other times I want to call you a fucking idiot."

"Janice, I'm at the point where I don't care if someone calls me a fucking idiot. I wish I'd had the courage to take a few more risks along the way, go my own way more often, not worry so much how it would appear to others."

"But don't you think you'd regret not accomplishing what you did do?" she asked.

"Hard to regret things that never happened," I said.

"Then how about I tell you I'm willing to accept your decisions on how to die," Janice continued. "The reason I want you to live longer isn't for you, it's for me."

I had gotten up to resume walking, but now I sat back down. "Come again?"

"I care about you," she said. "Can't you see? Sure, I respect your decisions. It's just I've gotten so comfortable with you. This relationship is a two-way one. Sometimes I don't think you see that. It makes a difference to me being with you. I'd hate to think we might never have met."

"Then remember," I said, "if I hadn't made my decision to forego treatment, I wouldn't have been on that road in Michigan."

"Wisconsin," she corrected.

[184]

"Whatever! Those Midwestern states are running together in my mind. "

She put her arms around me. "See, you need me more than you admit. You have to count on me for historical accuracy!"

I hugged her back. For a fleeting moment, I wanted the embrace to last forever.

As we resumed our stroll to the ballpark, Janice broke the silence. "Well, if I'm not going to talk you into more therapy, maybe I can talk you into a beer at the game."

"Now that's a command I can follow!"

Traffic had picked up. We had to weave between cars stopped in the intersection when the light changed.

"You know," Janice said, "you spend lots of time telling me what you haven't done, but from my point of view, it sounds like you've done quite a bit."

We were just about at Babe Ruth's home, ready to cross over to Camden Yards. "I guess to me it's a matter of what's lasting. And I can't claim much of that."

"Hey!" Janice said. "Only so many people can invent the electric light bulb, or build bridges, or walk on the moon. Doesn't it occur to you billions of people still lead useful lives?"

I stopped to buy an Oriole Gazette. "Here, read this during the game. Along with all the usual stuff, like batting averages, they list each player's salary. You can decide if they're earning their keep."

"That's the problem with you," she concluded. "You won't think you've accomplished anything in life unless you end up in a box score."

Valenzuela battled gamely, leaving in the seventh tied 3-3. Bottom of the eighth. Two on, two out. A huge roar went up.

"What was that for?" Janice asked.

"Look at the scoreboard," I told her. "They just put up the Oakland-Toronto score." The Athletics, down 1-0 from the first inning, had pushed across two runs in the ninth. "Plus the Yankees are losing. If the Orioles somehow win, they could be just one game from first."

The fans wanted action. Most deafening noise I've heard in the stadium all year.

Pinch-hitter Hulett walked. Bases loaded. Chris Hoiles at

[185]

bat.

"Hey," exclaimed Janice. "Didn't he hit that home run to tie the game? Maybe he'll do it again."

"Might be too much expecting lightning to strike twice in the same game," I cautioned. Almost as I spoke, he grounded the ball into left field for a single. I jumped to my feet cheering. "No complaints. A single's as good as anything right now."

The rattled Seattle pitcher uncorked a wild pitch, letting in an insurance run. Jim Poole set the Mariners down in order in the ninth.

Fans were unusually slow to leave. Another roar arose from the crowd. Scoreboard showed Oakland held on to win their game. Baltimore only one game behind Toronto. Yankees losing. If they fall, too, Orioles pull even in the loss column. Twenty-two games to go. Could there be a better way to spend a September night? Or any night? It's a feeling worth dying for.

I woke up feeling rotten and congested. Tried the usual treatments I had squirreled away in the medicine cabinet. There was a certain pleasure in taking the same medicines other people in America take when they get sick. Sudafed, Chlortrimeton, some Mylanta. No chemotherapy drugs with deceptive names, no high-powered antibiotics.

Thing is, when other people get colds, they battle on. It's just a cold. If I don't get better, I worry it's the beginning of the end. Couldn't shake my symptoms, but when I didn't get a high fever or otherwise deteriorate, I decided not to mention anything to Janice. No way I was missing this party with the kids. I certainly wasn't dying before trying one of those famous cookies.

Janice and I bantered nervously as we drove over to the hospital. She seemed edgy, worried that the guest of honor wouldn't show up. I tried to reassure her. "Hey, Janice, he's an Oriole. No Oriole is going to let a bunch of kids down."

"I hope you're right," she said. "I almost can't believe I called him. He could have thought I was just some loonie playing a joke."

"Oh, come on," I laughed. "It didn't take more than a sentence to make it clear to me you were a force to be reckoned with. I'm sure it was the same for him."

[186]

I parked the car. We took the elevator up to the children's wing. As we got off, I saw a sign-- "Orioles fans only on this unit."

We looked around the reception room. The nurses had decided with even a minimal risk of rain predicted, it would be best to plan the party indoors. That also gave time to decorate. Orange and black crepe paper streamers hung from the ceilings. The kids had painted pictures of Oriole players and put them on the walls. Someone made a decorative collage of box scores and newspaper photos. There was a large framed caricature of the Oriole mascot in one corner, with a strobe light pulsing on it. Two mothers manned a punch bowl; another doled out cups of soda. They'd set up a buffet table; a huge bowl bulged with potato salad. No visitor would have recognized this as a hospital ward were it not for the IV fluids lofted atop their rolling stands.

No Mike Devereaux yet, so Janice and I began mingling with the group.

"Why do you root for the Orioles?" Samantha asked me. She was wearing a pink dress, a far cry from the fading hospital gown she usually had on. "I mean, are you from Baltimore?"

"No, I'm not from Baltimore originally, Samantha," I began my reply. "It's kind of a long story. When I was growing up, all my friends rooted for the Yankees, and the Yankees always won. I guess I figured they didn't need any more fans. So I rooted for a team that did."

"Like your rooting for them would help," Ricky chimed in. He had a jaunty Panama-style hat hiding his bald scalp. I now noticed that no one had on hospital garb.

"Well, I liked to think it did," I said. "I guess I still like to think so. If everybody decided it didn't matter going to the ballpark, or watching on TV, or listening on the radio, do you think the guys would play as hard?"

"I don't think they'd care a bit," countered Johnny, "as long as they got their money." He wore an Oriole cap and a baseball shirt with Cal Ripken's number 8 on the back.

Perhaps he's right, but that didn't keep me from advancing my argument. "I guess I don't feel that way. I don't care what anyone does in life. Whether you're a ball player, a doctor, a policeman, or whatever. I still think it matters to them that what you do means something to somebody. And that feeling leads them to try just a bit harder. Don't you think?"

Samantha again. "My Mom always told me and my brothers that no matter what you do in life, it's your responsibility to give it your best. So shouldn't they always play their hardest?"

"I think your Mom's right, Samantha," I agreed. "They should. But I think deep down we all manage to give a better effort when someone shows us they appreciate what we do. I think my adrenaline would flow just a little more if fifty thousand people were out there cheering me on."

"Even if you're right," injected Billy, "how would they know when you're watching TV?"

"You've got me there," I admitted. "I don't know how to prove it. But there are things in life you can't prove. Somehow, I think the energy still gets sent out and reaches the players."

A strange quiet suddenly came over the room. The kids had spotted Mike Devereaux at the door. Their reactions were unbelievable. They greeted him as though he was a movie star. The way they might have swooned thirty years ago if they had met the Beatles. He shook hands, signed baseball cards, gave a friendly comment to each one.

Samantha came over to offer a glass of punch and say a few words of welcome. Johnny looked too much in awe to utter so much as a single syllable, but he did manage to hand him a notebook to autograph. Eventually the ballplayer went with a few of them to grab hamburgers, then sit down at a table.

Debbi Madison came over. "This is so great for the kids. It's amazing. He's so friendly, making them feel the party was for them, and they were wonderful to invite him."

I grabbed a burger, chips, and some potato salad myself, then sat between Samantha and Billy. It wasn't long before Janice brought Devereaux over to meet me.

I stood up and shook hands.

"Now didn't I meet you in an elevator once upon a time?" he asked.

I smiled. "I'm sure I made quite an impression."

"Well, actually you didn't," he laughed, "but now I think I'll remember it a long time. You've really seen us play every day this season?"

"Not quite," I said. "I missed the west coast swings, and I

[188]

was sick for a few home games."

"Still, that's being pretty faithful for a fan." He stopped and used a felt-tip pen to autograph Ricky's Panama hat.

You have no idea, I thought to myself. "The Orioles are therapeutic for me, I guess."

"Well, you need to know we appreciate our loyal fans," Devereaux responded. "There's nothing like playing in front of a big home crowd."

"Wow!" said Ricky. "You mean you guys really do notice how many people are in the stands, like Mr. Jameson tells us."

The ballplayer put his hand on Ricky's shoulder. "You know, if there weren't fans, we wouldn't be working. It's all of you that make it possible for us to play. I think every day I've got one of the best jobs in the world. I could never forget all the people who support us."

Ricky beamed. So, for that matter, did I.

Later I saw Devereaux at a corner table immersed in animated conversation with Janice and a couple of the kids. I hoped they were asking him the same challenging questions they threw at me. He broke into a smile as he caught my eye. Then he turned back to his new fans.

For the record, those cookies were as good as Jamie promised.

The Blue Jays lost again to Oakland Thursday night, falling into a tie with New York for first place. Orioles a half-game back. All even in the loss column.

I woke up Friday with a fever; I didn't need a thermometer for confirmation. Had to sweat it out. Literally. Made excuses for why I didn't want to go out for lunch, go to the zoo, take in a movie. I felt guilty. Janice was on such a high after yesterday afternoon's party. The kids had a great time. She told me Devereaux enjoyed himself, too, and was glad she'd arranged it. Hey, I had a great time. It's not fair being sick so soon afterwards.

Janice lingered in the condo and began reading *The Southpaw*, Mark Harris' prologue to his novel *Bang the Drum Slowly*. I found it faintly gratifying she was choosing baseball rather than, say, Danielle Steele. Usually she'd go out for a while if I felt lousy. The fact she hung around gave me this funny feeling she

[189]

knew something I didn't. Wondered if she had some insight I lacked into exactly when I'd die.

She didn't argue when I decided to go to the game. Admittedly, I was dragging. As soon as I got out of the car, I became lightheaded. Made a mental note– no beer tonight.

The team seemed to play with new confidence. Down 4-0 in the second, but no sense of defeatism set in. Three innings later, we were up 6-4. In the eighth, Oakland put two runners on against Mark Williamson. Not Jim Poole's night, either. He gave up a long double and a two-run single, then threw wide to first on a sacrifice bunt for an error. Alan Mills came in and was greeted with another bases loaded single. Down 10-6. Won't win this one.

I woke up again with fever, then a shaking chill. This time I knew I needed treatment.

"No, I'm not allergic to anything," I patiently told the emergency room nurse. She might have been the thousandth caring professional to ask that question since this whole ordeal started. Should I have given her a gold watch or something to commemorate the occasion?

"Well, this is an antibiotic you'll be getting. It'll run in over about an hour. In the meantime is there anything else I can do for you?" Besides taking me outside and shooting me?

"No. Thanks for being so attentive." It hasn't been easy being unfailingly polite. Especially since so often I want to scream out loud. I've come to accept that life's not designed to be fair. I never smoked, I exercised regularly, I kept my weight stable. Sure, I could have eaten less red meat and worked harder to develop a taste for tofu. But there are limits.

I still get one of those bad diseases that fills a few pages in those thick textbooks on a doctor's bookshelf. One for which no one knows the cause. I couldn't have avoided it had I tried for a lifetime. Probably programmed from birth. Makes me wish I'd never tried to like soy products. Should have eaten more hamburgers. With lots of fries.

I must have dozed. Awoke to a clamor. All sorts of white coats hovered around the gurney in the next room. I couldn't even be sure a patient was there until everyone walked away, leaving a man about my age lying motionless. Bags of fluid hanging over

[190]

him, catheters coming from his arm and under his collarbone, needles all over the place, everything seemingly knitted together by an interminably twisting roll of EKG paper.

Wondered if the guy had any idea this was coming. Dying with such suddenness might be comfortable for the person going, but it's always a shock for family and close friends. At least he's not suffering anymore, they'll say. Meaning they no longer have to suffer along with him.

Whereas my mechanism of dying prolongs itself sufficiently to eat away at relationships, much as the cancer eats away at me. Everyone gets to see the deterioration of personality, loss of hope, and angry acceptance of fate. I suppose it'll help obviate the distress of others when I die.

Enter Janice, her hair blown out of place but a broad smile on her face. "So guess what I've been doing today!"

"Beats me,' I said. "But I can't think of many better ways to kill time than watching an IV drip drugs into your arm."

Her smile, if synthesized, would supplant shock therapy for combating depression. "I had an interview at the University of Maryland med school. They looked at my transcript and told me I only need a couple of courses before I can apply."

I came to attention. "You've got to be kidding. When are you going to start? How are you going to afford it? For that matter, why are you even thinking about it?"

Janice shook her head in frustration as she thrust the application form at me. "Only you would have to ask. Think you might be a factor? Anyhow, I told them I got interested after spending so much time around doctors and hospitals helping my best friend during his last days of lymphoma. If you can take a serious moment, though, I really decided after seeing how you light up when you're around those kids. Most of the time you feel sorry for yourself-- not that you don't have reason-- or you think about the Orioles. But with the kids, you think about them and move out of yourself. The way they respond is amazing. Kids know when someone's putting them on. You're not. That bit of selflessness puts sort of a glow around you. Plus, this might make me part of your legacy. Now that should piss you off some!"

"Yeah," I said, "the Orioles in a free fall, my ex-wife

working to develop her new life, and Janice Browning a doctor. I'll die knowing I left the world a better place."

"Let me tell you something," she said. "You're leaving those kids in a better place. They hang onto your every word, wait for whatever you're going to say next. You make them want to live. They get to think about dying enough. They see the solemn faces on the doctors, the tentativeness of the nurses, the fear in their parents' eyes. You make them look forward to something beyond more blood testing and chemotherapy."

"So what you're telling me is that I'm a good distraction?" I asked.

She thought a moment before replying. "Yes, that's exactly what you are. You're a great distraction. It's nice being around someone in this world who's a great distraction."

My nurse came back. "Sorry for all the ruckus. How're you doing?" She checked the antibiotic drip, put a thermometer in my mouth, wrapped a blood pressure cuff around my arm.

"Guess I'm doing better than that guy there." The body lay motionless amidst the tubing and paper. Must be a shortage of bus space to the River Styx these days. "Though just barely."

"Dr. Bell said to ask you about a transfusion. Told me you'd say no, but to try anyway."

"No thanks," I said. "At this point, I've had enough of other people's blood in me. I'd just as soon finish up with my own cells, weak though they may be."

"Well, it's a free world," she said. "Let me clean you up a bit and get you ready to go."

Death in the news again. It always is, I guess, or am I simply filtering too much? Eighth foreign tourist killed in Florida this year. Another Kevorkian-assisted suicide. Maybe I'm being selfish insisting on natural causes for my own demise.

Also a piece about Oriole wives doing an event for the Johns Hopkins Children's Center.

A beautiful Sunday evening. Wisps of cloud dotting the slowly darkening powder blue sky. Temperatures in the seventies, slight breeze. Huge crowd; likely another sellout. Game on national television. Let fans across the country sample what I've been seeing all season.

[192]

Naturally, I liked the drama of going almost right from the emergency room to Camden Yards. You want to imagine the players seeing you enter just as batting practice ends. How they'd talk about it in the dugout. Go out and win one for the Gipper, that sort of thing. Though one game wouldn't be enough. This is the kind of illness that necessitates a pennant.

My stomach had settled by early afternoon, and I'd managed to keep soup down. Didn't want to miss this game. Like I told the kids, I truly do feel that being there in person makes a difference. A scream, a rise to my feet, a pump of my fist– it had to have some kind of impact. That heavenly body exerting a gravitational pull, however small, on another heavenly body.

I've fully accepted Oriole games will continue after I die. No fans in rival ballparks will know I'm gone. Precious few will be aware even at Camden Yards. Certainly no player will know. In a matter of weeks– months? maybe days?– the Orioles would simply have one less fan. For the most part, society would move on with no discernible difference.

I had a sudden feeling of emptiness. Considered leaving. Going home to rest. Maybe to die.

Chords of "The Star Spangled Banner" began floating over the stadium. I swayed, working to remain steady on my feet. Guy in the next seat asked if I was okay. "Getting over the flu," I told him. "Figured seeing the team win would help."

By the seventh, O's led 11-2. Deveraux had a homer and five RBI's. Probably inspired by Thursday's party. Baines and Pagliurulo also homered. Moyer got the win. Yankees lost, but Toronto rolled past California. Game and a half behind Toronto; New York two back.

Nineteen more to play. The team's destiny is in its own hands. I couldn't complain.

Janice skipped last night's game in favor of spending a day in Philadelphia. I caught a morning train to Philly, then Janice drove rest of the way to Boston. Compazine helped combat my nausea. The Philadelphia-to-Boston corridor isn't a bad preparation for death. Had Dante been a highway superintendent, he'd have included this as part of Purgatorio.

I was still assessing our relationship. Had I a religious bent, I

[193]

might conclude Janice had been divinely assigned to shepherd me through my final weeks of illness. Because of her presence, I may not die alone. To my surprise, that's a source of solace. Maybe I should think of her as a relief pitcher, coming in to raise my spirits in the late innings of life. However, your best reliever is called a "closer". I better not take this analogy too far.

We stayed at the Copley Plaza. There was a fading grandeur to the place, but the bar still ranked as one of the best. It featured all the polished oak and cigarette smoke that you expect to find in a venerable men's club rather than a modern watering hole. Janice wanted a drink after the game. The way the Orioles had played tonight, it wasn't a bad idea.

Israel and the PLO manage to sign a peace agreement, but the O's can't hold a 4-0 lead against the Red Sox. Wasted home runs by Hoiles and Baines. Rhodes pitched well, but relief pitchers blew the game in the sixth. Red Sox won 6-4. O's go two games back.

I risked a bourbon while Janice sipped her Manhattan. Black guy played a blues piano. He was pretty good. During his break he nursed a drink at the bar. All of a sudden Janice was up there talking with him. After ten minutes or so, they both came over to our table.

"You're not going to believe this," Janice said. "This is Sam. He's played with B. B. King and Muddy Waters. Made some of his own records a while back, too."

We introduced ourselves and shook hands. He told us a little about his life. Grew up sharecropping in Mississippi, learned the guitar from his uncle, played house parties and the like. When a friend moved to Chicago, Sam went along. He taught himself to play piano up there. Got a few jobs in local bars, others heard him, and he got invited to go on some tours.

"Drank away all my money. Missed a few recording sessions. So instead of being a headliner, I do the best I can in clubs and all. My own fault. Didn't know what life was like when I had the chance."

"Who'd you record for?" I asked.

"Oh, anyone who'd have me. Mostly backing vocalists. But Mr. Chess, Leonard, liked my style and had me do a couple of piano solos, then put them on an album."

"The world's different now," I said. "Think people will still be playing the blues in twenty years?"

[194]

He laughed. I noticed the two gold teeth in front. "Hey, you can be sure I won't be doing it in twenty years. I doubt I'll be breathing in twenty years." Pointed to his chest. "I cut back on drinking to save my liver, but now the doc says my ticker's giving out. Don't matter much what you do, something's gonna give out."

"Oh, he's dying, too," Janice said. "Of cancer. And of a hard head. Won't let the doctors give him any more treatment."

"Well, little lady," Sam said, "Sometimes it ain't no fun being treated. I've been in the hospital a few times. Once they had me on a breathing machine. 'Nother time somethin' happened to my kidneys and I had to be on some kind of machine to clean out the blood. Had to go in three, four times a week, get hooked up, sit there doing nothing for five or six hours. Weren't no fun, I can tell you."

"Probably a blues song somewhere in there," I suggested.

"Oh, there'll always be the blues," he said. "Words might change, rhythms might change, they might play different instruments. But there's gonna be people who're sick, people who're poor, people who're being cheated or played for fools. There'll be reasons to sing the blues."

Janice cut in. "Tell him what you were telling me about the kids."

"Oh, that was just something I picked up a few months ago."

"Yeah," she said, "but tell him."

"Oh," Sam said, "sometimes guys from the hospitals come in here at night. Doctors, some nurses and orderlies. We strike up conversations. They convinced me to play a few afternoons over there. They got lounges on the floors, and a couple have pianos. Been a lot of fun."

Janice broke in, "The kids."

"Oh, yeah. One day they asked if I'd play for some kids. I told them, hey, I'm no rock-and-roller. Kids today aren't into the blues. But they insisted. And you know, the kids kind of liked it. Started making up their own songs and such." I saw the bartender signal Sam. Time to get back on stage, I assumed. "After a while I started giving some kids guitar lessons. And they got it fixed up so I could do it at one of the schools. It's been nice. Get a little bit of money from it. Feels good that I might pass on something that'll be good for them. If I can do something so their life ain't as rough as mine, it's worth it."

He rose to go back to the piano. I didn't need to see Janice's expression. I could feel it.

Three drinks the most I'd had in a while. Let me add a hangover to the list of reasons I felt shitty next morning. Tomato juice had no effect. Aroma of coffee made me sick. I had some oatmeal just to get something into me. Oatmeal for breakfast in a hotel. A dying man's breakfast.

Janice had gone for a walk. Her nightgown lay on the rumpled bedcovers, a reminder that the girl still has some sense of modesty left. Any day now she'll start arguing for king-size beds in hotels instead of two doubles.

Not that a little physical companionship wouldn't be nice. But I never cheated when I was married, and somehow the idea of sex now didn't seem right. Would think I'm using my illness to unfair advantage. Maybe Janice just comes a little too close to being the type of person with whom an affair would have been satisfying.

Browsing newspapers, I focused on the remarkable rapprochement of Rabin and Arafat. You see two people like them civil after all the rancor, and you begin to think Brooklyn might be welcoming should the Dodgers return. Another murdered tourist in Florida, a British traveler near Tallahassee. I give a moment of thanks the American League isn't represented down South.

I wasn't in the mood for wandering aimlessly, so I checked the tourist guide. Boston Public Library was just across the block and offered tours. Good enough for me. I marveled at the architecture, admired classical art work, scrutinized displays of old books. Afterwards I settled into an upholstered chair and read the first chapter in *Battle Cry of Freedom*. I'd always wanted to know more about the Civil War. Learn as if you would live forever. Even if forever has become more circumscribed.

The pace of change in the nineteenth century appealed to me. Inexorable progress, but every concept or advance could be made comprehensible. My ability to grasp new scientific principles hit a plateau with television. I think about CT scanners and MRI's and CD players, and I have trouble separating them from magic. You slide under this huge camera hovering over a cold table, and –poof– your body comes out depicted in an infinite number of slices. Julia

Child never had such a grasp of an onion.

I went back to the room. No Janice, so I headed back out and crossed the street to Turner Fisheries. One thing about Boston—good clam chowder on every corner. I sat at the counter, but away from the guy shucking oysters. I doubted my intestines could handle oysters right now.

"You from out of town?" the guy next to me asked. He carried a briefcase, looked harried.

"Yeah," I said. "Here for a few Red Sox games."

"That'd be nice," he replied. "I'm here for a conference. Think I could get tickets?"

I'm an expert on this. "There were a few thousand empty seats last night. No ballpark's full when the team's out of the running."

"I guess every fan is really a fair weather fan at best."

I mildly resented the opinion. Except for that time when I was ten years old and refused to look at scores for a month after the Orioles lost a heartbreaker to the Yankees, I've been pretty steadfast. More steadfast than in any other aspect of my life.

I was barely able to finish the chowder.

Down 3-2 that night despite a Baines home run, Orioles took the lead on a two-run Hoiles round-tripper, then added seven more for a 11-3 victory. Fernando Valenzuela gained strength from the cushion and posted a complete game win. Glad his comeback continues to bear fruit. Yankees won easily. Toronto beat Detroit. Orioles hovering two back. Still in the race. They need to play consistently well, but they clearly have a chance. That's all I can ask.

We went to the exercise room next morning. Janice spent time on the treadmill. I rode a stationary bike. The exertion felt good. Relaxed in the spa before going back upstairs.

I could hear my heart beat while I soaked in the warm water. At one point, the sound ceased. A reminder? A harbinger? A preview? The interlude couldn't have lasted more than a couple of seconds, but it made me take notice. A silence. A sense of floating. Not at all unpleasant. Could I expect death to come that quietly?

When Janice suggested walking the Freedom Trail, I figured,

why not? I dragged a bit, but that gave her time to read the brochures. "How come they couldn't make history interesting in high school?" she spouted. "I mean it's really impressive seeing all these places you learned about, instead of just memorizing them."

"Maybe it would be interesting if you lived where it all happened, and history could be a series of field trips," I said as we rested inside Old North Church. "Of course, kids in Boston probably find this stuff boring, probably complain they've seen it too many times."

"That's too bad," she said. "Experiencing this stuff firsthand should make you want to pick up a book and read about it."

"No argument, Janice, but you're doing this on your own, not because someone's making you do it. Maybe society has it all backwards. We should work first, then when we're mature enough to get something out of it, we get the chance to go to school."

"There might be something to that," she agreed. "When I think of all the classes I skipped, or slept through, I'm not sure my parents got their tuition money's worth."

"There's that old adage that education is wasted on the young," I noted. "I figure at least I learned the basics, then if I got interested enough in anything, I had the ability to understand it."

"They should use you as an example," Janice replied. "You spend half your time hanging around waiting to die, but you still brighten up when you're learning something new."

"Maybe I find learning something new to be a good diversion," I said. "Take my mind off the disappointments of the present by focusing on the past."

We headed toward the Granary Burying Ground, resting place of John Hancock, Paul Revere, Sam Adams, and victims of the Boston Massacre. The place felt too enclosed amidst the tall buildings of a growing city. It wasn't much past noon, but the day was sufficiently overcast that the atmosphere felt funereal. Gravestones were heavy on symbols– skulls, winged cherubs, willow trees, urns. Many were highly eroded, their inscriptions difficult to read.

"Look at all these names," I tell Janice. "People you and I have heard of, whose names linger in the textbooks, if not the minds, of Americans. A bit of permanence, some proof you've made a difference somewhere along the way. Most of us don't get that.

We'll die, get buried, be forgotten. Discouraging, don't you think? Maybe I should rob a bank. Dying man turns to crime, not to feed his family, but because it's the only way he can make an indelible mark on the world. I mean, who wants to be simply forgotten?"

"Carrying this a bit far, aren't you?" Janice suggested. She began peeling an orange.

"Probably," I said. "But think about it. Every guy who ever played in the major leagues, even if only a year, or a day, gets his name in the record book. I used to pore over baseball registries. Found all sorts of unfamiliar names; some had played in just a handful of games. But they're in there. People in the future will find them just as I did. Will wonder about them. At least they've left a mark."

"You don't think you've left a mark?" she asked. "Taking care of people, teaching future doctors, and all that? Shit, you're still leaving a mark. Don't you think those kids at Hopkins– and their families– will remember you, will try to pass on some of your values?"

I wandered off to another row of gravestones. "Hey, Janice, I love this one. James Otis. He'd written that 'I hope when God shall take me out of time into eternity, that it will be by a flash of lightning.' And in 1783, it says, that's just what happened!"

We walked toward Faneuil Hall, still functional after two and a half centuries. "In truth, it's a little late to ponder leaving my mark," I said. "If my frustration drives you to doing a better job of making a mark yourself, I'll take it as a compliment. I'd be satisfied now just to see the Orioles win the pennant, so I can go to one last World Series. Then I'd die happy."

"I suspect it would take more than that to make you die happy," Janice argued.

We spent an hour at the New England aquarium. Worth the price of admission just to see the huge cylinder of jellyfish by the entrance. Life at its most amorphous. Won't be long before mine doesn't even amount to that.

"Janice, we're in Boston. How about we find Boston baked beans for an early dinner?"

"You're on," she answered, "at least if I can have Boston cream pie for dessert."

We settled on Parker House for our meal. I got my baked

[199]

beans, and a Parker House roll in its place of origin. Janice got her calorie-laden pie. Gave us a certain achievement of authenticity. No wasting my final meals on chain restaurants and fast-food places.

By now, Janice was fully energized by the pennant race. Her frustration matched mine when Mussina blew a 4-1 lead next night and the team lost 6-5. Toronto won. Yankees lost. Three games out. I cycled back from optimism to despair. A couple of drinks in the bar, listening to our new favorite blues player, tempered my disappointment only minimally. I'm still alive, but next week's games may not even matter. I may outlive the pennant race. Then what?

Open date after the Boston series, so plenty of time to reach Milwaukee. Janice suggested breaking up the monotony with a few rules. "How about each day, one of us picks something to do, and the other has to go along with it?"

"I'll buy that." I turned off the Mass Turnpike toward the Connecticut border. "How about I start, so if I die on the trip, I'll at least have had my turn?"

"Glad to see you haven't lost the ability to think about yourself first," she said. "Probably means you already have something chosen. But okay. I'll go along with that."

"Well," I said, "I've never visited Mark Twain's home in Hartford. And it's close-by."

"Why Mark Twain?" Janice asked.

"I've always loved his writing," I answered. "So many passages I wish I'd come up with. Like in 'Puddinghead Wilson' when he says more fools are killed on the Fourth of July than any other day, which means maybe we need more Fourth of July's."

She laughed. "All I've read is 'Huckleberry Finn' and my teacher spent so much time analyzing it that it stopped being fun to read."

"That's an irony Twain would appreciate," I said. "I'd love to see his reaction to knowing his books are classics that get picked apart in school."

"Can you believe this place?" Janice whispered as we exited the third floor billiard room.

"It really is something," I agreed. I hadn't expected such an ornate and opulent Victorian home. Multicolored brick atop a sandstone foundation, turrets, porches, solarium complete with fountain attached to the rear. Elaborately carved woodwork throughout.

"I mean, I think of him as so down to earth," she continued. "And then Tiffany himself comes to design." Stencilled walls, paneled ceilings, stained glass tiles on the fireplace.

"I wouldn't mind having that library," I added. "All those built-in book shelves, the octagonal sitting area, that mantle from a Scottish castle."

"I thought you'd like the 'stepping out' deck best," Janice suggested. "So his butler could honestly tell visitors he'd just 'stepped out'. That kind of sounds like you."

We pondered all this as we sped west on I-84, crossing the Hudson near Newburgh en route to Pennsylvania. Janice had her head buried in the Triple-A books we picked up yesterday.

"Hey, want to stop at Punxsutawney, Pennsylvania?" she piped up. "I mean, you'll get us to history and baseball places. I figure it's my job to make sure we see a few other slices of life."

"It's September," I pointed out. "I doubt the groundhog will be up and at it."

"So what?" Janice said. "There'll have to be something in the town on him. If nothing else, I bet I can get a great Punxsutawney Phil t-shirt." I should get one, too, I began thinking. An oversized one. Then no one will have to worry about finding an outfit for my funeral.

Suddenly I heard Janice remark, "Sure, it'd make a great shroud."

I didn't realize I'd been talking out loud.

Looked at my watch. We got an early enough start; maybe we could hit Punxsutawney before supper. How much can there be to see? It couldn't take that long to pick out a t-shirt.

"Why were you so surprised when I agreed about the shroud?" she asked.

"Why'd you think I was surprised?"

"Saw your expression." She was chewing away on another piece of gum. As always, she carefully put the wrapper in the ashtray.

"I guess I didn't realize I was speaking out loud," I said.

[201]

"Would this be a good time to tell you I've learned to read your mind?"

"Sure," I answered. "Just what I wanted to hear."

"You know, Dan, I'm not sure I'm that far from being able to read your mind. I certainly know what you think about baseball, I can guess your opinions on politics, I know what you like to eat. I sure know what you think about death. I'm not sure what you think about me, though."

"Don't worry about that. I'm not so sure what I think about you, either." I paused. "There is one thing I do wonder about, though."

"Shoot!"

"Why have you really wanted to hang around me for so long?" I asked. "I can't be particularly inspiring to you. It can't be fun to hear me talk about death. It certainly can't be fun to be around on the days I'm vomiting and can't do anything."

She stayed silent a moment before responding. "I don't know. Maybe I'm just fascinated by the passion you show for this team. I seem to run into too many people who don't give a shit about anything. It's kind of reassuring to find someone who cares, who really cares, and will follow through on that caring." She twisted her head, and looked directly at me. "A lot of my friends in college were spoiled. They didn't care about school, or the fact their parents were forking over thousands of dollars. I got kidded a lot for actually studying almost every night. And since school, I've been pretty good at picking shitty boyfriends. Once they get beyond partying and getting laid, they've got nothing they care about. If I talk about settling down– shit, if I even say the word future– they just withdraw. Some I never even hear from again."

"You know, Janice," I said, "you're pretty young. You'll rebound from bad experiences."

"I know that," she replied. "To be frank, I've never been down for long after something does go bad. But I guess my last bad relationship made me rethink how I want to approach life."

"You want to tell me about it?" I ventured.

"I'm happy to tell you but I'm not sure you need one more sad story to push you toward the grave." When I stayed silent, she brushed the hair out of her face and continued. "You know how when you first picked me up, that I was coming from Colorado? "

[202]

"Yeah."

"Well, I'd been going out with this guy about a year," she went on. "He was getting his master's degree. I was pretty much floating from one job to another since I didn't know what I wanted to do anyhow. Then he got a teaching job in Colorado. He'd grown up there and always wanted to go back. We'd gone out there once for a week to camp. I mean, it's so beautiful in the Rockies. It easy to see why everybody loves it out there."

Janice's countenance changed. Her expression turned serious, almost grim. "I got jobs waitressing. The first place wasn't much fun, but then I started at another one. Couldn't believe how many big tips I got. We talked a little about getting married. He wouldn't commit to any time frame, but he'd give me all the usual stuff about wanting to be with me, and all that."

She wriggled a bit in her seat. Undid her seat belt, smoothed out a twisted strap, re-attached it. "Well, I got pregnant." She looked to judge my reaction. "I knew I'd have to get an abortion. Even if we got married, I knew I wasn't ready to raise a kid. Plus, I didn't want pregnancy to be the only reason I got married. And then." She stopped and got rid of her piece of gum.

"And then he just dropped me. Fucking wouldn't even talk to me. As if I'd suddenly gotten leprosy and he was afraid he'd catch it. Here was the one guy I thought was stable. It's not like I was putting any pressure on him or anything. I told him right off that I'd get an abortion. But it was just like 'poof'– he wasn't there."

Her jaw muscles tensed; her hands tightened into fists. Janice didn't look this upset after she'd been shot. "I'm really sorry, Janice. You don't have to talk about it if you don't want."

"No, it's good to finally let it out," she said. "I mean, look how good you've been to me, and you didn't even know me. Here's a guy I finally trusted enough to think we could have a life together, and he turns out to be the biggest asshole of them all. I'd already seen a gynecologist and scheduled the abortion. He wouldn't even take me to the clinic on the day I was having it done. He moved his clothes out of the apartment, took the stereo and his books. Wouldn't tell me where he was going. Just said he needed a break.

"I'd always been so independent. I was used to being alone. But this was the first time I felt lonely. There's a difference. A couple of friends would have helped, but I was too embarrassed to call them. I got a room in a motel near the hospital. I mean, the hospital was a good half hour from our apartment, and I was scared. I'd never had an operation, not even my tonsils or appendix, for God's sake. I didn't know what would happen after. I wasn't going to let myself bleed to death or something just because of that asshole. I stayed in the motel three nights, went for my checkup, then finally went back to our place. Which had rapidly become my place. He'd taken some furniture but not very much. Left his shampoo, razor, and shaving cream. Just like a man. Not knowing what he'd need first in a new place. Not decent enough to leave a note. Just a receipt for a month's rent. To show me how generous he was, I guess."

I didn't know what to say. Janice struck me as the most self-reliant woman I'd met in a long time. I was outraged to think how she'd been treated. "And the next thing was that you met me."

She smiled. "Yeah, sort of. I got over the abortion pretty quickly. You already know how fast I heal. Two days of soap operas on the motel TV was enough to convince me not to let some jerk spoil my life. Soap operas are awful, you know. I'd doze off, another one would come on, I could never tell the difference. All the characters are the same, all the plots are the same, I think they even use the same music. How can people spend day after day watching that shit?"

"They don't call it an idiot box for nothing, I guess."

"Right," Janice said. "Anyhow, I had the manager change the lock. He was terrific about it, didn't charge me. I went back to work. I already had a bunch of money saved, and I changed it into travelers' checks. Gave my month's notice. Shipped some clothes and books and kitchen stuff home to my mother. I had my grandmother's silverware, and I wanted to keep it. So I sent that, too. I put ads in the paper for the furniture, gave the manager a third of anything that got sold if he'd show the people in and take the money. There were only a couple of things unsold when I finally left. Though I did have to spend a few nights on the floor in my sleeping bag."

"And your mother didn't get worried about what you were going to do?" I asked.

"No," she said. "She'd pretty much learned to let me find my own way. I told her Jim and I had broken up, that I had no reason to stay in Colorado, that I might travel around and see some more of the west before coming back home."

"Goes without saying you didn't tell her you were going to hitchhike?" I interjected.

Janice chuckled. "You can be sure she asked. And then warned me not to do it."

"When was all this?" I asked. "How long were you traveling before I picked you up?"

"Let's see, I left Denver early April. Went with my friend Darlene to Mesa Verde for a few days. Boy, is that a neat place! All those ancient Indian ruins. It's amazing I never learned anything about it in school. Came back, went out and saw Neil Young play in Red Rocks."

"Red Rocks?"

"Red Rocks Amphitheater. It's this park about an hour from Denver, where you can hike and everything. They have a great outdoor stage for concerts, right by these incredible rock formations. Sometimes I'd go for the day, run laps up and down the theater steps." She tilted her head toward me. "Do the Orioles ever play in Denver? Maybe we could see a game there."

"No," I said. "Denver's a new team. They're in the other league. So go on."

"Yeah," Janice continued, "so I headed out. Actually, I headed to Nebraska. Bought a bus ticket to Omaha, just to keep Darlene off my back. She freaked out when I told her I was going to hitchhike, so I told her, okay, I'll take a bus. Told her I had a friend in Omaha. Promised to keep my thumb in my pocket until I got to familiar territory."

"And I assume there was really no friend in Omaha?"

"Of course not." She grinned. "Until I checked a map, I wasn't even sure if Omaha was in the right direction. Took only one ride to decide I didn't want to spend much time on buses. I called a friend near Minneapolis, told her I was sort of free-lancing my way around, and could we get together? She picked me up in Des Moines. I spent four or five days with her up in Minnesota. It was after leaving there that I ran into you."

"Your savior," I said.

"Well," she went on, "to a certain degree. It'd taken me the better part of two days to get that far, and I'd waited quite a bit before you pulled into that gas station."

"Guess I had no idea of what you'd gone through before you met me," I said.

"But you know what?" Janice said. "I think it changed me for the better. When I was in that motel after surgery, I prayed. Two nights in a row. I hadn't prayed since I was a kid."

"And what did you pray for?" I asked.

"I really didn't ask for anything," she said. "I prayed to heal up after the abortion. And I swore I'd never do anything to anyone like that guy did to me. That I would work my whole life to make other people's lives better, sometimes hopefully in big ways, but all the time in smaller ways. That I would set an example of what one ordinary person could do with a good life."

"Let me guess," I said. "That's why you're on my case so much to make a difference."

She laughed. "Probably, yes. You came into the action while I was cheering myself on for the challenge. I guess it bummed me out that you, with your education and everything, had given up on helping people, while I had to accept the fact I had really nothing to offer anyone."

My turn. "You know, you're too hard on yourself. You're young, you've got plenty of time to make a difference. You're simply impatient. Not that it's bad." I hesitated a moment. "But being hard on yourself led you to be hard on me, too, I guess. I mean, Janice, there are times you're just unreasonable in your expectations."

"I'm beginning to see that a little," Janice continued. "But I have to say, you're a different person since you began spending time with those kids. You've been inspiring. Now I'll always think of you as someone who didn't stop helping people even during your last dying days."

"Believe me," I said, "there were times I thought your nagging would bring me to death's door a little more quickly."

Janice took a deep breath before speaking again. "Okay, enough of all this heavy stuff. You haven't missed our exit, have you? Have I maybe earned a good dinner tonight?"

We proudly wore our Punxsutawney Phil shirts the next morning– mine blue, hers pink– and set out. Typical tourists ready

[206]

to invade the upper Midwest. When I looked in the mirror, however, I saw a scarecrow. My arms were as thin as I'd ever seen them. A sunken appearance to my face made my eyes stand out. I had that look I'd seen so often in patients dying of cancer.

We sped out of Pennsylvania on I-80, merged onto I-90 somewhere around Cleveland. I felt unusually good, so I drove the first leg, getting us past Toledo. Janice decided Punxsutawney didn't count for a full stop, so she asked to get off at South Bend and see Notre Dame.

It's a beautiful campus. Half the college-bound Catholics in America– even more of the football-playing Catholics– must yearn to go to school here. Janice stopped in the bookstore and bought *The Confessions of St. Augustine* and *Travels With Charlie*. Needed something spiritual, she told me, plus wanted to compare my travel habits with those of Steinbeck.

The end is near.

Not my end. Though that's probably near, too. The team's end. When you're three games out, you're convinced there's still a chance. A five game deficit makes it different.

What did I ever do to Milwaukee that they wouldn't let the Orioles score a single run in the first two games? O's lost 2-0 and 3-0. McDonald and Moyer pitched well, but no one hit. I can bring this team only so far myself. Then I have to depend on the manager and the players.

Meanwhile Toronto won its seventh in a row, and New York took two of three in Boston.

On the advice of people sitting next to us at one game, we went to the Pfister Hotel for a drink. The place exuded luxury, from the red awnings out front, to the high arched lobby with its gilt-edged ceilings, to the marble staircases, etched glass mirrors, and museum-quality art work. A suit of armor stood guard alongside the entrance to the English Room. I told Janice this would make a good reception center for the dead arriving in heaven.

We stopped at a history museum and learned Milwaukee was a center of the cyclorama industry. In an era before movies, giant circular paintings would be mounted inside round buildings. They'd depict great battles, or Christ's walk with the Cross, or something else momentous. Music would play, perhaps an orchestra. A

[207]

narrator told an epic story while lights directed one's gaze to segments of the giant picture. Like watching a feature film but you moved your head circumferentially instead of depending on a projector flashing images to one spot. This once reigned as the entertainment of the day. I found the quaintness appealing.

Saturday was my turn to pick. I decided on the Pabst legacy. See the fruits of making a fortune in the production of beer. First, we toured the brewery, a complex of weathered brick buildings. We learned the secrets of the Malt House and Brewhouse, then the more utilitarian aspects of bottling and distribution. Afterwards we sat at an umbrella-shaded table in the courtyard and sampled the products that earned Pabst his wealth.

Next we visited his mansion. Unlimited money comes in handy when you're building a house. Lets you hire all the best woodcarvers and stonemasons, buy the finest materials available. You don't just build a house; you make a statement. A statement that lasts longer than you do.

Sometimes I wondered what archaeologists will think in, say, the twenty-fifth century. Fabulous mansions from the Gilded Age will still be around. So will plenty of New England stone and brick farmhouses, and brownstones in Brooklyn and Georgetown. People who wanted to build only once, so they dug sturdy foundations and gave them thick walls.

There won't be many examples from the mid-twentieth century. Too flimsy. Two-by-four framing down to one and three quarters by three and a half. Plywood and wall board instead of lath and plaster. Researchers will wonder why there's such a void– plenty of 18th and 19 century places, plenty of new buildings from recent decades, not much in between.

The evolution of a disposable society.

Maybe that's good. Maybe one's abode shouldn't last long after death. Let each new generation remake the world to its own taste. Skip the historical context. People aren't learning history anyway. Let them repeat mistakes that have been made before.

Ballparks disappear, too. Philadelphia's Shibe Park. Ebbets Field. The Polo Grounds. In Baltimore, Memorial Stadium still stands, waiting to be torn down. "New" ones– cookie cutter places in Pittsburgh and Cincinnati, domes in Seattle and Minneapolis– will run their course. Wrigley Field will last. Chicago fans would preserve it brick by brick if it started to crumble.

What would baseball be with every rough edge honed to such regularity there's no character left. You need some asymmetry, like the Green Monster in Boston. Not having an even playing field is part of baseball, as it is of life. Science could assure every baseball field has fixed dimensions, constant temperature and humidity, and a limit on wind variation. I suppose someday genetic potential could be manipulated so that each team has shortstops with quick reflexes, strong-armed relief pitchers, and first basemen with enough weight to propel batted balls a fixed distance. But who would want baseball with no errors, no bad bounces, no wind blowing in from right field, no fusillade of emotions?

Instead of having a baseball season to sustain me thorough my final months, I'd have a carefully controlled environment where I would decay at a precisely determined rate.

We asked a hotel clerk to suggest a unique restaurant. She gave us a blank look. One of her co-workers offered an idea. "I'm not sure you'll like this place, but it's pretty different."

"Sounds good to me," I said.

She continued, "It's way uptown. You'll need a taxi. The place is called Fourth Base."

"What's the address?" I asked.

"Don't worry," she said. "If he's not a brand new driver, he'll know."

I tried again. "Well, just for my peace of mind, tell me the address."

She had to look it up.

We changed clothes and came back downstairs to get a cab. I told the driver Fourth Base. He flashed us a funny look.

"Sure, I know the place. You sure you really want to go there?"

"Dangerous?" I asked.

"No, not really," he said, "though I wouldn't walk the streets looking for a cab when you want to come back."

"Is the food decent?"

"Didn't know they served food."

This didn't sound auspicious.

Fourth Base was packed. The only open spot was a high

[209]

round table along one wall. A friendly server came over to ask about drinks. This being Milwaukee, I stuck to beer. Janice had a glass of chardonnay. As I ordered beer number two, I asked if we could still get dinner.

"Sure, what d'ya want?" the server asked.

"Is there a menu?" Janice said.

"Oh, come on. A menu? Here?" She shouted over to the other side of the room. I looked, but couldn't find a receiver for the pass. Eventually a guy poked his head through the window to what must be the kitchen. I envisioned a microwave and a pile of ready-to-heat sandwiches. "Whattaya got to eat tonight?"

"Oh, almost anything," he replied. "What do you need?"

By now the whole place was watching. I didn't see a dinner dish anywhere. Pondering a default to Slim Jims and beer nuts, I asked if they had any fish. Our waitress relayed the message to the guy in the kitchen. He yelled back, "Yeah, tuna. Want tuna?"

"Is it fresh?" Waitress echoed my question: "Is it fresh?"

"Sure it's fresh." He sounded as though I'd insulted him. Safe in the security that if I got sick I could blame my disease as easily as his fish, I ordered the tuna, broiled, with French fries. Janice got the same. The waitress asked if we wanted salads. Well, if they carried lettuce in this joint, maybe they could have a few slabs of fresh fish.

"Once Mary and I came to Milwaukee for some kind of a conference," I said. "I remember we ate at a weird place called the Public Natatorium."

"What's a natatorium?" Janice asked.

"I didn't know either," I said. "It was an old bathhouse. They had this huge pool, with tables on two levels around it. Dolphins swam around while we ate."

"Yeah, that is strange," she agreed.

"That's not the weird part," I said. "The menu had these exotic species. Lion. Giraffe."

"What'd they taste like?"

"A lot like beef," I said. "We wondered afterwards if it was really lion and giraffe. Maybe it didn't matter. In a city built around beer, people would probably swallow anything."

My tuna tasted like tuna. Perfectly cooked. As were the French fries. I put a few on my napkin. Not a spot of grease. Didn't know how long the bartender had been at my side when I looked up. "From out of town?" I think it was declarative, not interrogative. My fifth grade teacher would be proud I remembered so much from my days of diagramming sentences.

"Yeah, from near Baltimore," I told her. "Came to see the Orioles play."

"You gotta be kidding," she said. "All the way to Milwaukee for a ball game?"

"Well, three games, actually," I said.

"Lonely at the stadium?" Crowds had been small, half the size of those in Fenway in a place twice as big.

"There were quite a few empty seats," I admitted

She thought a minute. "Jesus, I don't think I've been to a game since I was a kid."

After swallowing the last ounce of beer, I walked over and asked the bartender if she could call us a cab.

"Sure, you're a cab."

If I had more time to live, I think I could enjoy spending some of it in this city.

Maybe it was the tuna at Fourth Base, maybe not. Either way, all I could handle before Sunday's game were a bowl of oatmeal and a piece of toast. The appetite of the sick and dying.

"I resent you calling oatmeal food for the sick and dying," Janice said. "I like oatmeal."

"Janice, trust me," I said. "If it was all you could eat, you wouldn't like it as much."

"Maybe not," she said, "but spare me the need to shed tears about it. Maybe you should have beer for breakfast. You seem not to have lost your taste for that."

She's right. Wonder why I'm able to tolerate beer so well. Just another grain product, sort of like cereal? I can get my carbohydrate quotient with it. Add a couple of protein bars a day, take a vitamin, and maybe I could get along. Carnation should market an instant drink that you mix with beer instead of milk. Think how many people would have better balanced diets.

Orioles won the getaway game, 8-4, but we remained five games out of first. Team went from a single game back, just ten days ago, to what now seems an insuperable deficit.

[211]

Cleveland would be a six or seven hour drive. We could have waited until morning, but we both felt like moving. Janice drove a while, then we found a motel a couple of hours beyond Chicago. Once in the room, I didn't stay awake long enough to see the sports report.

Right after we crossed into Ohio next morning, Janice picked up tourist literature. She'd been rapidly turning pages ever since. We were on side roads, and I was enjoying the drive.

We stopped for a break. "Shit," Janice began, "my turn to pick and nothing to see."

"Let me look at the info while you're off to the bathroom," I told her. I'm easily entertained. I'll find something in the books."

Janice came back as the waitress arrived with coffee and our muffins. "Any luck?"

"As a matter of fact, yes. We'll stop in Fremont for Benjamin Harrison's home."

"Hey!" Janice exclaimed. "Thought it was my turn."

"Now don't be petulant," I said. "I'm just trying to fill some time on the way to Cleveland. You can have the next two." Easy for me to say, knowing I've got a shot at not being around for them. I did struggle with the idea that the last thing I learned on earth might be about a President nobody remembers. Aside from the fact that he ran twice against Grover Cleveland, winning once and losing once, making Cleveland the only Chief Executive to serve two non-consecutive terms, I knew nothing about the man.

"Remember that, because I'm going to find a couple of places worth seeing around Cleveland," Janice said. "The city, not the president. By the way, where was he from?"

"Who?" I asked.

"Cleveland."

"Buffalo, I think."

Fremont was a small place, population around twenty thousand. They could use a more exciting "favorite son" than Benjamin Harrison, but his Victorian mansion made for a pleasant enough tour. He's distinguished as the first grandson of a former President to be elected to that office, we learned. And he boasts the first Presidential Library, for what that's worth.

We hit Cleveland in plenty of time to get a hotel before the game. I'd thought about going back to the Radisson, maybe meet more players in the elevator, then thought better of expecting lightning to strike twice in the same place. Once we were set up in our bland accommodations outside the city, I regretted my hesitation.

The team's inglorious collapse continued. Got ahead of Cleveland 3-0 in the first game. A couple of innings later we're behind 6-3. When the 6-4 loss hit the record books, it left us 2 and 5 on the road trip. Six back in the loss column. The horses aren't there.

Janice began wheezing soon after we went to bed. She told me she's had asthma off and on since she was a teenager, but it hadn't flared up in a while. Our choice became one of breaking into a drugstore in a strange town or making a trip to an emergency room. She didn't laugh when I suggested we order up an inhaler from room service. Guess you have to be closer to death to find humor in illness.

I couldn't let her go alone to the hospital, so I got dressed and grabbed a few sections from the day's paper. At least I'd be an observer, not the featured attraction. By the time we arrived, Janice was wheezing audibly. A second year med student should have recognized her distress, but first came the requisite paper work. She listed me as her contact person. I could envision someone tracking me down in a week or two to check on her, and being told, I'm sorry, he's dead.

We weren't back at the hotel until three in the morning. By late afternoon Janice felt fully revived. "You know, I think I know how it feels now, wondering if you're going to die. I mean, that's how I felt when I couldn't catch my breath."

"Except for one big difference," I responded. "Asthma is treatable. At least it's treatable if you're not too bullheaded to be prepared for it. How come you don't carry an inhaler?"

"Hey, I haven't had any trouble since I left college," she said. "Why drag medicines around when you don't need them?"

"Well, you needed one last night," I responded. "Ever occur to you when you were hitchhiking the country that it'd be nice to avoid going to a strange hospital in a strange town?"

She lashed back. "You, the poster child for refusing treatment, have the balls to tell me how to take care of myself. Give

[213]

me a break."

"Damn it, Janice, you've got a problem that's treatable. I'd trade a lot for that."

I really would. These last few weeks I've felt more alive than I have in a long while. I'm realizing how in certain ways I've been lucky. In practice, I had always respected the maxim that no one wants to die alone or in pain. I've been weak enough, and I've certainly had enough nausea, but pain hasn't been much of a problem. Guess as I've been wasting away, I'm taking nerve fibers with me. Gives me hope I'll fade away, not go down in torment.

Janice has helped avert the loneliness. It's more than simple companionship. She challenges me, listens to me, argues with me. There are limits to what I can do physically, and they grow every day, but she's reawakened me mentally. There's pleasure in feeling a spirit thrive. Perhaps I've contributed to her life. It's terrible knowing what her ex-boyfriend did to her in Colorado. But anything I may have done for her is dwarfed by what she's meant for me.

Guess I could just suffer through the losing streak and wait till next year. I might do it more gracefully if I thought there'd actually be a next year. While Janice went to a movie, I caught glimpses of a baseball documentary on television. Reminded me of the hold baseball has on society, how intertwined it is with the history and sociology of America. Its heritage and mythology cement it in place. Sure, there's selfishness, a growing focus on money, and plenty of bad behavior. But it's baseball. It'll outlive all the adulteration.

The Orioles finally won a game. Lucked out with two runs in the ninth, beating the Indians 7-6. Toronto won, too, their ninth in a row. Magic number, that concocted term for sum of the first place team's wins plus others' losses needed to clinch the pennant, only seven. For those of us behind in the chase, you may as well deem it the tragic number.

Janice woke me around nine the next morning. "Hey, rise and shine. We're packing up."

"Hey, nothing." I yawned and rubbed my eyes. Janice was already dressed in her Punxsutawney shirt and a pair of jeans. "There's another game here tonight."

"I know," she said, "but that doesn't mean we have to sit

[214]

around all day waiting for it. My turn to decide what we do, remember?"

"Yeah, I remember," I said. "But what's that got to do with packing up?"

"I've got our outing planned," she continued. "You'll like it. It's about more presidents."

"Janice, let me relax, will you? I'm still beat from the other night in the hospital."

"More likely you're beat because life force is dwindling down inside you." She'd already started on her gum. "I'm not going to watch you slowly die in some hotel room."

"Then go to another movie," I pleaded. "Take the car. Go to a museum. Anything. But leave me alone." I pulled the pillow over my head.

"Bullshit!" She pulled the covers up from my bed. "We made a deal. We alternate choices on what we do during the day. And I've got today planned."

"Okay." I resigned myself to getting up. "What president?"

"Presidents. Plural. McKinley and Hoover."

"Hoover's from Iowa," I claimed, "not Ohio."

"Damn, you really do know everything, don't you?" Janice was frustrated. "I was hoping I could surprise you with that."

"Surprises I don't need," I said. "Where do we go for McKinley?"

"Not far," she said. "His grave's in Canton. Figure you need to be seeing where people are buried these days, not where they're born."

"Thanks for the uplifting sentiment."

"Then we can go to Hoover's home," she added.

"Have they moved Iowa a little closer?" I asked.

"No, they just have other Hoovers."

I groaned. "Please, not J. Edgar. What if he collected a dossier on me during the sixties?"

"Actually," she said, "it's the Hoover who invented the vacuum cleaner."

Sorry I hadn't begun traveling with her sooner. She handles aimless nomadic life well.

Janice continued. "We're staying in Akron. Only a forty minute drive to the game."

[215]

"And we're staying in Akron because? Because it's more scenic?"

"No," she insisted, "because it's my turn to pick places. There's a hotel in an old mill."

"Oh, fuck that–"

"Shut up!" she said. "I'm sorry. That's rude. Let me finish. Really, I just read about it. It's the mill where they used to make Quaker oats. After it closed, they made it into shops and a hotel. You've been reduced to eating oatmeal. Why not sleep for a night where it was made?"

"Nice use of irony," I said.

"Maybe," she added. "I guess. But you're the one who keeps saying that when you die, you want to know the last day had been interesting."

I splashed water on my face, then squeezed the last dollop of toothpaste out of the tube and brushed my teeth.

"You might want to shower," Janice said.

"Not if all I'm doing is visiting a dead president."

We skipped the McKinley Memorial. I didn't need to see more graves. But we did go to the Hoover home, where we learned about Boss Hoover, and about the history of cleaning a house. For good measure, we toured a chocolate factory, too, before checking into our hotel.

Janice handled the registration. "Hey, I picked this place. This one's my treat."

We took the elevator to the eighth floor. On opening the door, I immediately noticed there was only one bed. King-size, but one bed. "Okay Janice, what's with this?"

"What's with what?"

"Don't give me that crap. What's with the single bed? You planning to sleep on the couch?" I looked around. An upholstered arm chair. No couch.

She pointed to the clock. "Hey, it's five-fifteen. We've got a game to get to. We can figure this out later."

"I think we can figure this out now." I picked up the phone, called the front desk. No other rooms, I was told. A convention, or something. "You knew this before we got down here?"

"Yeah," she admitted. "But what could I do? It's not like I'm going to attack you in the middle of the night or something.

[216]

Let's go to the game."

"Okay, but we'll figure this out later," I said.

"Didn't I already say that?"

Cleveland won the finale 4-2, stopping another Oriole winning streak at one in a row. Some self-destruction. Two runners were waved home by an overeager third base coach, then easily thrown out at the plate. What remained of the announced attendance of 17,000 went wild.

"Is that so unusual?" Janice asked as we were leaving the stadium.

"Is what so unusual?" I echoed back.

"Throwing a person out at home plate."

"Yeah, throwing someone out at the plate is pretty exciting," I responded. "Now that baseball uses designated hitters, so that pitchers no longer get unexpected hits, a play at the plate is one of those few moments that can make a mediocre game memorable. I'd just prefer not to see it happen against my team."

"Why's it so unexpected for a pitcher to get a hit?"

"Mainly because they don't take batting practice. They put all their time into pitching."

"Wouldn't teams do better by making them take batting practice?" she asked.

"Some would agree with you," I said. "When you're young, pitchers are often the best athletes. They hit as well as anyone. It's specialization, like in anything else. Once you become a pitcher, you concentrate on that. It's like medicine. Take a cardiologist who specializes in heart disease, well, you wouldn't want that person taking care of your asthma or your pneumonia."

"And a designated hitter just hits?" she asked.

"Yes," I said. "Sometimes you have a guy who doesn't field well, or has gotten slower running but can still hit. The National League doesn't have a designated hitter."

"Why not?"

"Guess they didn't want it," I answered. "They wanted the game to stay the way it was, letting the pitcher bat and all."

"Jesus, how do you learn all this and keep it straight?"

I laughed. "It takes a lifetime, Janice, it takes a lifetime."

She clapped me on the shoulder. "And just when you finally

know it all, you die, huh?"

Toronto and New York both lost. It barely matters. Six games down, only ten to play. No longer does the team hold its destiny in its own hands.

Of course, neither do I.

Cal Ripken played his 1887th consecutive game. At least let me die before Ripken's streak ends, I told myself for perhaps the hundredth time. Much as I'd hoped to last long enough to see him break Lou Gehrig's record, I couldn't bear the idea of seeing him fail.

I woke up in Akron amidst a conglomeration of grain silos. We walked around the complex, then had an early lunch in an old railroad car. It probably hauled oats once upon a time.

"Well, want to talk about how I attacked you in the middle of the night?" Janice asked.

I put my Coke down. "What?"

She laughed. "You were so worried about us sleeping in that king bed. I'm reminding you that it worked out fine. Nothing bad happened. Though I guess that's a matter of opinion."

"Am I supposed to applaud you for noble behavior?" I asked.

"You could, I suppose," she said.

"Then thank you. I'm pleased you could resist coming on to a dying man," I said.

"Dan," Janice started.

When she didn't continue, I started to get up.

"No, wait," she said. She sipped a last bit of soda through her straw. "There was a time in the middle of the night. You were asleep. I put my arms around you, just so I could feel closer to you. And then I fell asleep, too. I wanted you to know that."

"Thank you for telling me," I whispered. "It lets me say how much you've meant to me, too. I never knew if I would begin to feel lonely during this trip. Because of you, I've never had to find out. I wish I could do something in return."

Janice looked thoughtful. "You already have. You somehow manage not to see it, but you've helped me tremendously. You've helped me regain a sense of direction. You've got me focused on what I might someday accomplish."

[218]

She pulled her chair around, so that she was next to me. After taking my hand, she continued. "Let me tell you something. I wasn't around when my father died. I was at college when he got sick. Mom called to tell me. But I already had plans to go to Florida for spring break. She tried convincing me to come home, but I was your typical self-centered young college student who wanted to be with her friends. Besides, when you're that age, who ever thinks that one of your parents could die?"

"And he did die, I assume?"

"Yes," she said. "I called from Florida my third or fourth day down there. He had died the night before. They had no way to get in touch with me, so I didn't find out until then. My friends took me to the airport so I could fly home. But I felt like I was just going through the motions. I should have been there before he died."

"That's a hard thing to carry around, I'm sure."

"You bet it is." She was weeping. "And you can be damned sure I'm going to be with you until the very end."

I smiled and hugged her.

Today was my turn to pick a place. I would have chosen a tire factory tour, but they don't offer those anymore. Liability issues, I guess. I'd have signed a waiver. It's not like I could blame my soon-to-come demise on some chemical in their process.

Instead, I suggested we drive on to Johnstown and learn about the flood. Janice already knew a fair amount about it. "I did a history paper on it in college."

We didn't arrive at the National Park Museum until almost three o'clock. Just as well. Fewer hours to dwell on how many people drowned or lost their homes, or how much property was destroyed. For me, the lesson was simple. Man can attempt whatever he wants on this earth, but if nature decides to contest the issue, nature will win. Humankind can invent trains and automobiles, build dams and bridges, erect tall buildings and detonate atomic bombs. But if some higher power chooses to produce an earthquake, erupt a volcano, or unleash a flood, man's contrivances may well fail to contain the damage. I suspect part of it is man's lack of humility. Human race takes itself a bit too seriously. God, if there is one, can better take a joke.

[219]

"You're sure the name is Stoltfus?" Janice asked again from the phone booth as she riffled through a tattered phone book. We'd driven to Amish country in search of a nutritious dinner.

"Yeah, I'm pretty sure." It was one of those strange names that sticks with you.

She turned to the white pages. "Jeez, there's dozens of Stoltfus. But none's a restaurant."

"Oh, I don't care," I said. "Let's go get gas, ask there for advice on a good place to eat."

"That's not fair," she said. "We drove all this way to eat Amish food."

"Why do you care so much about it?"

"I wouldn't," Janice said, "but you always make a big point about trying something distinctive. So why settle for Shoney's or McDonald's now?"

I tried to contain my sarcasm. "Janice, I doubt it'll be of any great cosmic significance if we change our minds and grab hamburgers somewhere."

She tried to suppress a smile, couldn't, broke into a laugh. "Okay, you win. But you were holier than thou an hour ago when I was hungry. I made the compromise. I waited. Now you tell me it doesn't make any difference. You're not playing fair."

"Okay, I'm not playing fair. But it's my rules. By definition, however I play is fair."

"No! That's not fair," she said. "It's like Nixon claiming if the President does it, it's not illegal. Remember, you told me none of this 'honoring the last wish of a dying man' crap. You told me you may as well continue living the best you can, following through on life the same way you would on a golf swing, or something like that."

Arguing by a phone booth made no sense. We checked listings and found a restaurant offering the traditional Amish seven sweets and seven sours. I didn't want to fight anymore.

We stayed that night at another of those chain motels you can find anywhere. It almost made me nostalgic for the oatmeal mill. By now I understood a few consecutive days on America's interstates offered a good sense of death, or at least of purgatory. I'd come to realize I could pick any exit, find the nearest Econolodge or Best Western, go across the street for McDonald's or Burger King, maybe Pizza Hut for a vegetarian meal, go to sleep, wake up to find *USA Today* slipped under the door, and have no fucking idea whatsoever where I was.

Nothing the least bit distinctive, nothing the least bit unsatisfactory about this particular choice. If God didn't plan to use a huge abyss for purgatory, but instead house people one or two to a room, these would fill the need.

I'd gone to sleep feeling sick, then awakened twice to vomit. Janice got up, helped me clean up, sat beside me until I fell back into a fitful slumber.

Janice went to the exercise room after breakfast. I listlessly browsed a newspaper, seeking some signal to make it worth living another twenty-four hours. We were barely two hours from the condo, much less distance than the O's were from the playoffs.

I was finishing a crossword puzzle when Janice returned and reminded me it was her turn for our tourist event of the day.

"Let's go to York," she suggested. "York Peppermint Patties were my favorite candy as a kid. Do you think the factory's there?"

"How should I know?"

"Well, shit," she said, "you seem to enjoy pretending you know everything."

The idea of biting into the soft white center of that silver-wrapped confection made me feel only sicker. "Well, we can drive there and see."

"If it's there, then that's my pick, the Peppermint Pattie tour," she said. "It's close enough to Baltimore. If we run late, we can drive straight to the game instead of going home first."

"You've gotten so comfortable you're calling it home," I commented.

"You're right. I am so comfortable there. With you. If you weren't so determined to avoid sex, it'd feel like this grand secretive affair. No one knowing I'm there." Janice looked over my shoulder to the puzzle and pointed to fourteen-down, villain in Othello. "That's Iago."

"Thanks," I murmured.

"No, really," she picked back up on the conversation. "We both come and go as we want. There's no pressure. I mean, I've lived with guys before, and it's a hassle. After a while, they think they own you. That you lose the right to do anything they don't

[221]

want you to do. You don't even have friends over, because it doesn't seem like your place. Now I can read, go for a run, go to a movie, and it's okay. I'm spoiled. Maybe you're sort of that older brother I never had."

I finished my cup of coffee and sat mute. Janice stared, waiting for a response. She was right, it was comfortable. I felt no need to fill in silences, no need to retrieve nuggets of gossip to keep conversations going. I like not having that pressure. That's part of the reason I went on the road in the first place. So I could read the paper at breakfast without feeling guilty. So I could be moody without inconveniencing anyone else.

Is it God's final irony to have me meet the right person just as I'm dying, when nothing can come of it?

"A penny for your thoughts." Janice woke me from my musing.

"Not sure they're worth that much these day," I said.

"Okay," she rephrased, shaking her head, "three thoughts for a penny."

I laughed. "All right. I was thinking about what you said. I'm trying to decide whether I like being portrayed as your older brother as opposed to your lover. I guess either is better than being looked at as a father figure. Even if I'm going to die, I don't need to think I'm old."

"You're not old," she said. "In college, I dated a professor twenty years older than I was."

"Bottom line," I cut in. "I like thinking of us as roommates. The kind of roommates you have in college if you're lucky, the kind you can talk to about anything, the kind that become lifelong friends."

"Just not the kind that screw?"

"No, probably not. Sorry. Is that always a requirement for you?"

"No, I guess not, at least not now. Since we haven't." She grinned. "Not even after sleeping in a king-size bed together!"

The waitress refilled our cups. Breakfast crowd had left. She probably wished we would, too. I pulled out some cash, left my hundred percent tip, and we went on our way.

Jamie Moyer pitched reasonably well in a 2-0 loss to Detroit,

[222]

but otherwise the team looked flat. It's time to face facts. The Orioles are at least a year away from winning a pennant. Which means I won't see it.

I read *Ballpark,* a book about the planning that went into Camden Yards. I found it sad reading about the Orioles' glory days, and how an organization once among the best in baseball began to unravel. That's the problem with organizations. They take on lives of their own and forget their roots. Connection to mission gets lost. There's no institutional memory left. New players have no idea who Brooks Robinson was, what he meant to the team. I want to scream, you know that maple tree in your backyard, the one whose leaves turn a brilliant red every fall, no matter how drab all the other foliage might be? That was Brooks. You could count on him. Every day. He might not get a hit, he might not make a great fielding play, he might even make a crucial error. But you could count on him playing his hardest, trying his utmost to win, whether it was the World Series, or a season ending contest against a last place team.

Minor leaguers coming through the ranks now have no concept of the "Oriole Way," that consistency of instruction once preparing prospects for the climb up the ladder to the majors. Too many guys don't accept they have so much to learn after being stars in high school or college. I suppose someday managers will make their decisions with computer programs, not from experience or baseball sense. At which point, I'd ask why play the games at all? Just slide in the punch cards, or spin the dial, like I did on the All-Star Baseball game I played as a kid.

Am I merely getting more bitter as the days run out? If Brooks Robinson and Cal Ripken aren't going to leave permanent marks, why should I expect to leave one?

The rain perfectly fit my mood. Postponed game means a doubleheader tomorrow. Once that represented the best of all possibilities. Hour upon hour of baseball. Now I've got the feeling of a man who won't– can't – die because he's got a machine sustaining his breathing. But the life it's giving him has become meaningless.

I think back to days camping along river banks, the tumbling waters blotting out all but the closest background noise. I'd hear the gentle clanging of my dog's ID tags, perhaps the occasional flitting of a bird, but little more. Surrounding me was fragrant forest canopy – gleaming white birches, cedars with fringes of late season brown edging the green clusters of flattened needles– and foaming water headed downstream toward its outlet.

It's not easy accepting I'll never again hike to a remote lake, scamper through a dense forest glade, or go back north for the vibrant palette of orange, yellow, and red leaves of autumn. There won't be another canoe ride, my paddle gently breaking the glassy surface of the water. Nor that sense of triumph upon a mountain top, looking all around with the earth under my feet.

Rain left me too much time for introspection

"Want to go to a movie?" Janice asked.

"No, I just want to lay low. I feel kind of lousy." I lay on the couch in sweat clothes.

"Feverish?" she asked.

"No, I just feel like shit," I said. "Queasy stomach. Aching all over. That kind of stuff."

Janice put her hand on my forehead. "You don't feel warm. Want me to call Eric?"

"Absolutely not!"

"There's no game today anyhow. Why not get checked out?"

"I'm not going anywhere," I insisted. "I've got enough pills for whatever comes up."

She emitted an exasperated sigh. Probably the same sound my mother would emit if she were alive to face the situation. "Why do you always have to be so stubborn?"

"Guess it's in my genome," I said. "I promise, if I'm not better by Monday, I'll get checked out in Eric's office."

"What if you're dead by Monday?"

"Just a risk I'll have to take," I said

"And that I'll have to take?"

"You're under no obligation."

We heated soup for lunch, then Janice headed out for a movie. The apartment felt so empty once she left. I forget how her presence fills the space around me. We all want to fade away peacefully when our time comes, but we don't think much about how peace will come if we're alone. Her companionship has provided assistance when I've felt weak, distraction when I've had the energy to stay active, solace when I've begun to feel sorry for myself.

I found myself wishing I could live longer just to be around her.

Next morning, Janice went for a jog, leaving me to drink too much coffee and overanalyze the sports section. Rest of the news left me cold. A cheating scandal at the Naval Academy. A peek at our nation's future? Five hundred test-tube babies to have a reunion at Greater Baltimore Medical Center. Another view of the nation's future.

I tried walking but had to stop. Not short of breath, just lightheaded, ready to pass out. It had to be the weather. Damp, overcast, ground wet. A sense of miasma all around. Back inside, I picked up a *Sporting News* to read until Janice got back.

The dreariness improved to a haze by game time. Mist gave a dreamlike quality to Camden Yards until a hitting barrage by the Tigers sharpened the focus. Detroit cruised to a 9-4 first game victory.

"Sure glad I didn't miss that one," Janice cracked.

Game two went no better. Orioles battled back from a 4-0 deficit, took the lead on Brady Anderson's triple and Mark McLemore's single. But Detroit came back in the ninth to win.

Brady Anderson threw out a runner at the plate, and teammates gave high fives. Youth and vigor from players to whom it still matters. From such roots, hopefully, will come the Orioles' future.

"See, Janice," I said. "A play at the plate is exciting even for the players."

"Guess it'd be even more exciting if they won because of it," she said. No argument.

Exhausted after five hours of baseball on this dreary Sunday, I gazed around-- at the emptying seats, at the Bromo Seltzer tower muted by early dusk, at the promenade alongside Oriole Park with its flow of people, at the long brick railroad warehouse, at the expansive green playing surface. Defeat notwithstanding, I still couldn't conjure up many places I'd rather be.

The stadium had come to feel as comfortable as home. I began to wish I'd had a dog, just so I could name him Camden.

I wanted to close my eyes a few minutes before getting up to leave.

EPILOGUE

April 4, 1994

I'd gone over to the hospital that night after Dan died. Visiting hours had ended, but the nurses let me talk to the older kids.

"He stayed in his seat after the game, went to sleep, didn't wake up," I told them. "In a way he was lucky. Not much was as important to him as the Orioles. I think he'd like the idea that he died in the stadium."

"It sucks that they lost a doubleheader," Billy spurted. "Who wants to die a loser?"

"He always used to say that when his time came to die, he just wanted the week before to have been worth it. And it was." I choked up and averted my glance for a few seconds, then turned back to the kids. "To be fair, I don't think it was the losses that killed him! Losing would never have killed him. The only thing that could have done that was feeling the team had stopped trying. And I think he died knowing they never did."

"I hope so." It was Jamie, who so rarely talked, but who always looked forward to the visits. "There's something romantic caring about the team that much. Sort of like going down with the ship. It's almost chivalry."

"I never thought of it that way," I said. "But I know he had no patience for fair weather fans. He argued a real fan stands by the team no matter how it's doing. That like anything you do, you should do it thoroughly and passionately, the best you can. So no one loses faith in your actions."

"What are you going to do now?" Jamie asked.

"You know," I said, "we'd only known each other a couple of months. I'd been thinking about going back to school, but I was in no hurry. Now I'm thinking of going to medical school."

"Wow! Where?" they chimed almost simultaneously.

"I'm taking classes right now at Goucher," I answered. "I'll be ready to apply in a year. I've only just started thinking about where. I've sort of gotten used to following baseball. I think I'll have to go to school in a place that has a team."

"He'd like that, wouldn't he?" asked Jamie.

"Probably," I agreed. "Most of all, he'd want me to care

[227]

about what I was doing. To do it well, to be special. He'd also be a bit surprised. He thought I never really got into baseball."

"Would you stay in Baltimore?" Billy queried.

"Would be nice, I think. After all, I'm an Oriole fan now." I smiled. "It's easy to trade in a car, but I'm not sure it's so simple to start rooting for another team."

Billy and Jamie were waiting in front of the Babe Ruth Museum today when I arrived. Attempts to act cool couldn't mask their excitement. Opening Day! And they had tickets for the game. Or rather, they knew I had tickets for the game.

Kansas City. A team the Orioles could beat. They could be one and zero. As long as the standings are put in alphabetical order, they could be in first place after day one. It would also be Cal Ripken's 1898th consecutive game played.

Both kids had achieved remissions in their diseases. They'd gone back to school and were both getting good grades, impressing both parents and teachers with their newfound discipline. I presented the game as some sort of reward. I think their families liked that.

Really, though, I wanted them there because I couldn't go through with this alone.

Dan had stipulated no funeral, no memorial service, no hoopla whatsoever. His parents had died years earlier. He didn't want his ex-wife involved in any arrangements. The only other people needing notification were his brothers and his attorney. I'd called them.

He wanted to be cremated. Dan had talked about a crematorium high on a hill overlooking the Hudson River near Troy, New York. A wealthy manufacturer built it in memory of his son. Dan described it as a work of art– architecture reminiscent of an armory or castle, with lots of marble and tile mosaics inside. Most of all, he focused on a room of urns. Ashes that families had never picked up. It haunted him that so many people could have died and not mattered enough for their closest relatives or friends to retrieve their remains.

I arranged for the cremation. His brothers went along with the idea. I wasn't quite sure how I'd explain my relationship when I called them, but they were great. One lived in Tampa, the other in

Atlanta. They flew up to meet me in Baltimore. I told them our strange story. The next day, they came by the apartment, asked to keep a few photos and mementos. They told me to keep Dan's Toyota. We had a late lunch at Obrycki's before they left to meet Dan's attorney.

The will held a few surprises. It left money to pay for four years of education for me, saying I should use the opportunity to benefit society as a whole, especially those who tend to be left behind when wealth accumulates. He also left money for those kids he visited in the hospital. So they "could fulfill a few dreams," as he put it.

Most of the rest, after modest bequests to his brothers and his alma maters, went to create a fund for sick or injured children to be administered by Johns Hopkins Hospital. Oriole fans were to have priority. Since Hopkins attracted patients from all around the world, some benefits could go to kids rooting for other teams-- "even kids who never heard of baseball, who thought perhaps no sport could matter as much as soccer."

And he left the ashes to me. Me, whom he'd known barely a few months. That was the clause that most mystified his family, who'd never heard of me until then. I guess I knew why. He didn't want the ashes abandoned for someone to find in a year, or a decade, or a century.

Dan wouldn't have approved, but I arranged for a small headstone in the graveyard where his parents lay. However, I knew the ashes shouldn't be buried there.

"Hey," yelled Billy, bringing my mind back to the present. "Let's get some peanuts out here. They're cheaper than in the park."

I bought two bags, plus the Oriole Gazette. We wound our way through the throng to the gate. Our seats were way up top, but we jockeyed for position in the lower deck to watch batting practice for a while. As batters lofted balls toward the outfield, I reflected on Dan's memory of his first home run. I silently prayed that each of these kids, who had already suffered so much in their short lives, would someday get to enjoy as glorious a moment.

Jamie and Billy sat mesmerized. They knew every player's name, including the rookies who'd just made the team. I bought them programs, and we headed for our assigned seats.

We all kept score. Jamie knew baseball well, but she only understood the bare minimum of using a scorecard. It gave me pride being able to teach her what she needed to know. I taught her a strikeout swinging was a backward "K", just as Dan had taught me. Years later, maybe she'll wonder why I had her use that symbol differently than others did. I would simply tell her that's how I'd been taught. But I really did it to give a small bit of immortality to Dan. Maybe Jamie will teach her kids the same foible.

The game went by in a blur. I barely remember a thing about it, although I know we won. Afterwards the kids and I stayed in our seats until our section emptied. Then we slowly made our way down to field level. Attendants tried to keep us from moving toward the box seats. I made up a story about how the kids came all the way from Florida to see their first major league game and wanted to see the field up close.

We stood by the Oriole dugout for a while. Without a word, we pulled small paper bags out of our pockets and sprinkled the contents onto the field. Dust to dust, for the most part, with a few coarse granules that would require a little more weathering. For all anyone knew, we were getting rid of peanut shells.

Peanut shells could have been vacuumed up. Dan couldn't be.

He'd forever be with the Orioles.

Rbf – March 2017

ABOUT THE AUTHOR

Rich Frost grew up in upstate New York. After earning degrees from Wesleyan University and Duke University College of Medicine, he completed a residency in internal medicine at the University of Kentucky.

In addition to his medical career, he wrote a regular travel column for over 25 years, and now authors a regional history column.

He has published three compendiums of regional travel, and two books on topics of upstate New York history. The most recent of these tells the story of a nineteenth-century resort on New York's Lake Champlain that served as President McKinley's summer White House, then later became transformed into a Jesuit seminary, and now a college.

He also wrote the book and lyrics for the musical *Battling in Plattsburgh,* based on a crucial confrontation near the end of the War of 1812; it was produced in conjunction with that event's bicentennial in September 2014.

Final Season marks his fiction debut.